PRAISE FOR SALLY KILPATRICK

Little Miss Petty

"Smart, hilarious, and surprisingly poignant, *Little Miss Petty* is the cozy revenge fantasy I didn't know I needed. I'd follow Stella Stark anywhere . . . especially to Waffle House."

—Valerie Bowman, bestselling author

Nobody's Perfect

"Hilarious and heartfelt. I flew through this book. I love Kilpatrick's easy style and achingly real characters. A must read!"

—Brenda Lowder, award-winning author

"Hooray for a new Sally Kilpatrick book. Per usual, you can expect quirk and humor in this homage to motherhood and womanhood and all the ways we sacrifice ourselves and feel misunderstood and underappreciated, yet also the ways we have our own blinders and unrealistic expectations and need to own responsibility for our choices and happiness. Vivian's journey to striking that balance is riddled with antics, sure, but also with heart and wisdom. An enjoyable read that goes down like sweet tea."

—Jamie Beck, *Wall Street Journal* and *USA Today* bestselling author

The Happy Hour Choir

"This book made me laugh out loud, cry until my eyes puffed up, and think about deep things like the meaning of life and why bad things happen to good people. It reminded me of a Southern *Gilmore Girls*."

—Valerie Bowman, bestselling author

"It is hard to believe that this is Kilpatrick's debut novel. The characters are honest, lively, and heartfelt. Beulah deals with a number of relatable challenges. No character is wasted, and they remind the reader that anything worth having is not easy. A good takeaway is that family is what we create, not restricted to bloodlines. Kilpatrick mixes loss and devastation with hope and a little bit of Southern charm. She will leave the reader laughing through tears. This is an incredible start from a promising storyteller."

—*RT Book Reviews* (4.5 of 5 stars)

"Kilpatrick is a debut author with a distinctive voice who deserves an audience."

—*The Romance Dish*

"This book got to the point where I didn't want to put it down and couldn't wait to get back to it each night. I'll always keep reading an author that makes me laugh, and Sally definitely did that."

—*Well Read Southerner*

"*The Happy Hour Choir* is a beautiful, inspiring tale of faith, forgiveness, second chances, and hope."

—*Wondrous Books Blog*

Bittersweet Creek

"Fans of Southern contemporary romance will be charmed."

—*Publishers Weekly*

Better Get to Livin'

"Don't miss this quirky, fun story. I couldn't put it down."

—Haywood Smith, *New York Times* bestselling author

"Kilpatrick and her signature, quirky Southern characters are back! This is a fun story about following your heart—even through life's unexpected detours—and not letting fear hold you back."

—*RT Book Reviews* (4 of 5 stars)

"Resident ghosts, a reluctant mortician hero, a down-on-her-luck actress heroine, and a solid supporting cast all wrapped up in Sally Kilpatrick's heart-tugging emotion and quirky Southern humor? Yes, please."

—*The Romance Dish*

"In short, this one is pretty much as close to perfect as a reading experience can get."

—*Nashville Book Worm*

Bless Her Heart

"Do yourself a favor and grab this book and hide away with its laugh-out-loud and cry-out-loud moments all mixed up in one place. Kilpatrick enthralls us again with her trademark quirky humor and vivid characters."

—Patti Callahan Henry, *New York Times* bestselling author

"Captures all the sweet and sassy of a cozy Southern town . . . Takes the story beyond a romance to a novel about self-discovery."

—*Booklist*

"A little bit Flannery O'Connor, a little bit Fannie Flagg, but most delightfully and originally Sally Kilpatrick."

—*The Romance Dish*

"Kilpatrick is back with another tale full of sassy Southern characters. She writes in a way that makes readers feel as if they are hanging out with their best friend."

—*RT Book Reviews*

Oh My Stars

"Charming . . . a yuletide treat that will warm readers' hearts."

—*Library Journal*

"*Oh My Stars* hits all the right emotional beats. If you can walk away from this book without getting a bit of a lump in your throat or misty eyed, then you're a better reader than I am."

—*Nashville Book Worm*

"This is one of my favorites."

—Kim, Sally's spiritual adviser

LITTLE MISS PETTY

OTHER TITLES BY SALLY KILPATRICK

Nobody's Perfect

The Happy Hour Choir

Bittersweet Creek

Better Get to Livin'

Bless Her Heart

Oh My Stars

Much Ado about Barbecue

Novellas

Orange Blossom Special

Snowbound in Vegas

The Not So Nice List

LITTLE MISS PETTY

Sally Kilpatrick

This is a work of fiction. Names, characters, organizations, places, events, and incidents are either products of the author's imagination or are used fictitiously. Otherwise, any resemblance to actual persons, living or dead, is purely coincidental.

Published by Montlake, Seattle

www.apub.com

EU product safety contact:
Amazon Media EU S. à r.l.
38, avenue John F. Kennedy, L-1855 Luxembourg
amazonpublishing-gpsr@amazon.com

ISBN-13: 9781662532474 (paperback)
ISBN-13: 9781662532481 (digital)

Cover design by Ploy Siripant
Cover image: © Piotr Piatrouski, © Olga_Rusinova, © New Africa / Shutterstock

Printed in the United States of America

For Lorelai.
Who helped me create many of these scenarios
because
they aren't as mean as they would like to be
and we should all appreciate that.

Origin Story

My career in karmic facilitation began at a young age.

Age six, to be exact.

Back then, my mom would drop me off at my nana's house anytime she had to work but I didn't have school. Often that meant going to Nana's bridal shop, where I could hide under the dress racks and pretend I lived in a frothy tent. Or I could peek in between the full skirts and watch women try on dresses that made them look like princesses. Future brides with misty eyes would clasp hands with mothers who similarly couldn't see through their tears.

Of course, that was back when I believed true love and magic and happily ever after might exist somewhere outside the animated movies I watched.

On Sundays and Mondays, however, Nana's shop was closed. On those days, I stayed with her in her antique-filled Queen Anne home, a house where children were to be seen but not heard. Absolutely no running. No touching. Nothing above a whisper because Nana lived with her aunt Edna, a woman lost in another era, both literally and figuratively. Looking back now, I can see she suffered from dementia, which probably explained why the house was kept pretty much as it must've looked when she was younger.

Hardwood floors, plush rugs, and ceramic knickknacks perched precariously on small tables—they didn't believe in childproofing back then. Or, to be more accurate, their idea of childproofing was to teach children not to touch or to run or to knock about the house. To my credit, I did a good job of *not* being a bull in a china shop.

One day, Aunt Edna wobbled into one of those little tables, which caused Nana's favorite vase to topple over to the floor and shatter into pieces too small to be reassembled with superglue.

I, it should be noted, was in a different room entirely at the time. I heard the crash and ran to the parlor, a.k.a. the scene of the crime, only to have Aunt Edna throw me right under the bus just as Nana arrived.

"Look what this little girl did!"

Shock and hurt reverberated through my tiny body. *What this little girl did?* This little girl had a name, Stella, and she had been watching *Mister Rogers' Neighborhood*—that's what she had been doing. I could think it, but I couldn't make the words come out of my mouth.

When Nana turned narrowed eyes and a frown on me, I froze in the face of her disappointment. After a handful of excruciating seconds that felt like hours, she slowly shook her head and left the room to find a broom.

I looked at Aunt Edna, whose expression was self-satisfied, to say the least. "*You* don't have to live with her," she said before stepping gingerly over the vase's remains and leaving the room.

Maybe the stutter I hadn't quite outgrown kept me quiet. Or maybe it was the harsh realization that adults didn't always do the right thing. Whatever the reason, the outcome was the same: I never said a word.

Instead, after I'd received an unjust spanking from my mother, I crept into the front parlor, where Aunt Edna always kept a puzzle on a little table. As my mother apologized profusely to Nana, I grabbed a piece of that puzzle and stuck it in my pocket.

I'm not entirely sure what made me do it, but I think it was simply that I knew Aunt Edna found great joy in putting together elaborate thousand-piece puzzles. She took pride in still being able to see well enough to do so despite being ninety. In truth, she had very few hobbies, so the puzzle was the only thing I could think of.

As to what kept me in the petty business?

The beautiful schadenfreude that came a week later, when I happened to be at Nana's house because school was out for the day.

I heard my aunt Edna's cry of distress and left the television to stand in the doorway of the front parlor as she walked around the little table, then crouched down with a grunt to look underneath. With great effort and the help of the table, she got back to her feet. "Uh, little darlin'"—she'd forgotten who I was again—"I'm missing the very last piece of this puzzle. Would you get down on the floor and look? It has to be around here somewhere."

I hid my smile while I easily complied with her wish. I even scooted around the small room and looked under the writing desk and the chairs she'd lined against the walls so she could walk around her puzzle table with ease. Finally, I sighed. "I don't see it anywhere, Aunt Edna."

"Huh. Must be a manufacturer's defect," she said with a frown. "You go on back and watch TV, then, like a good girl."

I bounced out of the room and finally allowed myself to grin.

Many's the day I thought back on that puzzle of a mountain scene with one tiny piece missing from the middle. Many's the day I took that puzzle piece out of my top dresser drawer to run my fingers around its now-softened edges.

But where is that puzzle piece now?

Framed.

On my apartment wall.

Because if there's one life lesson that has been drilled into me, it's that you're never too young—or too old—to be petty.

Chapter 1

40 Reasons Not to Fear Your 40th Birthday

My fifty-six-year-old mother sent me this article via text.

I growled at my phone and started to put it down but then thought better of it and added a thumbs-up emoji to the text, even though I had no intention of reading the article. That deed accomplished, I put my phone in the passenger seat beside me and trained my eyes on a town house a block away.

My mother had a lot of nerve trying to establish a normal mother-daughter relationship at this late date, especially on a night when I was on a stakeout of sorts. My partner in both love and business, Ken, had bet me twenty bucks I couldn't serve papers on a particularly squirrelly man. I'd taken the bet.

One, my quarry had gone more than a week without frequenting his favorite watering hole. Two, he wasn't expecting a woman to serve him papers. Three, he especially wasn't expecting a ringer for Kate Beckinsale—plus twenty-five pounds and only if you squinted—to serve him those papers in an Irish pub at ten o'clock on a Monday night.

At least that's what I hoped.

Just as I was about to give in to boredom and read the article from my mother—or rather, have the phone read it to me so I wouldn't have to take my eyeballs off the town house—John Dalton emerged from the front door. He looked both ways and tiptoed to his car.

I let him get a good head start because I knew where he was going.

Nothing better than allowing one's target a false sense of security to help one get a job done. Dalton's wife had tipped her hand about sending him divorce papers, and he had been keeping a rather low profile ever since. Ken had given up, but he detested serving papers and would've found just about any excuse to push that job off on me. While I *could* serve these papers late, I didn't want to. I'd given myself the same deadline the state of Georgia gave to process servers: five days.

In twelve hours, my time would be up.

Would that invalidate the service? No. Would it drag the lawsuit out even more? Probably.

Most importantly for me, I would lose the twenty-dollar bet, and I hated to lose.

He drove past the Marietta Square, then made an abrupt turn.

I kept going but then doubled back to a mostly empty parking lot often used for people who had to go to court. Sure enough, as I walked up the cracked sidewalk toward the old Carnegie Library, I spotted Dalton's car in the next lot over.

Casually, I took a right and walked toward Finnegan's Pub.

It didn't take me long to find him sitting at the bar chatting up the bartender, an older lady with smooth olive skin and short spiky silver hair. He leaned forward to ask her something, and she arched an eyebrow. She had no time for his bullshit.

I liked her.

When the guy to my quarry's left slid from his stool, I ambled over and took his place. John Dalton looked me up and down, his eyes lingering on my cleavage before bouncing back up to my eyes.

"Hi," I said with just enough smile to encourage him.

"Hi," he said with a grin.

Oh, Stella. No matter what Ken says, you've still got it.

The bartender placed a pint glass in front of him, then asked me, "What'll you have?"

"Something red, please," I said, my eyes not leaving Dalton's.

She walked away muttering, and I reached inside my leather jacket to act as though I were looking for something. I pulled a stack of papers from the inner pocket and asked, "Could you hold this?"

"Sure." He took what I offered.

"Thanks. Oh, and by the way? You've been served."

His eyes widened, then narrowed before he washed all emotion from his face and said, "Uh, no comprendo inglés."

"Ha sido notificado."

At least I hoped that was right. Since I wasn't required to say anything when I handed over the papers, it was literally close enough for government work.

He sighed. "Fine. You can't blame a man for trying."

He put a ten on the bar and then took his papers and his beer and headed to the other side of the bar, muttering all the while.

"I was afraid you were actually interested in that guy," the bartender said as she placed a glass of wine in front of me.

"Oh, heavens no," I said. "Just proving to my partner that anything he can do, I can do better."

She chuckled. "In that case, this glass of Malbec is on the house."

"Thank you," I said with a bright smile.

She nodded and moved to the other end of the bar to take an order. I sipped my wine, all the better because it was free, and thought about how I would collect on my bet with Ken. I could simply take him for twenty dollars, but I was thinking about calling in a sexual favor because we'd been a little out of sync in recent weeks.

As I sipped, I considered a plan involving a piece of lingerie I'd been saving for a special occasion. Maybe, to quote the great poet Janet Jackson, "Someday Is Tonight." The more I thought about it, the more determined I was to reconnect with Ken. We'd each been doing a lot of work for our PI firm, and one could expect to hit the sexual doldrums from time to time in a long-term relationship—especially if there was a significant age gap—but that was no excuse for letting things get stale.

I pushed away thoughts of my fortieth birthday.

The good thing about being so much younger than your paramour was that if you were turning forty, then he was well ahead of you. Sure, gravity had necessitated push-up bras, but his body was beginning to show signs of wear and tear, too. We were both beyond a search for the Fountain of Youth.

We'd also decided not to have kids and had saved our money judiciously, so we would be able to retire in ten years or so. Then we would finally travel to the South of France, just as Ken had promised me—an entire month, he said.

I was lobbying for a trip to Champagne as well. Surely there were trains that could take you all around France. Maybe Paris or Bordeaux, too. Heck, why not spend a week in the South of France and spend the other three weeks traveling all over Europe?

I daydreamed about the logistics of this new plan for a good long while and looked down to see my glass empty. I left a fiver as a tip and walked to my car, still working on ways to get things going between us once again. Buoyed by thoughts of France, I drove out of my way to duck into Kroger only minutes before it closed and grabbed a bottle of champagne.

Ken would be beyond surprised to see me.

He'd been sure I couldn't serve this particular set of papers, and he knew I would stay in my car all night if I had to. I couldn't wait to slide into bed with what we used to call "No Reason Champagne" while wearing my new lingerie.

We'd go through our comedic bit for the first time in a long while. He'd say, "What's that?"

I'd say, "Champagne."

"Why?"

"No reason."

Then he would smile and kiss me and say, "I love 'No Reason Champagne.'"

I parked my car just down the street from our bungalow and practically tiptoed into the house, choking back giggles. As I neared the bedroom, I grew bolder.

Why bother with lingerie?

I might ruin the surprise with the creak of my ancient dresser's drawers, and I definitely didn't want to turn on the lights.

Instead, I paused in the hall and put down the bottle so I could strip down to nothing.

As I opened the bedroom door, it whined. I froze.

Snoring continued.

Exhaling with relief, I gave my eyes a minute to adjust, but it was beyond dark in our bedroom because Ken couldn't stand to have the sun hit him full force in the morning. I held a hand in front of me even though I knew where I was going—stubbing my toe would put an end to all my romantic plans, so better safe than sorry.

I crept to my side of the bed and pulled back the covers, sliding in and immediately hitting a body. Why was Ken on my side of the bed? And why did he smell like vanilla? Most importantly, why did he have boobs?

"Don't stop now," a woman's voice said as I removed my hand, then froze.

Move, Stella. At least get back to the hall, where your clothes are.

But my body didn't listen.

Ken yawned. "Don't stop what?"

"What you were doing," she said.

"I wasn't doing anything," he said.

"Yes, you were."

His hand moved under the covers, finding my hip, then disappearing, then reappearing.

He shot up in bed, then ran to the lights.

"Uh, Stella," he said as we all blinked to adjust to the light.

Now his girlfriend sat up, flashing her boobs before pulling up the covers. My eyes hadn't completely adjusted, but she looked disturbingly young.

The lump in my throat made it difficult to form words. The pounding in my ears made his voice seem far, far away. Even so, some survival instinct deep, deep within knew I had to play this situation carefully. I shocked myself by saying, "And to think, I've always wanted to have a ménage à trois. The least you could've done was invite me."

Bolstered by the words, I slid slowly from the bed, dressed only in what dignity I could muster. Posture straight, steps slow despite the racing of my heart, I sauntered over to Ken and paused. Despite my supposedly advanced age, at least one part of him was happy to see me.

"Aren't you going to introduce us?"

"Stella, this is Eloise. Eloise, Stella."

"Can't quite say it's a pleasure, Eloise."

Her mouth opened and closed, but nothing other than a squeak emerged.

Now that I was standing in front of him and had adjusted to my new normal, I understood Ken perfectly when he said, rather hopefully, "Ménage à trois, you say?"

I glared at him. "I think we need to have a chat tomorrow."

Ken sighed and ran a hand through his thinning hair. As my posture improved, his worsened. "Yeah. Tomorrow."

Head held high, I walked out of the bedroom and gathered up my clothes from the hall floor.

Only when I was sitting in my car, waiting for tears to come, did I realize I'd also picked up the bottle of champagne. I couldn't seem to find any tears, but condensation from the warming bottle did the job for me.

Chapter 2

Thus, on the second-worst day of my life, I shuffled, zombielike, into Finnegan's Pub for a second time and plopped a lukewarm bottle of champagne on the bar.

"Uh, this isn't a BYOB sort of place," said the bartender.

Oh yeah. I liked her. Free glass of wine earlier. Spiky hair that was aspirational. Only, she might not be my friend, based on the expression on her face.

I couldn't find the words, and her scowl faded into a concerned frown. "I can tell you're not the same woman who came in here about an hour ago. How about I take this bottle and chill it for you? Maybe get you something stronger while you wait."

I nodded.

"Vodka?" she asked as she placed a cocktail napkin in front of me.

I shook my head.

"Rum?"

Shook my head to that one, too.

"Bourbon?"

At my nod, she turned her back to me, and I clasped the bar to steady myself. Sound and light were both a blur. I couldn't be sure how I'd managed to drive back to the square or even why. Nor did I know where my car was. Where had I parked it? Would my heart ever leave my throat? If it was in my throat, then what was banging around in my rib cage?

"Come back to add insult to injury?"

When I looked to my left to see who'd spoken, I saw John Dalton himself had returned and was sneering at me. Only an hour before, I'd served him with papers. I missed the woman who'd done that. She'd been confident, sexy, so sure of herself.

Truly, I was not the same Stella Stark as before.

With a deep sigh I gave him the meanest stare I could muster. "Dude, I am insulted and injured enough for both of us. Now go kick rocks."

"You heard the woman," the bartender said as she placed an Old-Fashioned on the cocktail napkin in front of me. "Move along."

Her eyes didn't leave him until he walked out the door. Then she cocked her head to one side to study me. "What the hell happened to you?"

Bourbon was required to answer that question. It burned its way down my throat and pushed my heart back to where it belonged. "I touched a boob."

Her mouth twitched. "Is that all?"

"The boob belonged to a naked woman sleeping next to my partner. On my side of the bed."

She whistled. "That's a hard one. I'm going to guess the champagne was originally for him? Or her?"

"Him. He'd bet me I'd never be able to find that bozo I served with papers earlier."

She wiped at a spot on the bar. "You run on spite. I like that. Heck, I resemble it."

I took a sip of my drink. Gradually, bar chatter overtook the buzzing in my ears, as did the gravity of my situation. I wasn't just without a partner; I would soon be without a home and without a job. "Too bad spite doesn't pay the bills."

"Huh. I've been running this place on spite for over twenty years," she said with a shrug before moving down the bar to tend to a new customer.

After another sip, color joined sound. Sure, the interior of Finnegan's was a bit dark, but enough bric-a-brac lined the walls to distract me from my current situation. Several Santas nestled in among the liquor bottles along with tiki mugs, action figures, and a creepy baby doll that had to be haunted. Above me hung a sign for a tire shop that was so old it actually used the word "emporium."

I sat with my back to the door, a rookie mistake I wouldn't make again. On the wall to my right hung soccer flags and signs for Irish beers. Apparently, the team of choice for this bar was Liverpool. The quaff of choice? Guinness, Harp, Smithwick's, Strongbow—you could pick your poison there.

The place reminded me of a Southern Cheers, but no one knew my name.

Yet.

A presence on the other side of the bar had me looking up. My bartender was back.

"What's your name, kid?"

Kid? I was turning forty in less than a year. "Stella Stark."

She held out a hand. "Nice to meet you, Stark. You can call me Havisham."

Chapter 3

Six months later

Finnegan's was a surprisingly good place to do my homework. I'd found a new seat, of course, because I had that private investigator urge to sit in a corner where I could see all the comings and goings. In this case, I took the last stool at the bar, a spot in the corner that gave me a clear view of the entrance, the other side of the room that held booths and soccer memorabilia, and, of course, everyone who'd bellied up to the bar.

"You a paralegal yet?"

"No, Havisham. I'm about halfway through all the classes I need," I said without looking up from my laptop. "But Attorney Lawless has me doing odds and ends and is holding a spot for me."

"Well, hurry up. I can't believe I've made it this far without legal trouble."

I could.

She might've been petite, but anyone who wasn't at least a little scared of Havisham didn't have any sense in this world. The woman could stop a bar fight by raising her left eyebrow one millimeter.

I'd incurred her wrath once by asking her if she'd been named for the Dickens character in *Great Expectations*. No answer but a hard stare and intense eye contact while she put the cheap bourbon in my Old-Fashioned. Considering how rare the last name was, I wondered if she'd legally changed her name at some point, possibly out of the spite that had bonded us.

One thing I did know was that she, much like me, had vowed to never marry, something she'd told me on the night that would live on in infamy. She hadn't volunteered her rationale, but we'd been kindred spirits ever since, despite my ever-growing curiosity.

"Any luck working things out with the Douchecanoe?" she asked.

Havisham called most people by their last name. I suspected she'd spent some time in the military, but mainly she wasn't that keen on her first name, Aurelia. She called my former partner "the Douchecanoe" because she said he was both harmful to women and exceedingly unnecessary.

"Not exactly."

"Oh?"

"He owns the house. He owns the PI business. All I have are my car, my student loans, and my freelance connections."

Another woman might lecture me on the stupidity of being in such a position, but Havisham merely pressed her lips together tightly. She knew. We all knew. It was always easier to blame women for the precautions they didn't take than it was to blame men for the harm they caused.

"Well, that's enough of him, then. May his pillow never have a cool side, and may his bare feet find any Legos that happen to be on the ground."

I snorted. "You are a paragon of kindness."

"I only wish for him what he so richly deserves."

With that she sauntered to the far side of the bar to tend to a new patron. I turned my attentions back to my online course on legal research. Thanks to my prior training as a private investigator, I knew more than the basics of research—just not the specifics of *legal* research. As for writing? I hadn't done formal writing since college, but I had written tons of reports for our—scratch that, Ken's—PI business, and I'd also kept a self-indulgent blog once upon a time.

Legal research reminded me of the proofs we used to do in geometry class: Identify the jurisdiction, write down the facts, and figure out the legal issue—then make your case, step-by-step, using statutes and case law. I was parsing the details of my sample case in an effort to define the legal issue when a guy reeking of cologne slid into the seat beside me and glanced over his left shoulder to the hallway that led to the bathroom.

I took a sip of Malbec, but his aroma—like a cheap car air freshener but somehow bergamot?—interfered with the taste of my wine.

"Bruh! I can't come over now!"

Of course he was also on his phone. As if his cologne weren't loud enough.

"Make it quick. I'm at Finnegan's with this girl . . . she says she's a virgin . . . naw, man. I think she's telling me the truth, and get this: She's foreign."

I cringed, but he laughed.

"Bro. If I can hit this, then I get bingo. Are you not listening? She's both 'virgin' *and* 'from another country.'"

Gross.

"Okay, okay. Fine." He looked over his shoulder again. "She should be back from the bathroom in five minutes—you know how women are. Give me fifteen to get her back to the apartment and another twenty to get her naked . . . then it's ten minutes over to your place, let's see . . . I should be there before the seventh-inning stretch."

Disgusting.

"So help me, if you tell Chelsea about this and she breaks off our engagement, I will kill you with my bare hands."

And he's got a fiancée? With those soft hands? And even softer morals?

I was standing before I knew it, taking my drink with me because my mama, whatever her faults, hadn't semi-raised a fool. No drink was safe around that guy, but Havisham would keep an eye on my laptop. Casting a glance over my shoulder, I could see he hadn't even noticed

I was gone. Probably hadn't registered my presence at all since I was almost twenty years older than he was and decidedly *not* a virgin.

I squeezed down the narrow hallway to the bathroom and tried the door.

Locked.

Tapping my foot, I craned my neck to check on Soft Hands just in time to see him end his call. He looked at me. I resisted the urge to glance away—that's what a guilty person would do. Sure enough, he was looking for his date, so he turned around and motioned for the check.

The handle jiggled, and I wasted no time pushing the woman back into the bathroom before he could turn around and see us.

"Hey! What do you think you're doing?"

"Did you come in with a blond college boy wearing a camo ball cap?"

Her eyes narrowed. "Yeah?"

"Well, he sat next to me at the bar, and he was on the phone telling his buddy about how he's going to win the world's most disgusting game of bingo by sleeping with a girl who was both a virgin and . . ." How did I say the next part without being just as gross as he was?

"Let me guess," she said as she crossed her arms over her chest. "Not from around here."

"That was the gist," I said. "Also, he has a fiancée named Chelsea."

"What?"

I checked the mirror to make sure her shriek hadn't shattered the glass.

Her eyes flashed. But then suspicion replaced anger. "Why are you telling me this?"

"While it would've been easier to sit there and drink my wine and not do anything, I've called a moratorium on watching men take advantage of women. It really chaps my hide."

She took in my age—advanced—and my attire—baggy T-shirt, holey jeans, Converse—before nodding.

"Fair enough," she said with a sigh. "I can't believe I stopped working on my presentation for this."

"Some guys can pour on the charm when they want to."

Oh, how I'd learned that lesson the hard way.

"For what it's worth," I said, "you're really making that outfit work for you."

She looked down at her miniskirt, knee-high boots, and slouch-necked sweater that fell off one shoulder to reveal a lacy bra strap, then tossed her jet-black hair over her shoulder. "Thanks."

It was just the sort of outfit a woman agonized over before a first date. Sexy, but not too sexy. Comfortable, but not too comfortable. Dressy, but not too dressy. Perfect for a cooler-than-usual spring date night.

Just the thought of having to go through that whole dating rigamarole again made me want to look for a cave where I could be a hermit. Bonus points if I could also yell indignantly at the sky from time to time.

She took a deep breath and rolled her shoulders back. "I guess I should go kick him to the curb."

"You can definitely do better," I said.

"I *know* that," she said with a dazzling smile.

Envy gave a visceral tug in my belly. I'd kill to get my old confidence back, but ever since the night that would live on in infamy, I'd seen only wrinkles and single strands of silver peeking out from my auburn hair. "Tell the bartender to get you a glass of whatever you like and to put it on Stella's tab."

"Thanks," she said before we did an avoid-the-toilet dance in the tight space so she could exit.

She left the bathroom, and I took advantage of the facilities. I poured what was left of my wine down the sink and resolved to get a new one. Rationally, I knew the drink couldn't pick up germs just from *being* in a cleaner-than-the-average-dive-bar bathroom, but . . . nah. No need to chance it.

The first thing I noticed upon exiting the restroom was an unnatural quiet.

Patrons no longer chattered but instead studied the couple at the bar. Havisham stood tensely coiled, like a lioness about to pounce. Soft Hands should've been grateful that looks couldn't kill. Instead, he appeared to be in double-down mode.

"And why would you believe *her*? I really thought we had a connection, Daisy, but I can't trust you if you're going to question me like this."

Bold attempt to salvage your plan, Broseph.

My new bathroom buddy's shoulders slumped.

"Hey, hey." He laid a hand on her shoulder, then inclined his head to where I stood. "She's just jealous. Look at her. I'd never go for a woman like *that*."

All eyes in the bar found their way to me.

"She's old enough to be my mother."

Rude.

But technically accurate, and I would've probably been a reasonable twenty as opposed to my own mother's sixteen.

Mortification threatened to fell me, but if I could discover my partner's infidelity by touching a stranger's boob and walk out of my own bedroom with my head held high, then I could handle a prick like Soft Hands.

"Oh, I'm not jealous," I said as I sauntered back to my stool and then motioned for another Malbec. "I'm sure at least one other person in your vicinity could back me up on the conversation you were having because you, much like your cologne, are loud."

He stiffened, then turned to face me, his expressions contorting. "Why don't you mind your own business?"

"Funny, I was minding my own business, but your disgusting phone call made it very . . . challenging. Then you made me a part of your business when you singled me out just now."

He blinked twice as if surprised I had the ovarian fortitude to give as good as I got. Finally, he said through his teeth, "Well, it's not too late to butt out."

I looked at my watch, then back up at him. "Hmm. I think we've used at least ten of your fifty minutes, so you might want to head on over to your buddy's house for the game."

He started, his eyes widening at the proof I'd overheard his conversation. My presence hadn't registered for him earlier. It had been as though I was invisible, and I guess I was to him.

"Speaking of," I said, before taking a sip of the wine Havisham placed in front of me, "I think your future calculations should probably include more foreplay. Maybe some cuddling afterward. Or do you reserve that behavior just for Chelsea?"

If his face got any redder, he might explode. He looked from my bathroom buddy to me and then got up from the bar muttering, "Saggy-ass bitch."

He made it all the way to the door before Havisham growled, "Stop. You haven't paid your bill."

"I'll take care of that," my new friend said sweetly, her voice echoing through the still-stunned bar. "I wouldn't want to owe him one single thing. Oh, and Tanner?"

He turned, his eyes hopeful.

"I was born at Kennestone. I'm just as American as you are."

He took a step backward, stumbled, and then turned to rush out of the bar. I faced Daisy as she jabbed a thumb in my direction. "I'll pay for her drink, too. It's the least I can do."

"Well, thanks," I said as I extended my hand. "I'm Stella Stark."

"Daisy Salcedo," my bathroom buddy said as she shook my hand.

"Salcedo, what do you want to drink?" Havisham asked.

"Uh, I'll have a Strongbow." She turned to me. "Does she call everyone by their last names?"

"Only the people she likes."

We sat in companionable silence for a few minutes. I told myself not to let the man-child's insults get to me, but they were a little too close to some of the things Ken had said. He'd told me I was getting too old for the honey-trap cases, that no guy would want to cheat with me. I hadn't thought much of it at the time because I didn't like those sorts of cases, the ones where women—or usually some well-meaning family member—wanted to see if a man would hit on another woman or be susceptible to her charms.

Don't get me wrong, it was fun to flirt, and sometimes I got to wear a tiny button camera, but it always felt pretty sleazy, and no one was ever happy with the results either way.

"You know," Salcedo said, "you're pretty good at putting people in their place."

"Thanks. Too bad I can't make a career out of it, because I could use the money."

Chapter 4

A week later, movers left me with the chemical scent of new carpet mixed with the mustiness of an old building under new paint and the oppressive beige of my new apartment. After months of squatting in my nana's basement, I'd finally saved up enough money for my own place. I surveyed my domain: a tiny table with four mismatched chairs, a love seat Nana didn't want anymore, and a coffee table as scarred as my heart.

I walked down the hall to the main bedroom, where the movers had set up the double bed and dresser from my childhood. A glance into the closet, and I realized I'd used only one side of the closet for my clothes, as if waiting for Ken to use the other one.

Well, that simply wouldn't do.

I moved a few of my blouses and dresses to the other side of the closet. One of the perks of being single had to be taking up as much space as I wanted to.

Yes, I was going to take up space. Literally and figuratively.

Saggy-ass bitch.

The words from the college boy still haunted me from time to time, coming out of nowhere as if my subconscious blamed me for everything that had happened. Havisham said I needed to find a good therapist, but therapy required money, so I'd have to stick to my do-it-yourself mantras for now.

Slow inhale: *I am worthy . . .*

Slow exhale: *of love and happiness.*

After a few repetitions, the unsettled feeling in the pit of my stomach subsided.

I intentionally bypassed the bathroom so I wouldn't see myself in the mirror and pick apart every part of my reflection that I didn't like. It was a new hobby inspired by Ken's harsh words, my mother's well-meaning articles, and my left eyebrow's sudden and inexplicable decision to go rogue no matter how much eyebrow gel I applied. Instead, I plopped down on the love seat in the living room and tried to give myself a pep talk about living in Bel Air Apartments, a moniker far fancier than my current digs deserved, with no Fresh Prince anywhere to be seen. The complex had been built in the sixties and hardly updated since then, but the rent was something I could cobble together from my assorted freelance jobs while I went to school to get my paralegal certificate, which would open me up to more and better-paying freelance jobs.

If you'd finished law school, you wouldn't be in this predicament.

Yes, and if frogs had wings, they wouldn't bump their butts when they jumped—at least, that's what Nana liked to say. Sure, I'd dropped out of law school to join Ken in the private investigator business. Yes, I was still paying off my loans from that year as well as my undergraduate degree. Absolutely, I should've kept up with my payments instead of skipping two months' worth so I could get out of Nana's basement and move into my own place.

Silly me to think that making every payment religiously since 2007 would've bought me some grace. Oh no. Now I was two months behind, and I had fees on top of that. The kicker? The form letter alerting me to the extra money I now owed had arrived that very morning, when it was too late to call off the move.

Theoretically, I could take some extra jobs from Ken, but I'd rather sit in a fire ant hill than ask him for help. I could check around with some of my favorite attorney friends. There always seemed to be more papers to serve, more spouses to surveil, more insurance claims to validate.

Or I could sell feet pictures.

One look at my knobby toes, and I knew that wasn't an option.

My past decisions had put me in this present predicament, but I refused to beat myself up for believing in love. I'd been young and stupid, foolish enough to believe that my life story might turn out differently from those of the other women in my family. Sure, every chapter of our history should've convinced me otherwise, but I'd always been one to learn things the hard way.

That trait ran in the family, too.

Suddenly, the oppressiveness of the apartment's beige silence made sense. I was living alone for the first time in my life. I'd gone from my parents' house to my nana's, from Nana's to a dorm with roommates, from the dorm to living with Ken. Mom once told me that crappy apartments found us all eventually. I hated to think she was right about anything, but broken clocks managed it twice a day, so it made sense something she'd told me would be accurate.

The urge to leave had me back on my less than photogenic feet. I could go to Finnegan's to do my homework. Maybe see if Havisham and Salcedo would join me for a housewarming party—that would motivate me to make my new space more of a home.

Or not.

Why have a party in this sad apartment when we could hang out at Finnegan's, as we usually did?

I marched out the door and straight into a man who smelled of bourbon vanilla and spice.

Large hands landed gently on either upper arm to steady me.

Not soft hands, either. Warm, capable ones.

I meant to say "Sorry about that," but as I looked up a suited body, past broad shoulders and a bearded jawline, to my reflection in mirrored aviators, what I actually said was, "Are you the 'Man in Finance' I ordered? That delivery was fast."

When he realized I was referring to the song, he laughed out loud. "Not six five."

"Are you sure?" I asked. "You seem pretty tall to me."

"That's because you're fun-size."

I smiled in spite of myself. I wanted to be offended by his remark, but his inflection of "fun-size" was simply too good-humored. "If you're sure . . ."

"Afraid I also don't have blue eyes or work in finance."

"Damn."

One corner of his mouth twitched upward. "No trust fund, either."

"Double damn."

I should've moved, but I didn't seem able to. I couldn't see his eyes, but I liked everything I could see: full lips, closely cropped brown hair, broad shoulders, strong hands. But mainly it was his intoxicating smell, his willingness to play along with my silliness, his voice, the mischievous upturn to his lips.

And you want to jump out of the fire and into his frying pan because a part of you doesn't want to live alone.

"I guess I should let you go," I finally said.

"If you must."

"I must," I said with a sigh.

It had to have been my imagination that he wasn't in any more of a hurry to leave than I was, because he then headed to the parking lot with purpose. He looked over his shoulder at me once more, still smiling. Then he paused briefly at the side of a newer-model, silver Lexus to take a phone call. "Malone here. What's the problem now?"

I stepped behind the stairs that led to the upper floor and studied him through the gap between the concrete steps while pretending to check the mail I most certainly didn't have yet.

Tall, tailored navy suit, expensive shoes. Those aviators cost as much as what my monthly car payment used to be. If he wasn't in finance, then he was in something lucrative.

Not that it was any of my business. Or that I was in the market. Or that I even wanted a rich guy. Something about his height and suit had brought that silly song to mind.

"No, no. This is a delicate operation," he said.

I studied the mailboxes so it wouldn't look like I was eavesdropping. They were so old they had slots for the name of each person above the apartment. There was Malone. He lived in the apartment across the breezeway from me.

Taking my keys from my pocket, I opened my own mailbox—just in case he looked over to see what I was doing—and took out a collection of flyers for "Current Resident" as well as bills for people who'd lived in the apartment before me. Pretending to peruse a Lands' End catalog, I ambled over to my Corolla.

"I'll be there in a minute," my handsome neighbor said as he ended his call and slid into the Lexus. "No, I'll handle it."

Handle what? Could I volunteer to be handled?

I shook those thoughts away. Sure, his baritone voice exuded calm confidence, but I was on a hiatus from men. For heaven's sake, I'd left Ken only six months ago. Before that I'd been with him for almost twenty years. And before that it had been my high school boyfriend. Basically, I'd been involved in a relationship, juvenile or otherwise, since age sixteen.

I owed it to myself to learn who I was and what I wanted from life. I owed it to myself to learn to love my own company.

No more compromises.

No matter how intriguingly handsome my neighbor might be.

A part of me whispered, *You're just scared he sees you the way Soft Hands did*, but I told that part of me to shut up and recited a new mantra.

Slow inhale: *I may not be able to touch . . .*

Slow exhale: *but I can most certainly look.*

"Oh, Stark," Salcedo sang as I walked into Finnegan's. "I have a gift for you."

"You didn't have to do that," I said. "My birthday's next month."

"Oh, but I wanted to. Don't worry. It's neither expensive nor anything you'll have to dust." She slid from her barstool and held her phone in front of me before pressing play on a video. From the angle I saw Ken in his office, which meant Salcedo had been filming from the building across the street.

"How did you—"

"Watch."

In the video, Ken took a poster tube from the top of his desk, turning it from side to side before inspecting the mailing label. He opened one side, and bam! An explosion of glitter.

I slapped a hand over my mouth to keep from laughing.

For a moment I thought the video had stopped. No, he'd only been shocked into momentary stillness before he began frantically brushing at the glitter on his suit. The video shook with what had to have been Salcedo's laughter.

"You sent him a glitter bomb?" I asked.

"Oh, absolutely," she said. "Guess what else?"

"I'm afraid to ask."

"There among the glitter were hundreds, perhaps thousands, of little golden penises. And I added a note: 'Tools for a tool.'"

"So, last week I told you about my greatest humiliation, and you concocted this little plan? This is why you wanted me to teach you about surveillance, isn't it? So you could capture this beautiful moment." I wiped an imaginary tear from my eye. "That's beautiful, Salcedo. If you ever want to be a PI, I'd say you're a natural."

She clapped a hand on my shoulder. "Seriously, it was the least I could do since you exposed my date for who he was last week. When you told me your own story, I simply had to."

"What in the blue hell are you two up to?" asked Havisham.

Salcedo showed her the video, but the bartender frowned. "With that boutonniere, he looks dressed for a wedding."

"Maybe," Salcedo said, her eyes darting to one side and then the other.

A laugh burbled forth. Oh, this was too good. Ken had told me to never expect a proposal because he didn't want to marry and he didn't want kids. I'd felt the same way, since marriage had never once worked for a woman in my family. *Why chance it,* I'd thought.

Only, *not* marrying hadn't worked for me, either, now had it? It was almost like the system was rigged against certain people from the start . . .

Havisham grimaced. "It's not wise to mess with people on their wedding day."

Her reaction sobered me. I still didn't know what past trauma had caused her vow against marriage, but I now suspected it had something to do with a ruined wedding day.

Salcedo didn't know anything about Havisham's history. She must've taken the comment personally, because she said, "It's better than what she did to Tanner," as she jerked a thumb in my direction.

Havisham's gaze turned to me. "Dare I ask what you did to Tanner?"

I schooled my face into an expression of innocence. "Why, Havisham. I was in possession of certain knowledge of, say, a certain hidden website, and I shared that information with a certain interested party. Think of it as a public service."

"Stella found the secret page on his fraternity's website, the one with the pictures of scantily clad women and the giant bingo board that informed Tanner's fiancée that he'd been sleeping around on her."

"Really?" Havisham said over her shoulder as she deftly managed the tap for two beers at once.

"Yeah, wanna know what's even better?" I asked. "Chelsea, his erstwhile intended, is on the university newspaper staff and wrote a feature on the fiasco, so the fraternity has been suspended. A few of the guys are headed to court."

Havisham studied me for a moment, her head tilted to one side. "Impressive, Stark. Logical consequences are always more satisfying than random revenge."

I couldn't help but preen. "Thank you. It's true I wanted to avenge Salcedo, but once I saw the scope of what Tanner and his buddies were up to, I knew I had to shut that down."

"Excuse me," a woman two seats to my left said. "Did you say you can figure out secret websites?"

I gave her an apologetic look. "Sometimes? I'm not a computer person, per se, but I'm good at following the electronic breadcrumbs people leave behind. Discovering information from social media is more my speed."

"I will give you fifty dollars right now if you can figure out my husband's password for this dating site."

Stunned, I stared at her, taking in her ash-blond hair, stylish glasses, and steely gray eyes.

"Fine. A hundred."

She picked up a large purse that probably cost more than my monthly rent and dug around in it as she walked to my back corner of the bar. "I know what his username is, but I can't figure out his password. He's somehow blocked me, but I know he's having an affair. When I confronted him about having a profile, he said he was doing research for the marketing firm where he works. Research!"

Finding what she sought, she slapped a Benjamin Franklin down on the bar. Her eyes locked with mine. "All I need is his password. It isn't one of the ones he's used in the past—at least not the ones I knew about."

I looked at the hundred-dollar bill, then back at her. I was about to refuse her money, but it was the look in her eyes that stopped me. Here was a strong woman, a woman probably ten years older than I was, give or take. This was a question of pride.

"I'll give it a try, but I can't make any promises. Which site, and what's his username?"

She gave me his Tinder username, and I looked him up on my laptop.

"That's him," she said as she peeked over my shoulder. "Can you catfish him or something?"

I stiffened at the memory of Ken telling me I was too old for honey traps. Of course, he now had a child bride, so what did he know?

"Eh, I've done the honeypot thing in the past," I said with a shrug, "but it's not my favorite. Besides, I'm behind with my homework and don't have time for an elaborate sting operation. Let me see if I can figure out his password instead. What were the ones he used in the past?"

From there, we spent fifteen minutes doing an impromptu interview. First, she told me the old passwords—variations of pets' and children's names, mostly—and what passwords she'd tried. Then she told me his favorite color, favorite food, and favorite sports team. When we got to his favorite television show, inspiration struck.

"Oh. I may have an idea," I said. "May I?"

She passed over her phone, and I typed in a password made famous by an episode of *The Office*, a show I'd watched all the way through more than once because Ken was obsessed with it.

Winner, winner, chicken dinner.

I returned her phone. Her lips trembled as she looked through his now-unlocked account. She glanced up at me. "It's not all in my head! It's all right here. Oh, thank you!"

She jumped up and threw her arms around me, slapping my back with the huge purse she still had on her arm. When she withdrew, she sniffed a bit, blinking back tears. "Wait. What's the password. Just in case it logs me off."

I hesitated, but we'd come this far. "It's from an episode of *The Office*: 'big boobs' with a *z*. All one word."

She froze but then laughed out loud. "Oh, he wishes."

She placed a fifty under her mostly full wineglass and hurried from Finnegan's. I put the hundred in my back pocket, shaking my head and chuckling. When I looked up, Havisham was studying me in a rather speculative manner.

"What?"

"Did you just make a hundred dollars in less than thirty minutes?"

I couldn't help but grin. "Yep."

"Impressive."

"Well, good thing I did, because I fell behind in my student loan payments, and I have fees and payments and rent, oh my."

She opened her mouth to say something but was interrupted by a loud, familiar voice saying, "Stella Stark, I know you're in here."

The Douchecanoe had found me.

Chapter 5

I couldn't help but compare how Ken wore a suit to how my neighbor did, and the comparison wasn't kind to Ken. First, his suit was definitely off the rack. Second, it hung too loosely on his shoulders but strained over his waist. Third, it had a patina of gold glitter, and a tiny golden dong clung just behind the pocket square.

"Of all the lowdown things you could've done, ruining my wedding day has to be worst."

"I didn't—"

"Oh, but I know you did. You are the pettiest woman I have ever known—"

"Obviously, you don't know a lot of women," Salcedo muttered under her breath. "Or that men can be ten times as petty as any woman ever thought of being."

I shot her a look that said, *You're not wrong, but you're also not helping.*

She held up her hands in surrender.

"—a regular Little Miss Petty. Always sticking your nose where it doesn't belong because you think you can be the arbiter of justice. What do you have to say for yourself?" Ken asked, his face now dangerously red.

"Well—"

"There's nothing you can say for yourself. Maybe behavior like this is why I was planning to break up with you."

"Ken, really—"

"No, you listen. You've always asked too much of me. Maybe I should've ended things before I started seeing Eloise—that's on me—but our relationship had been over for a while. Falling in love with Eloise . . . just happened. Maybe I want to have a wife to come home to, did you ever think of that?"

"You told me—"

"Just like you to pull one of your childish pranks. Eloise was in tears. She'd engaged a photographer to take pictures of us in the square after the ceremony. Did you know that?"

"No, I—"

"Sure it was a justice of the peace wedding, but she still had expectations, and it was very difficult to explain to her why I was covered in glitter. You ought to be ashamed. You—"

"Ken, so help me, if you say one more word without letting me answer—"

"No, I'm not done here! You—"

In a haze of anger, I walked up to Ken and performed a perfect leg sweep. He landed on the floor, the wind knocked out of him. The crash of the stools he knocked over as he went down silenced the pub.

"Now, you listen to me," I said as he gasped for air. "I did not send the glitter bomb. Honestly, I wish I had, because listening to you just now has shown me exactly how much of our personal history you have rewritten. Also, there is no excuse—none—for not breaking up with me before starting a relationship with Eloise. You can rationalize your actions any way you want, but that's the truth."

"Stella—"

I put a foot on his chest. "Nope. I'm talking now. You told me you didn't want to get married. That was fine with me. You told me you didn't want to have children. Also fine with me. You told me you were looking for someone to be your partner in all aspects of life and then convinced me to leave law school. That is why I trained to be a private investigator. So we could build a business together. That's also why I took those courses on accounting, a subject I detest. So I'm sorry Eloise was in tears, but maybe that's because you married a child. After taking up with me when I was little more than a child. Only having relationships with younger women won't keep you from growing older, you sad little man."

At first I thought the noise in the bar was the pounding in my ears, but no. It was applause.

Stunned, I took my foot off Ken's chest. He scrambled to his feet, but his face, now a dangerous shade of red, twisted into an expression of pure anger.

A chill washed over me, and it was all I could do not to take a step back. As someone who'd done surveillance for a lot of divorce cases, I knew better than most the truth behind Margaret Atwood's observation that men were afraid women would laugh at them while women were afraid men would kill them.

People in the pub, including women, had laughed at Ken. If looks could kill, his glare would've already ended me.

His lips upturned in a Grinchian grin, and I had to wonder if he'd thought of a punishment worse than death. "You'll be apologizing to me for everything if you want the title to your car."

"Excuse me?"

"You heard me."

The pounding in my ears was back. Apologize to him?

"No."

"How about a thousand bucks, then. For handling your paperwork."

"I don't have a spare thousand, and you know it."

"Fine. Good luck when they come to repossess *my* car."

Satisfied that he'd found a way to get the last word, he turned on his heel to leave.

He might've won this skirmish, but he wasn't going to win the war.

"He can't do that, can he?" Salcedo's voice held the outrage of youth.

I sighed deeply. "Unfortunately, he can. Know how we have to pay our car registration every year before our birthday?"

"Yeah."

"Well, we financed the car in his name, so I need to have that title changed to mine in less than a month so I can keep my tags current."

"Stella, I'm so sorry," Salcedo said.

"Don't be," I said as the crowd dispersed, ready to get back to their own diversions. "I'll think of something."

"You're not going to pay him, are you?"

"Hell to the no."

"Apologize?"

"Very unlikely."

I took my seat at the corner of the bar, and she sat beside me. Havisham joined us to ask, "I only heard part of that. Why does he have the title to your car?"

I sucked in a deep breath. "Long, long ago and far, far away, a man sired me and lived in the same house and answered to 'Daddy.'"

"Was he Darth Vader?"

"No. His name is Willie Stark, and he used my Social Security number to open a bunch of credit cards that he had no intention of paying off."

"Sounds like a winner," Havisham said as she wiped at a sticky spot on the bar. "So, when you and the Douchecanoe were together, you financed the car in his name to get a better interest rate?"

"Correct."

"Ah," she said. "Is the car paid off?"

"As of two months ago, but my birthday is next month, so . . ."

"She needs the title to pay for her vehicle registration." Salcedo took a sip of cider, looking for all the world as if she hadn't just been asking me all the same questions.

"Bingo." I picked up my wineglass, only to discover that it was empty. Havisham instinctively turned around to get a new bottle. When she returned, I confessed something I hadn't even told my nana. "Here's the thing: I'm two months behind on my student loans due to moving into the apartment. I can't pay him any money to bribe him. I'm *not* going to apologize, either. That hundred dollars earlier was welcome because, between student loans and moving expenses, I gotta come up with at least seven thousand dollars in the next month."

Salcedo almost choked on her drink, her eyes wide.

"And I'm only telling you this to say . . . don't defer your loans unless you absolutely can't help it. And don't borrow more than you need. Seems like a good idea at the time, but the money's gonna come due eventually. Oh, and be careful who you finance things with. I thought my relationship was rock solid, but it was a pile of gravel over a sinkhole."

She nodded. "What are you going to do?"

I sighed. "Maybe take a break from my paralegal classes and look for extra jobs? Maybe take in a roommate. Or sell feet pictures—how are you with lighting and photography? Do you think there's a market for knobby toes?"

I didn't last long after my heart-to-heart with Salcedo and Havisham. My rage monster could deal in only brief bursts of energy, so the adrenaline crash left me both shaky and cranky. I retreated to my apartment half expecting to cry, but the tears never came. Instead, I felt numb, exhausted, no longer enthused about my paralegal courses.

Sadly, no ideas on how to get the title to my car materialized, either.

I was staring at my framed puzzle piece and trying to decide if it was level when Havisham texted me:

Meet Salcedo and me at the Waffle House at one.

"What? You can't even add a 'please'?" I asked myself as I plopped down on the love seat.

I had more coursework to do, but I dedicated quality time to moping instead. I couldn't even muster the energy to watch television, which was just as well because Ken had changed all the passwords to our streaming services.

And to think he was calling *me* petty.

But of all the bullshit I might've expected from Ken, barging into Finnegan's hadn't been in my top five. If nothing else, his appearance had reminded me to stop sharing my location with him. Since we were no longer friends, he didn't have any need to find me. There was one problem easily solved.

But his irrational anger over the glitter bomb?

Sure, Salcedo had sent it on his wedding day. She was in college. Her frontal lobe hadn't fully developed yet. Besides, it wasn't as if he and Eloise were having some expensive shindig at the Marietta Country Club. He'd said himself they went to see the justice of the peace and then were taking pictures in the square.

Probably at the same fountain where Eloise had posed in a prom dress mere months before.

If I thought she'd listen to me, I'd have told her to steer clear of him. She wouldn't, though. I wouldn't have listened at her age.

Mom had tried to tell me not to drop out of law school, said I would need a law degree to pay back my student loans. Not that she knew exactly how predatory those loans were, thanks to the fact that my father's credit card stunt had ruined my credit.

I'd handled that situation by getting whatever debt I could forgiven and then consolidating the rest. Slowly but surely, I'd paid off those bills, but that meant I was left with deferred student loans. My father's debts: the gifts that kept on giving.

Or taking, as the case might be.

My rage monster wanted an encore performance at the mere thought of such injustice, but she was too tired from her earlier demonstration.

A thud and a cry of pain in the breezeway had me on my feet, with what little adrenaline I had left, to see if anyone was hurt.

Could it be my neighbor? Why did that thought have me reconsidering the concept of playing sexy nurse?

No, Stella. You promised yourself a sabbatical from men. Don't even think about it.

When I opened the door, my neighbor was nowhere to be found. Instead, an older woman half sat and half lay on the ground in a way that suggested she'd missed a step and fallen backward.

Lord, please tell me she didn't break a hip.

"Are you okay?"

"I think so," she said, clearly still stunned.

"Do I need to call for help?"

"Oh, for heaven's sake, no," she said as she attempted to climb to her feet.

I offered a hand even as I wondered if she should try to stand. But what could you do with an adult who refused help?

I got her to her feet, and she tested putting weight on one foot and then the other. She gently pressed her left wrist and hand. "I think I'm okay."

"Maybe we should take you to the doctor," I said. "Just to be safe."

She patted my cheek. "Sweet girl, I'm not going to the emergency room at this time of night. That would be a fool's errand. If anything is swollen in the morning, then I'll reconsider, but ain't nobody got time for emergency room tomfoolery."

"If you're sure . . ."

She put her hands on her hips. "You are just the kindest, but I can handle myself. You're new around here, aren't you?"

"Stella Stark," I said, extending my hand.

Her hand was little more than veins and sinew, but she had a hearty shake. "Marcia Quattlebaum, but you can call me Mrs. Q. I've been here since the place opened."

Wow. That would mean—

"Yes," she said, as though reading my mind. "Eighty-two years old next September. So you can see I've been handling myself for a good long while."

"Yes, ma'am."

My response mollified her. "I like a young person with some manners. Why don't you come up and see me tomorrow? I've made a lemon pound cake, and I can't eat it all myself."

"Sure."

"Apartment two-fourteen. Sometime after three. But before seven because I won't miss *Wheel of Fortune* for anything or anyone."

"Yes, ma'am," I said.

She'd already made it to the second step, but her progress was slow. It took effort to lift each foot up enough for the next step, and she clung to the railing. Was she hurt, or did she have arthritis?

"Staring at me won't make me go any faster." Her voice might've been sweet, but her intent was clear.

Pride was an emotion I recognized. No matter how much I wanted to reassure Mrs. Quattlebaum that I only cared about her safety, I retreated to my apartment to will the clock to move faster so I could see why Havisham had requested my presence at the Waffle House.

Chapter 6

Ah, those black letters on yellow squares, that beacon in the night: the Waffle House.

A glance at the car clock told me I'd arrived ten minutes early, and I weighed whether I wanted to enter a clean, well-lit place or wait in my car.

Well, Ken's car, if I couldn't come up with a way to get the title from him.

Studying every law reference my paralegal course allowed had led me to the conclusion that I was in another situation where what was legal and what was just were two very different things. Legally, the car was his. His name was on the title. If life were fair, the car would be mine because I'd paid for it. There was, of course, the possibility I could persuade a judge of my point of view, but that would require even more money I didn't have to take the matter to court, and I couldn't be guaranteed that I would win.

It was all so exhausting.

To date, every man in my life had been exhausting.

I'd heard that good men existed, but I was beginning to suspect they spent their free time with Bigfoot, the Easter Bunny, and chupacabras, because I'd never met one.

In the meantime, I would leave *my* car and enter the Waffle House, a place Ken hated but I loved. Unlike him, the Waffle House had never let me down.

Out of habit, I chose a booth in the far corner, my back to the plate glass window so I could surveil the entire restaurant, empty though it was.

"Couldn't you just sit at the bar?" huffed the waitress as she limped toward me.

"Sorry," I said. "Habit."

"My feet are killing me," she said as she reached my table. Her face was a road map of experience, and her name tag declared her to be Betty.

"Plantar fasciitis?"

"What's that?"

"Deep, soul-sucking ache in your heels?"

"Sounds about right."

I was showing Betty some calf stretches while talking about proper orthotics when Havisham and Salcedo walked through the door. Everyone settled into the corner booth and made their orders before I finally asked, "What's this all about?"

Havisham nudged Salcedo.

"I, uh, I feel bad about what happened, but I've thought of a way to get the money you need," she said.

"Oh, hon, you don't have to feel bad about anything. Your glitter-bomb idea was hilarious. Unfortunately, Ken doesn't have a sense of humor."

"Still, I want to help." Salcedo reached into her satchel for a folder and slid a piece of paper across the table. At the top was a grinning blob of a cartoon character who resembled the Mr. Men / Little Miss stories Nana used to read to me when I was little. The design was obviously meant as a parody of those books. Below the cartoon it read:

LET ME BE YOUR LITTLE MISS PETTY!

Is karma not working fast enough for you?

The patriarchy got you down?

Need some payback?

Let me be your petty personal assistant.*

Ask Havisham at the bar or scan this QR code to fill out a form, and someone will get back to you as soon as possible.

*I only deal in logical consequences. No random revenge.

"I added that last part," Havisham said, as if I didn't remember her words from earlier.

"How is this going to help me?" I asked as Betty passed around cups of coffee and did the Waffle House ritual of napkins with silverware on top for each of us.

Salcedo's eyes glowed. "*You're* Little Miss Petty, and *we're* going to help you."

"This isn't a job," I said, "and 'pettiness' isn't something you put on a résumé."

"But it *is* a skill," Havisham said. "And we've seen the demand. Remember how easily you made a hundred dollars earlier today?"

I waved away her compliment. "A fluke. Basic private-investigator stuff, along with a fair amount of luck."

She arched an eyebrow. "Tell her what else you've been up to, Salcedo."

"Well, I did some informal market research," the younger woman said, "and by that I mean I asked around in the bar and on social media. I already have several potential customers—"

"In the mere *hours* since we last saw each other?"

"—including the woman you helped earlier."

"Really?"

"Yes, really. She took a picture of the flyer and asked about your services right before we closed up. Said her neighbor might be interested. You gotta strike while the iron is hot. But also . . ."

"But also what?"

She scrunched her nose up most adorably, but I felt a sense of foreboding, nonetheless. "I have a confession to make."

"Dare I ask?"

"You're kinda going viral? Well, viral-ish?"

"What?"

"I, uh, recorded your interaction with the Douchecanoe, and I may have edited the video down to just the part where you took him down to the ground, and it may have a bunch of views."

"Daisy Salcedo, you didn't!"

"I didn't show your face! I pasted Johnny Lawrence's head over yours."

"*Karate Kid* Johnny Lawrence or *Cobra Kai* Johnny Lawrence?"

"*Cobra Kai* Johnny. Duh."

I pinched the bridge of my nose. "I'm not sure that's better."

"Someone else got your speech on video. That's where it all started."

If I could've sunk below the floor, I would have. "Oh, for crying out loud."

Salcedo cued a video, and I winced as I heard my own words: *Only having relationships with younger women won't keep you from growing older, you sad little man.*

"I really dislike the sound of my own voice," I muttered.

"Well, lots of other people must like it, because I have a waiting list of potential clients, some of whom are willing to pay up to fifty dollars for a DIY option."

"What?"

"At a discounted rate, you give them the idea, but it's up to them to implement it."

I looked from Havisham to Salcedo and back again. Words failed me.

"Come on, Stark," Havisham said. "All you have to do is meet with the first client on the list. See if it works."

"I have a job, and I'm already doing homework for my paralegal classes!" My excuses sounded hollow to my own ears. My job was on my own time, and I would have to take a break in my paralegal classes if I didn't get my money situation straightened out.

"Which you're able to do at a bar," Havisham, the traitor, was saying. "So I think you can handle it."

"I have my freelance gigs, too."

Salcedo's eyes brightened. "But I'm going to help you."

Betty chose that blessed moment to slide plates of food in front of us. She topped off our coffee, and I was glad for the interruption, so I had a moment to think.

Salcedo tucked into her hashbrowns, closing her eyes and savoring the greasy goodness.

Havisham, meanwhile, was skewering me with one of her signature looks. "Come on, Stark. What have you got to lose?"

"Not a lot, but I'm sure this viral video will be forgotten by next week."

She pointed her fork at me. "For heaven's sake, when did you get to be such a pessimist?"

"Would you like a chronological list or one in order of severity of trauma?"

"Anyway," Salcedo said in a tone that suggested we would get back on topic and we would like it. "I got the idea for 'Little Miss Petty' from what your jackwagon ex said. We can consider the glitter bomb as my audition for being your assistant."

"The petty personal assistant to me, the petty personal assistant?" I asked, my chicken biscuit held midair.

"Yes!"

I nibbled at my chicken biscuit while I considered. Finally, I said, "Listen, I may be a millennial, but I'm getting too old for side hustles."

Havisham looked up from her hashbrown bowl. "If you want to come up with seven thousand dollars in a month, then you need to take your vitamins and hustle."

"Don't remind me."

Havisham and Salcedo started a whisper campaign of "you tell her" and "no, you tell her."

"Just spit it out," I said as I put down my biscuit and picked up my water glass. Gotta hydrate along with my coffee and all that.

Salcedo took a deep breath, then blurted, "Your first client is willing to pay you three thousand dollars."

I had been taking a drink at the moment she said "three thousand dollars." That water went down the wrong pipe, which necessitated a coughing fit that brought Betty shuffling over.

"Ma'am, are you choking?"

I shook my head.

"If you can't speak, then I'm going to assume you're choking." She cracked her knuckles in grim anticipation of performing the Heimlich maneuver.

Waving her off, I finally managed to croak "No, I'm fine" between coughs.

She exhaled with a combination of relief and disappointment but then yelled over her shoulder to the cook. "Jasper, I told you those biscuits were too dry!"

"Ain't nothing wrong with my biscuits! And this is the *Waffle House*. People ought to be eating *waffles* anyway," said the wiry man standing by the griddle.

Betty hobbled in his direction, and the two got into an argument that I would've enjoyed a lot more if I hadn't been wondering what in the heck Havisham and Salcedo had gotten me into.

"What does she want me to do for these three thousand dollars?"

Havisham shrugged. "I don't know. You'll have to ask her tomorrow."

"Tomorrow?"

She arched an eyebrow. "Want your car repossessed?"

"No."

"Okay then. You're petty Perry Mason, I'm your Della Street, and Salcedo is your petty Paul Drake—"

"Who?" asked Salcedo.

"It's *Perry Mason*, look up the classics," Havisham said before turning back to me. "I'll keep up with your appointments. If none of this works, then we've lost nothing but time, but if it works . . ."

Unable to argue with Havisham's logic or the opportunity for almost half of what I needed from one job, I turned my attention back to the flyer. "This is really impressive, Salcedo."

"Thanks." She sat up a little straighter and beamed. I wanted to be mad at her for posting the video, but I didn't have it in me. Best I could tell, TikToks and memes were Gen Z's love language.

I sighed. "Okay. So I'm going to try this Little Miss Petty thing, I guess."

Havisham paused before taking a sip of coffee. "You can do or do not—"

"But Yoda says there's no try!'" said Salcedo in a respectable Yoda voice. "I get *that* reference."

When I got back to my apartment, I noticed the lights were still on in my hot neighbor's apartment. Through the vertical blinds, I saw that he was working out. Forty push-ups so far, and I'd started counting while he was in the middle of that particular activity. It was also possible I'd lost count while studying the musculature of his back and arms. You know, for science.

Next up were squats, which he blessedly did facing his door rather than the glass patio door.

Then burpees?

Wow. Who knew my neighbor was a masochist.

Stella, you're skulking out here like a Peeping Thomasina.

Reluctantly, I gave up my vantage point. My bed was calling, and I needed a good night's rest if I intended to add a side hustle to my usual schedule.

Chapter 7

What have you got to lose?

The next night, Havisham's question echoed through my head as I slid into the last booth at Finnegan's. I longed for my usual seat at the bar, complete with an unfettered view of the haunted doll. The booth seemed better for conducting my new petty business, but I liked to know where that doll was at all times. Just in case.

Most of the patrons around me were taking advantage of Winedown Wednesday. They sat in pairs, threesomes, quartets, leaning in to share work gossip or get to know each other a little better. I sat alone. It was just me and the larger-than-life Liverpool FC flag that hung above me.

I am not alone. I am flying solo. Intentionally.

"Can I at least have a glass of wine?" I asked when Havisham came around to check on the patrons in the booths.

"You can have your wine after you meet with your clients," Havisham said. "I'll bring you a lime and soda for now."

"Clients? With an *s*?"

"Clients. But first up is the big spender, so you'd best have your A game."

I saluted her. She scowled at me.

When she returned and set down a whiskey glass full of bubbles with a lime on the rim, I gestured to the pub around us. "We have a bar as a base of operations, so I don't think a drink would be out of place."

"And? People want to feel like you're taking their situation seriously. I said 'petty Perry Mason,' not 'petty Sam Spade.' You can't nurse bourbon until a dame comes to hit on you or a heavy comes to beat you up."

"More's the pity," I said as I took my lowball of very little flavor and absolutely no alcohol. In truth, there were few things I took more seriously than righting wrongs, but that didn't mean I had to be happy about forgoing my evening glass of wine.

At least I could rest assured that if anyone could take being a petty personal assistant from cottage industry to full-fledged business, it would be Daisy Salcedo, marketing major. After countless texts and emails, I was beginning to think she wanted to both create and rule a pettiness industrial complex. While I'd spent the morning serving papers and finishing up my paralegal homework, she'd made sure to reserve all socials under "LittleMissPetty." Part of me wanted to ask her if she was taking care of her own homework, but I let it be. She felt awful about Ken's reaction to her glitter bomb.

I was halfway through my nonalcoholic concoction when an impossibly slender woman with sleek blond hair walked through the door. Damned if she didn't look like a femme fatale from one of the noir films Havisham had referenced. She had to be my new client because she telegraphed "trophy wife," and only a trophy wife would have a spare $3,000 lying around to throw at me. Sure enough, Havisham pointed her in my direction. Everything about her screamed "money," from her exquisitely coiffed hair and tailored clothing to her understated manicure and overstated jewelry.

I smiled, despite feeling sloppy in my customary uniform of skinny jeans—sorry, not sorry, Gen Z—with an oversize button-down. Older than I was, but by an indeterminate number of years thanks to both makeup and a better gym regimen, my client had style. Of course, she also had money. Funny how style and money so often went together.

"You must be looking for Little Miss Petty," I said with a smile.

"Yes, I'm Trista," she said as she slid onto the bench across from mine. "And you are . . . ?"

"Your new petty personal assistant, Anonymous McGee."

She nodded. "Plausible deniability. I like that in a person."

"How can I help you today?"

"I feel like such a cliché, but I'm living the true tale as old as time. Girl falls in love with boy. Boy gets bored. Falls out of love with girl. Checks out of fatherhood and marriage. Almost certainly has a younger woman on the side. Girl decides to be proactive and get her shit together to serve him with divorce papers before he can serve her."

My eyebrow couldn't help but lift. "You would think life could find some new plots."

She chuckled. "You really would."

"Okay then. What is your vision?"

"My vision is to feed my husband through a sausage grinder, but he is the father of my children, so I suppose I could settle for some good old-fashioned karma. My friend, Jackie, is the person you helped with the Tinder password. She came back later to thank you again, saw your flyer, and sent me a picture. The part about how karma doesn't work fast enough? That really spoke to me."

"So, you don't want me to look for his side chick?"

She brushed her hair behind her ear, and a diamond stud earring caught the light. Well over a carat, best I could tell. "No. It won't do me any good to show that he's cheating on me. The state of Georgia doesn't care. Mind you, if *I* were the one cheating, then it could affect custody arrangements and my alimony, but since he's the primary breadwinner, he can sow his wild oats in anyone's field."

She paused as Havisham placed a glass of chardonnay in front of her. Warmth suffused her features. "Chardonnay?"

"Yep."

"How'd you know?"

"I have a sixth sense about these things." Havisham had observed that women of a certain age and income bracket tended to like oaky, buttery chardonnays—especially when single or about to become single. She'd taken to calling chardonnay "cougar juice."

I hoped the wine's nickname became a self-fulfilling prophecy for Trista. Didn't she deserve a future rebound fling with a younger man? If I were truly in charge of karma, I would make it so.

My client took a sip of wine, then closed her eyes before taking in a breath, holding it, then releasing. Either she was no stranger to yoga, she had her own mantras to chant, or both. Once centered, she met my eyes with a gaze that was once again steely. "Now, where was I?"

"You were about to tell me how I could help karma find your husband."

"Yes, that. It may be childish, but I need to see him reap at least some of what he's sown. It's exhausting and exasperating to see him get away with so much."

"Exhausted" and "exasperated": These were two adjectives I knew only too well. "And you saw the fine print on the flyer about logical consequences rather than random revenge?"

She sighed. "If we must."

"We must. A wise woman once said, 'Karma's only a bitch if you are,' so I'd rather . . . identify areas of improvement for your husband."

She snorted, and the sound was incongruous to her polished exterior. "Plenty of fertile ground there."

"Enlighten me, then. Other than his aversion to fidelity, what are some lessons your husband needs to learn?"

She took another sip of wine before looking out into the distance, tapping her chin while she thought. "He's the antithesis of gracious or generous. He wouldn't lift his pinkie to help someone in need."

"So a soup kitchen would do him good?"

"I wouldn't trust him to cook for others. He might accidentally poison them."

"Something more labor intensive, then?"

She spewed a bit of her wine. "I would pay dearly to see him do manual labor."

"Paying for what you want to see is the plan, isn't it?" I said with a grin.

"The filthier, the better."

"Challenge accepted. What else?"

"Ugh. He's so dismissive of any woman with power. Won't vote for a woman. Won't watch women's sports. We have three daughters, and he won't let them listen to Taylor Swift in the car if he's driving, much less buy tickets for the girls to see her in concert. And he has the money, I assure you."

It was on the tip of my tongue to ask why she'd married him in the first place, but I kept that to myself. Sometimes people showed you only one face until you were invested in the relationship. Sometimes being in love was like wearing blinders. Often, the truth of a relationship gone wrong lay somewhere in between.

"And another thing." She paused to take another sip of wine. "I swear he lost interest in me because I had the audacity to get 'old.' Being a few years older than him didn't seem to be a problem back when he was trying to get into my pants. Now he has no use for women over the age of thirty-five. Not even his own mother."

I thought of Ken's dewy-faced bride and how Soft Hands had muttered "saggy-ass bitch" with such rancor. "How dare we women age. How dare we?"

"Yes!" She continued in this vein, really warming to the topic with a colorful selection of four-letter words. I smiled and nodded while waiting for her to move on to the next topic. Finally, she said, "And he always wants things just so, with his clothes clean—all name brands, of course—his house neat, and a home-cooked meal the second he gets home. But no casseroles, heaven forbid! 'That's cheating,' he says, as if he's ever so much as boiled water."

Having worn herself out with her very legitimate grievances, she stared beyond me with glassy eyes. While waiting for her to compose herself, I mentally summarized what she'd said:

No casserole—noted.

Fastidious about clothing and surroundings—also noted.

Stranger to manual labor and not in the least charitable—most duly noted.

Total chauvinist. Oh, how much sweeter that made being the woman who'd be making his life difficult for the next few weeks.

When she looked up at the ceiling and began blinking furiously, I looked away. I had been known to use that trick to quit crying back when I actually could cry. After a few more deep breaths, she said, "Do you think you can get photos or video of him doing any of those things?"

"That's my plan, but I need to know *who* he is and *where* he lives."

"His name is Blake Malone—"

Malone? My heart sank in irrational disappointment. Surely, her husband wasn't my "Man in Finance."

"—and I think he's currently living in some dump of an apartment off Delk Road—"

Of course. A Malone in a dump off Delk? At least you found out who he was before you fantasized too much.

"Here's what I know: His company, Malone Construction, has an apartment that they've leased for years, supposedly for out-of-town guests. Perfect place for him to hole up. We visited it once or twice back when we were dating. Bell Something Apartments. He claims he needs to find himself. I'm just hoping—"

"Bel Air."

And why did I have to blurt that out? So much for anonymity.

She paused. "I think that's right. But how . . . ?"

"Because that's where I live. What does your husband look like?"

She hesitated, unsure now that I'd figured out something for myself. "Tall, brown hair, early forties—"

"White guy with aviators? Italian loafers? Drives a silver Lexus? Always on his phone?"

She almost choked on her wine. "Yes! But how did you know this already?"

"Haven't you guessed? I, too, am a woman who had the audacity to age. Twenty years wasted, and that's how I came to reside in a crappy apartment off Delk Road. There's a Malone who lives across the breezeway from me, in . . . Bel Air Apartments." I thought of those strong hands on my shoulders, and something inside me again ached with the disappointment of knowing he was not what he'd seemed. "I ran into him yesterday."

"Impossible."

"Ah." I held up one finger. "Improbable, but not impossible—"

"I'm so sorry," Trista said, all the blood having drained from her face. "I didn't mean to imply you lived in a dump."

I waved away her concerns. "Oh, it's a dump. Not my first choice, but needs must."

She lifted her wineglass, then frowned at its emptiness. "Is that going to be a problem?"

"Oh, no," I said with a grin. "Things just got a lot easier."

Slumping back against the booth, she allowed herself a tiny smile.

I grinned back. This ludicrous idea just might work. "Now, about payment . . ."

Chapter 8

After interviewing three more clients, I went back to Bel Air Apartments to rest and do my homework before the inevitable debriefing later that evening. A quick look at my watch told me I had half an hour before *Wheel of Fortune* started, and I wanted to make sure Mrs. Quattlebaum was okay.

I jogged up the stairs and knocked on her door.

"Come in, come in!" Her face lit up as though she'd never expected in a million years that I would take her up on her offer of lemon pound cake.

"I know your show is about to come on, but I wanted to make sure you were okay."

"Fit as a fiddle," she said, stepping aside and again gesturing for me to come inside. "Well, other than this one nasty bruise. See?"

Before I could politely decline, she pulled down the elastic waistband of her slacks to show me a gnarly purple-and-brown bruise at the top of her hip.

"Oh. That has to hurt," was all I could think of to say.

She pulled up the waistband and smoothed down her shirt. "While you're here, why don't you join me for supper? It's tiresome eating alone."

I hesitated, but I hadn't yet done a full grocery run, so a free meal wouldn't be unwelcome. "If you're sure I wouldn't be imposing on you."

"I insist!"

And how I wished she hadn't. Not only was supper a spiceless Midwestern casserole made with cream of mushroom and Tater Tots, but Mrs. Q talked my ear off. She gave me a complete history of the Bel Air Apartments as well as an unabridged biography of her now-deceased husband, Harold.

The lemon pound cake almost made up for it.

Well, that and when she said, "You know, I used to always make one of these casseroles when someone new moved into the complex. I should make you one."

"No," I said a little too quickly. "I mean, you already have. Even better, you invited me to eat with you, and I'd hate for you to go to the trouble of cooking another one just for me."

"It's no trouble at all," she said, launching into a detailed description of the ingredients, the community cookbook where she'd found the recipe, and why the store-brand Tater Tots were just as good as the name brand but the frozen mixed veggies really should be Green Giant.

"Maybe you could make one for the guy across the breezeway from me," I suggested. "I don't know how long he's been living here, but, uh, bachelors, you know?"

"Oh, good idea! No, he hasn't been here that long," she said. "Funny, that apartment usually sits vacant. Back when we first moved in, I think some guy was using it to have affairs, but he has to be my age now."

I opened my mouth to ask more questions, but from the television in the living room came three words that let me know I'd been dismissed: "Wheel. Of. Fortune."

Mrs. Q stood.

"At least let me help with dishes?"

She shook her head and patted my hand before gesturing toward the door with her head. "Gives me something to do later."

I thanked her for supper and made my retreat.

"How'd your first set of meetings go?" Havisham asked later, at our Waffle House confab.

"Great," I said as I stirred my coffee. "At least, I think it went great. These are uncharted waters."

"Did our biggest fish at least put down a deposit?" asked Salcedo, who'd opted for a burger rather than breakfast this time. Jasper had refused to drop fries, though, so she was having hashbrowns with her burger.

"Half down now, and half upon completion of three 'petty' tasks, complete with photo and video evidence. I'm working on a few ideas, and I installed a doorbell camera outside my apartment in some spare time I had between meeting the client and coming here. I even bought a spy camera that's hidden in a shirt button. All that and got my paralegal online homework done, too."

"Look at you! Next glass of Malbec is on me," Havisham said.

"That shirt button camera should be a good investment because I have more potential clients for you," Salcedo added.

"I hope so because I spent a chunk of the deposit money on the camera. I used to have one, but . . ."

I left the sentence unfinished because that camera, along with so many other things, was still with Ken.

"No need to dwell on such things," Havisham said. "I'm sure we'll be able to find you enough clients to make the money you need to get back afloat."

"I got another gig serving papers and doing a few other odd jobs for a law firm this weekend, too," I said as I lifted my coffee mug.

We ate in silence for a few minutes, eventually pushing away our plates and bowls.

Betty shuffled over to take our dishes. "Y'all gonna make a habit of coming in here like this?"

"Maybe."

"Fine with me. At least y'all tip," she said. "But seems to me you'd want to be at home in bed."

"That's where I'm headed next," Havisham said. "But running a bar means keeping late hours."

"College student," said Salcedo, complete with a yawn to undercut her argument.

"I'm just here for the hashbrowns," I said.

"Well, I've worked the night shift now for ten years," Betty said. "Don't ever be too good at a job, that's what I'll tell you. That and don't take the night shift because you figure you were waking up at oh dark thirty with night sweats anyway. Those will eventually go away, but the night shift will haunt you for the rest of your life."

Salcedo's eyes bugged out. When Betty turned her back on us to take the dishes away, she mouthed, "Night sweats?"

Havisham mouthed back, "Don't ask."

"It's awfully late for you women to be out and about," Betty yelled from her spot behind the counter. "Don't you have any burly boyfriends? Someone to improve the scenery around here?"

"I'm here," said Jasper.

"You're a string bean of a man with spiderweb tattoos on your elbows. I want to *improve* the scenery."

Naturally, Jasper took issue with Betty's words, and the two began their nightly argument. It had to get dull working the wee hours of the morning, so I could hardly begrudge them. In two visits, I'd seen only two other customers in the Waffle House at the same time we were there. Betty and Jasper had to amuse themselves somehow.

Havisham chuckled, but then it became a full laugh.

"What's so funny?" asked Salcedo.

"Just the idea of asking the three of us to bring burly boyfriends."

"Questions like that are why so few movies and books pass the Bechdel Test." Salcedo shook her head while stirring her coffee.

"What in blue blazes are you talking about?"

I was glad Havisham asked, so I wouldn't have to.

"You know, the Bechdel Test. Does a movie—or book—have at least two women characters? Do they talk to each other? And do they talk about something other than men?"

I opened my mouth to refute the need for such a test, but my brain scanned through all the movies I'd seen, and I had to close my mouth with a "huh."

"I'm not saying I'm opposed to a romantic relationship," she continued. "But even our petty project tends to focus on men."

"Because the patriarchy is a helluva drug, and too many men are getting high on their own stash," Havisham said.

"Well, I, for one, have no intention of dating anyone for another six months," I said. "I declare myself on sabbatical."

Even as the words left my lips, I thought of a certain man who looked good both in a suit and while doing burpees.

Both Havisham and Salcedo stared at me. The former finally said, "That seems like an arbitrary length of time."

"I promised myself not to date for at least one year from the day I walked back into your bar," I said. "I've had a boyfriend or partner for almost my entire adult life, and I'm gonna do that cliché where I work on me. I'd do the whole *Eat, Pray, Love* thing, but I don't have the money to travel. Obviously."

Salcedo whistled. "Except you said your intentions out loud. To the universe. You know what that means."

"No, what does that matter?" I didn't even hide the irritation in my voice. Salcedo wasn't yet twenty. What the heck could she know about these things?

"It means the universe is going to plop the perfect person right in front of you and dare you to break the promise you made to yourself."

"Oh, please." I rolled my eyes. "Maybe I'll extend my sabbatical to a lifetime. Become a cat lady or something."

"Fifty bucks says you get your freak on before a year's out." Havisham extended her hand.

"Deal," I said before shaking her hand. I turned to Salcedo. "This is gonna be like taking candy from a baby."

"Ha! That's what you think. Now the idea is in your brain, tempting you like chocolate cake when you declare yourself on a diet," Havisham said. "I've been on a relationship recess for over forty years. When needed, I scratch the occasional itch, but I've always been glad to kick him out once he's done his job. Let a man stick around too long, and he's gonna want you to either make his breakfast or do his laundry. No thank you."

Salcedo looked from me to her and back again. "Oh, you're both in for it."

"Say, Havisham, why did you swear off marriage?" I asked, both because I was curious and because I wanted all such conversations to avoid me.

She sighed deeply. "Back when I was nineteen—a stupid age, Salcedo, so you should find a padded room and stay there until your twentieth birthday—I got engaged. Planned a wedding. The groom didn't show."

My stomach roiled at the thought. "I'm sorry."

"Don't be. They'll never find his body."

Salcedo's eyes went wide.

"I'm kidding. I'm way too pretty for prison and definitely too bougie for toilet wine. Last I heard he was living his best life in Peoria."

"But what did you do when it became clear he wasn't going to show?" I asked.

"My mother, God rest her soul, offered to get in front of everyone and tell them the wedding was off, but I made the announcement. Figured I owed it to myself to start in the way I meant to go. Everything had been paid for, so"—she paused, and for a moment, I could see her as the vulnerable bride of nineteen—"I told everyone to go on to the reception and enjoy the party. I danced as though I weren't dead inside, then took a solo honeymoon to Cancún. Had such a great time doing whatever I wanted whenever I wanted that I decided to marry myself. Haven't looked back."

Seemed a good time to try out my theory, so I asked, "And then you legally changed your name to Aurelia Havisham?"

"No," she said with a grimace. "That's my government name. My mother's favorite college roommate was named Aurelia. My father saddled me with the extremely rare last name."

"Huh. So she didn't even know she was naming you after a woman who got stood up on her wedding day, and then . . . you got stood up on your wedding day."

"Don't rub it in, Stark."

"I would never!"

"Why didn't *you* marry?" Salcedo asked me, pointing the conversation exactly where I didn't want it to go.

"Marriage hasn't worked out well for my family," I said. I almost told her my darkest secret, but even the cozy emptiness of the Waffle House, with its drone of employee arguments and the hum of an overworked air conditioner, couldn't lull me into sharing that information. "Let's just say that my mother, grandmother, great-grandmother, and a myriad of aunts all married poorly. It may go back further, but that isn't the sort of information you can find in the family Bible."

"Statistically, fifty percent of marriages end in divorce," Salcedo said.

Havisham muttered something like "assuming you could get them down the aisle," and I sighed deeply. "Well, as it turns out, avoiding marriage did me no favors. I don't have a claim on any part of the business I helped build nor the house I helped pay for. You heard him demanding money to get the title for a car I exclusively paid for. I could kick myself for trusting him, but what was I supposed to do? I was in love. I was thinking in terms of forever."

"Damned if you do and damned if you don't," Salcedo said softly.

I lifted my coffee mug in a mock toast. "Hence, my new plan to become a cat lady."

"Stark, you don't have a cat."

"Well, it wouldn't take much to get one, now would it? I'm only thirty-nine. I have time."

"Thirty-nine. That's another stupid age," Havisham said.

Salcedo's eyes grew wide. "Are there any other ages I should worry about?"

Betty tore off the ticket and slapped it on the table. "All of them."

"I have got to find more friends who are my age," Salcedo muttered under her breath. "Y'all are depressing."

Havisham took the ticket and slid out of the booth. "The truth often is."

Once we were outside, enjoying how the Georgia night was warmer than inside the Waffle House yet cooler than the day had been, Salcedo paused by her little hybrid. "Sometimes I wonder if I should give up on the idea of love, but I'm sure as heck not going to declare it to the universe. That's how you end up going on dates with dudes like Tanner. But . . . is it worth it to even try for something other than . . . how did you put it, Havisham? Scratching an itch?"

I leaned against my Corolla. "Oh, I don't think this conversation is going to pass the Béchamel Test—"

"Bechdel Test."

"Whatever."

"Seriously . . ." She turned to Havisham. "You were stood up at the altar." And then she turned to me. "We all saw your ex. Then it turns out that the first guy I've tried to date in college was trying to use me for some kind of frat game? It'd be one thing if I were with a group of people my age, but we have three different generations here, only the story seems the same."

I looked to Havisham. She was squinting at the night sky, trying to find stars she wouldn't be able to see for all the security lights in the parking lot. Finally, she spoke. "I think it's tough to find a person you want to spend the rest of your life with no matter who you are or what age you are, but I think it's even harder for a woman to find a man who's comfortable enough in his own skin to allow her to be herself. Heck, for all we know, there's a poker game full of men somewhere, and they're all commiserating on how women did them wrong."

"Huh," said Salcedo. "But how do you know if you've found that person? Is there a sign from the universe that would make you take a chance on love?"

"At this point I'm kinda like Sally from *Practical Magic*," I said. "I need a guy whose favorite shape is a star, he can flip pancakes, and he has one blue eye and one brown eye and—"

"I think it was one green eye and one blue eye," Havisham said in a gruff voice that indicated she liked *Practical Magic*, but she also didn't want to admit it.

"Whatever," I said.

"Would you be serious?" Salcedo interrupted. "Please."

"Fine, if you're right about how I've provoked the universe, then I'll know he's not the perfect person for me unless"—here I stopped to think of something ridiculous—"he wears friendship bracelets unironically, reads self-help books because he's comfortable in his own skin but knows he's not perfect, declares his love for me under a blue moon, and—"

"Be serious," Havisham said.

"Has one brown eye and one blue eye," I said just to tick her off.

Salcedo turned to Havisham. "What about you?"

"I don't believe any of that mess."

"But if you did," Salcedo prodded.

"He would be a cowboy billionaire philanthropist."

"What?"

"Exactly. This whole exercise is silly, but you started it, Salcedo, so what are your requirements?"

"Oh, I don't have any," she said with a smile. "I'm currently open to whoever the universe wants to send me. I wanted to see what you two would do. That said, you can check back in a decade or so to see if I've narrowed down my requirements."

Havisham and I shared a look of mutual disgust. The youngster had gotten the better of us. Chalk one up for hope?

"Oh, look at the time," Salcedo said with a faux yawn that turned into a real one. "Night, y'all."

She was in her car and gone so fast, we didn't know what to do.

"Cowboy billionaire philanthropist?"

Havisham snorted as she opened the door to her pickup. "More useful than flipping pancakes in the air."

Chapter 9

A week and some later, I was ready to implement phase one of my big assignment for Trista. I'd called in a favor with a former client, and he'd set up the perfect comeuppance for a less-than-generous person who hated manual labor.

I was prepared for multiple scenarios. One way or another, I would capture photo and video evidence of Blake Malone hopefully having a terrible, horrible, no good, very bad day.

Out in the parking lot, a van door slid open. I checked my phone to make sure the app for the doorbell cam was capturing the apartment across the way and, more importantly, recording.

Showtime.

Two men in work clothes crowded my view of Malone's door. The shorter one hesitated before using the door knocker.

When no one answered, they looked at each other. I bit my lip, while drumming my fingers on the upholstered arm beside me. The only outcome I hadn't planned for was that he would refuse to open his door.

The taller man checked his phone. His short buddy gave the door knocker a more vigorous workout. We all waited. The men shifted their weight from side to side or front to back. My fingers drummed even faster.

C'mon, Malone. Open up.

The two men looked at each other, shrugged, and took a couple of steps toward the parking lot. I bit back a groan and scooted to the edge of my seat with a sigh of frustration and a fervent wish that I'd brewed more coffee.

But then Malone tried to open his door, only the chain was still attached, so it banged when it hit its limit. Malone cursed, closed the door, and then reopened it with a yawn. "Can I help you?"

At least that's what I thought he'd said. The door muffled his voice, and I had the sound on the recording muted so my eavesdropping wouldn't be given away. Blessedly, the workers had moved to the side, so I had a clear view of Malone leaning against the door, shirtless and wearing only boxers. He yawned while absently scratching the back of his head. Was that a hint of a tattoo? A thin line of writing on the inside of his right bicep, maybe? Definitely broad shoulders. Toned, but not to the point where he looked susceptible to roid rage or prone to giving a lecture on the evils of sugar.

My mouth went Death Valley dry.

Trista had said her husband worked out. I had even seen him working out, but . . .

Stella, you can't drool over your client's soon-to-be ex-husband. Highly unprofessional. Also, there's a reason why you're doing what she hired you to do. As Nana likes to say, pretty is as pretty does.

With that thought, I waited for him to wake up enough to cuss these guys out and slam the door in their faces. Then he wouldn't be so gorgeous.

If only I could get my eyeballs to believe that.

Sabbatical, Stella. Sabbatical.

I shook some sense back into myself in time to make out what Malone was saying: "Huh. I don't remember signing up for that, but if you'll give me a minute, I'll be right back."

He didn't cuss them out or slam the door in their faces.

Okay then. On to plan D, which I really didn't think we'd get to.

I grabbed my camera bag as well as a backpack that contained snacks and water. I'd pick up coffee on the way.

Implementing plan D didn't bother me; having misread the psychology of my target did.

Based on Trista's description of the one time she'd tried to talk him into delivering gifts to Christmas Angels, I thought for sure I'd come up with a perfect combination to incite his anger: manual labor, helping others, waking him up just as he would've been hitting his REM sleep. The little hairs on the back of my neck stood up, a sure sign that something was off.

Malone emerged in sweatpants and an impossibly tight T-shirt and followed the Habitat volunteers. A laugh echoed over the parking lot before a van door slammed shut.

Maybe coffee and some careful observation would give me the answers I sought.

Coffee helped, but surveillance was tricky. The Habitat for Humanity build site sat among a row of small homes a few streets over from the Marietta cemetery. Finding a place to park where I could see the workers but not be seen was a challenge but nothing I couldn't handle.

I kept Malone in the sights of my high-powered lens.

I soon felt like a Peeping Thomasina once again. I was not taking revenge photos. Nay, nay. These were thirst-trap snapshots.

So far I'd observed Malone lift heavy objects, joke with his fellow workers, and listen intently to the construction site leader, who happened to be a woman. With his neatly trimmed beard and lopsided smile, he was my aesthetic.

Salcedo's words haunted me: *The universe is going to plop the perfect person right in front of you and dare you to break the promise you made to yourself.*

Honestly, it wouldn't be the first promise to myself I'd broken.

Besides, I wasn't looking for forever. He could be Mr. Perfect-for-Right-Now.

No.

He is a cheater. You are on the rebound. Absolutely not.

I revisited my new mantra.

Slow inhale: *I may not be able to touch . . .*

Slow exhale: *but I can most certainly look.*

Sadly, my mantra didn't help much.

He had to have an angle, because he was acting nothing like the man Trista had described, and she was legit. I'd always prided myself on my bullshit detector, and she'd passed muster.

But my bullshit detector had missed Ken, now hadn't it?

With a strangled growl of frustration, I put away my camera. I needed to observe this man up close. Time to implement plan E, which I was already dressed to do—all that remained was pulling my hair into a ponytail and putting on a cap and sunblock.

As I approached the worksite, Malone paused in his work to study me. I couldn't see his eyes behind those mirrored glasses, but a twitch of his lopsided smile suggested he was happy to see me. "Don't I know you from somewhere?"

"From across the breezeway."

His smile bloomed into a grin. "That's it. You were looking for a 'Man in Finance,' if I recall."

"And, if memory serves, you really know how to wear a suit."

"But I would prefer to be dressed like this. Too bad the guy you were looking for didn't arrive."

I shrugged. "A man like that would be entirely too high maintenance."

"So you prefer someone a little more . . . down to earth?"

I drank him in: His shirt had a new rip, dirt streaked his sweatpants, and a smudge sat beside his nose. Not at all as Trista had described him. Did Blake Malone have a not-so-evil twin?

"Uh-huh."

So articulate, Stella.

He lifted the hem of his shirt to wipe away sweat, and I sucked in a breath at the flash of abs.

"Yo, lovebirds. Get to work," came a cry from the site manager. "Wait! Who are you?"

She pulled me aside to question me, politely blessed me out for being late, and then put me to work next to Malone, which was both a reward and a punishment.

I hit my thumb with my own hammer at least three times because he was that distracting.

Maybe it was just my imagination, but it felt as though each time I took a peek at him, he looked away suddenly, as if he had been studying me, too.

"Wanna grab a pizza together?" Malone asked when we reached the apartment complex. I'd offered to give him a ride home, and he'd accepted that, as well as my story about how the volunteers must've knocked on the wrong door.

"Yes, but no," I said.

We got out of the car, and he looked at me as if I had three heads. "You don't like pizza?"

"No, I like pizza."

"You don't like me?"

"No, I like you," I said, my words surprising me with their truth. "Maybe I like you a little too much."

An eyebrow arched over his aviators. "And that's a problem?"

By now we stood in the breezeway, each poised in front of our respective doors. I weighed whether honesty was the best policy.

"I just got out of a long relationship."

"Ah."

"And I promised myself that I would wait before I got into another one."

He leaned against his doorframe, and I was reminded of why women love to watch actors lean and to read about men leaning. Malone leaned especially well, with his arms crossed and his biceps straining at the cuffs of his T-shirt.

"I was just offering pizza," he said, his voice as innocent as his expression was not.

"Offering to get 'just pizza' with someone whose name you don't know," I said. "Right."

"Yes, because it's the neighborly thing to do," he said. "Besides, I do know your name. You're Stella Stark. I bet you're the one who doesn't know *my* name."

I lifted an eyebrow. "You're Blake Malone."

Was it my imagination, or did he flinch ever so slightly? I guessed hitting on a woman while technically still married would do that to a guy. Flinch or no, he definitely frowned for a split second before recovering his composure. "Yeah, but I prefer to go by Malone."

Maybe he felt guilty?

Not that he was wearing a wedding band.

Nor did he have that telltale lighter indentation on his ring finger that showed he'd been wearing one up until recently.

"This last-name business seems to be going around," I said. "I have a friend who only calls me Stark."

"I like that," he said. "Suits you."

"Well, Malone, thanks for the offer, but I'll have to decline. The only date I have is with my shower." I turned to unlock my apartment door.

"Let me know if you change your mind about pizza," he said. "Or, say, pizza with benefits."

My head whipped around, but he was already unlocking his door. He didn't even have the good grace to turn around and see my shocked expression.

Chapter 10

I showered, trying not to imagine what pizza with benefits might look like with Malone. The strains of "All Too Well" wafted down into my bathroom from the one above with some kind of Swiftie sorcery.

Good. I needed to be reminded of breakups and the general perfidy of men.

It should be noted that I had no problem with Taylor Swift, but the ten-minute version on repeat? Could we mix it up a bit? More importantly, I was beginning to worry about the mental state of my upstairs neighbor.

I was considering banging on the ceiling with a broom handle à la the eighties-sitcom cliché when I heard a tiny cry.

No, more like the mew of a kitten.

Great, first the anguished wail of Taylor Swift, and now I was being invaded by kittens.

Or, worse yet, rats.

I shuddered before googling "what sounds does a rat make."

Squeaky noises.

Relief washed over me, but the mew came again, this time more insistently.

First, I searched my bedroom and then my sparsely furnished living room. Nothing behind or under the love seat. Nor under the table.

I paused and heard . . . nothing.

"Maybe I'm losing my marbles."

Mew.

I looked in the cramped laundry closet, the bathroom, my closet. I even checked the world's tiniest kitchen. Still nothing.

Mew.

The sound seemed closer, more frantic.

Oh. The patio.

A quick peek beyond the blackout curtains showed a scraggly kitten sitting in the shadows of my patio.

No mother. No brothers and sisters.

My heart jumped up in my throat.

And this kitten doesn't even have a Nana cat to step into that void.

Shoving that thought away, I searched my phone for "what to do if you find a kitten" even as I wondered how the creature had managed to get over the waist-high wooden barrier. Maybe it had climbed over the top and then didn't know how to get out?

After gauging the age as somewhere between four and six weeks, I checked again for any sign of a mother or a nest and found none. Then I searched the web for a rescue shelter. Closed for the day, of course.

The kitten—a tiny calico, probably flea-ridden—stepped out of the shadow and looked up at me with sad eyes. My own words came back to haunt me: *Maybe I'll extend my sabbatical to a lifetime. Become a cat lady or something.*

I looked heavenward. "Very funny. I've never had a pet before, and I have no idea what to do with a kitten."

Even so, I couldn't leave it out there, could I?

What if a hawk swooped in? Or a big dog jumped onto my patio?

I yanked at the door before remembering the sawed-off broom handle I'd placed in the runner to appease Nana's anxiety about the safety of sliding patio doors in ground-floor apartments. With the help of a four-letter word, I removed the handle and opened the door.

The kitten backed away from me as if I might be a predator, but I scooped it up and hugged it close, fleas be damned. The little rascal nestled into the crook of my arm and began to purr.

"I don't know what to do with you, though."

The cat wiggled and mewed indignantly, as if to say, "Google is free. Make another search."

With a sigh, I began research on cat ownership before looking down at my new roommate. "Don't get too comfortable. I'll probably take you to a shelter next week."

The tiny creature gave an impossibly big yawn and promptly fell asleep. My resolve weakened ever so slightly.

At least I wasn't talking to myself anymore?

Despite my aching muscles, I made a quick trip to the store for a litter box, kitten chow, and everything else necessary for my new roomie. I even got a bag of flour, not because I wanted to bake, but because one website recommended dusting the ground with flour so I could search for paw prints later to see if the mother came looking for her baby. The whole way to the store and back, I pondered the probability that one kitten would magically land on my enclosed patio. My conclusion? Highly unlikely.

More probable? Either Havisham or Salcedo had decided to prank me because I'd said I was going to be a cat lady. Havisham seemed the likelier culprit—I knew Salcedo still felt bad about the fallout from the glitter-bomb incident.

I texted the former to come over and then went about combing the kitten for fleas as a precaution and to double-check the search I made before heading to the store. I found none, which was good since it was too young for a flea collar. It—I had no idea if I was dealing with a he or a she yet—could eat canned food, though.

It ate as though it had never eaten before, then looked over its shoulder with a growl once it had licked the dollop of food clean from the saucer.

"What?"

An indignant mew was my answer.

"I don't know how long you've been hungry, and Dr. Google says to give you only small amounts. Just in case."

The kitten stalked out of the kitchen, its pointy tail pointing skyward, and sniffed its way across the living room. When the doorbell rang, it jumped straight up in the air and fuzzed out completely. I scooped the creature up and answered the door to see Havisham.

"I have thirty minutes before my bar shift begins. What do you want?"

"Havisham. It's so good to see you, too."

"Seriously, Stark. Time. It's of the essence. The little stuff life is made of. Et cetera."

"I want to know why you tossed a kitten on my patio."

"What?"

She looked down at the miscreant, who was currently pricking me with its surprisingly sharp little claws. I put it down. "I made that joke about being a cat lady, and then I find a kitten on my patio. Very funny."

Havisham frowned. "I didn't do it. I haven't had time for such shenanigans, although I kinda wish I'd thought of it now that you mention it." She sat on the couch, and the kitten sniffed her ankles before climbing her pant leg like a tree and curling up in her lap.

Little traitor.

"You want me to believe that a kitten that's barely old enough for store-bought food just magically appeared on my patio."

She shrugged. "As you have seen, they have claws. They can climb."

"Then why didn't it climb *out*?"

"Oh, stop calling the kitten an 'it.'" She lifted the creature's tail. "I'm no expert, but I believe this is a she—seems to be missing some equipment. Also, every calico I've ever met has been female."

Why hadn't I thought to look that up?

Probably because you were busy worrying about fleas and food and because neither your mother nor your nana ever allowed you to have indoor pets. Well, any pets.

"Fine. Why didn't *she* climb out?"

"God has a sense of humor?"

"Well, you're older and thus in need of a cat sooner. You can have this one," I said. "I've got a starter kit for her for you and everything."

"Oh no. This kitten is yours." Havisham put the cat on the couch and stood. "The universe wants you to have it. You put out a request, and behold . . . the cosmic cat-distribution system has answered."

The kitten in question cocked her head and then mewed. Loudly.

"Good luck!" Havisham said as she reached the door.

"But what if I have to do surveillance? I can't leave her here by herself, can I?"

"Of course you can. You've got a litter box, right?"

"Yeah."

"Put her in the bathroom with food, water, and a litter box, and be sure to play with her when you get back. She'll be fine."

"But that seems so . . . cold."

Havisham snapped her fingers. "Good call. Put a warm blanket in there for her to curl up on. Maybe one of your sweaters so she'll have your scent."

"You're no help!"

"Au contraire, I've just been remarkably helpful, a fount of knowledge. Besides, you wanted to be a cat lady. Toodles."

Havisham left. The kitten ambled over to my feet and batted at my untied shoelace.

My heart contracted from the cuteness but then hardened. Nana had once said she wouldn't have another pet because losing her last dog had almost killed her. I vaguely remembered her bichon frise, Buffy, a fluffy sweetheart who had been too old to play by the time I came along.

Then, when I was ten, Mom had dated a guy with a golden retriever named Skip. We'd go to the park sometimes, and she'd hold his hand—the man's, not the dog's—while I played fetch with Skip. At one point she even gave me the speech about how I was going to have a stepdaddy.

Then poof! Both the guy and Skip disappeared from my life. When I asked my mother why we hadn't seen them in a while, she looked me in the eye and said, "No sense in getting too attached to anyone or anything. They all leave you in the end."

As if to prove her point, she promptly took herself off to Florida, leaving me with Nana once again.

Funny how I could remember the dog's name but not the name of the guy who'd almost been my stepfather.

The kitten rolled over on her back and grabbed my shoelace, chewing on the aglet while her little back feet kicked together against the lace. I started to bend and pick her up but thought better of it.

Mom and Nana never agreed on anything, but they somehow shared an opinion on the subject of pets and people: They all abandon you eventually.

I told the cat, "Don't get too attached." But I had to wonder if I was talking to her or to myself.

Chapter 11

The next morning, I drove to the mountains of North Georgia to serve papers on a preacher. As my favorite lawyer boss, Lawless, and I had suspected, the pulpit was the best place to find a preacher on a Sunday morning.

While it might've been fun to interrupt the service, I instead waited outside the doors of the church. To while away the time, I fretted over my kitten. By the time Brother John Fitzhugh finally wrapped up his sermon—complete with three altar calls—and shook the hands of each of his flock, not only was my stomach growling but I'd also imagined at least twenty scenarios in which the kitten could've hurt herself.

I practically threw the papers at him and then hightailed it back to Marietta, where I burst through the door like a SWAT team member with a key. Imagine my surprise when I found her in the bathroom, where I'd left her, curled up in the cat bed I'd placed on the vanity. She blinked at the light I'd turned on and then gave a ferocious yawn.

"Smug, aren't you?" I asked as I picked her up.

She stretched a little and purred as we took a tour of the apartment and looked outside to see if there were any paw prints in the flour that dusted my patio floor.

Not a one.

"I suppose you're going to need a name," I said.

She blinked again and began to make tiny biscuits on the arm that cradled her.

"Patches. No, that's not it. Annie . . . because you're an orphan? No. How about Callie?"

She yawned again.

"You have a point. That's a bit on the nose."

The cat with no name wanted down, which had me humming "A Horse with No Name." I even sang a verse about living in an apartment with a cat with no name. She toddled over to her food bowl, and I broke off mid-verse.

What are you doing, Stella? You absolutely cannot give this cat a name, much less sing songs about her.

I couldn't get attached to this cat. Nor to anyone—at least, not before I'd thoroughly vetted them. I wasn't going to go through betrayal again. I'd had enough of that, thank you very much. Between my parents and then Ken, I didn't have it in me to trust again.

With a sigh of resignation, I petted the kitten once more and headed out the door to check around the neighborhood whether anyone had seen a mother cat or kittens.

Maybe someone was looking for a kitten, and I could be an agent for the universal cat-distribution system.

I surveyed neighbors in the other two buildings of the complex first. No luck. Once back at my own unit, I paused in front of Malone's door.

Nope.

That would be a bad decision.

Upstairs, I got into a lengthy discussion with Mrs. Q, one that didn't have an end in sight. With absolutely no shame, I interrupted to ask her if she knew that Hulu had episodes of *Wheel of Fortune* that she could watch anytime she wanted. In less than an hour, Mrs. Q was signed up for Hulu, had a basic understanding of how to use streaming services on her smart TV, and was plopped down on her sofa shouting phrases at Pat Sajak.

I showed myself to the door.

No one else on the upper floor answered my knock, other than in the apartment directly above mine. When I heard someone taking down the chain, I felt a smidge of giddiness. Now I could find out who'd been listening to "All Too Well" on repeat.

A harried woman not much older than me opened the door.

"Hi, I'm Stella Stark from just below you and—"

Her brow furrowed. "Is Addie being too loud with her music again?"

"Well—"

Before I could finish my sentence, she turned and yelled, "Addie!"

"Oh, really. It's not a big deal," I said. "I'm mainly worried because someone's been playing the ten-minute version of 'All Too Well' on repeat and that suggests a breakup of epic proportions."

The woman sighed. "She had a crush on some boy who's now going out with her nemesis—at least, that's what she tells me. I'm April, by the way."

"Nice to meet you," I said just as she yelled, "Addison Amelia Trimble, get your happy self in here now or that phone will be mine."

Addie Trimble appeared in mere seconds, but the scowl on her face indicated she wasn't happy about it. "What?"

"This is our downstairs neighbor, Miss Stella, and she isn't keen on reliving the Eras Tour over and over and over again, which, as you will remember, is the reason why Mr. Turtleberry moved out of the apartment below us and into another unit altogether."

"Mom!"

"Don't 'Mom' me. Turn your music down. And apologize to Miss Stella."

She heaved the aggrieved sigh of teenagers everywhere before saying, "Sorry."

April cleared her throat.

The teen stood up straighter and adjusted her voice to something closer to contrite. "I apologize for playing my music so loudly."

Underneath the indignation lay mortification. I remembered that feeling only too well. Something about hormones meant life itself was embarrassing, much less mothers who made you apologize to strangers.

Maybe that empathy prodded me to say something to lighten the mood.

"Too bad you don't live above Mr. Malone. He hates Taylor Swift."

Her jaw dropped. "How? Why? But he's such a snack."

More like a whole damn meal, kid.

"Addison," April warned. "He's also old enough to be your father."

"Ew, gross, Mom. Why do you always have to go there?" She backed away from us disgusting adults, but then I remembered my real reason for being there.

"Are y'all missing a kitten, or have you seen any kittens or a mother cat around here?"

"No," April said at the same time Addie said, "Phillip's mom—they live over in building three—took a mother cat and kittens to a rescue society day before yesterday."

"Do you know which one?" I asked.

She shook her head. "I only heard him talking about it on the bus."

So my kitten really was an orphan.

"Well, thank you," I said. "And nice to meet you both."

April waited for Addie to disappear down the hall, then stepped out into the breezeway with me. "Does the guy downstairs really hate Taylor Swift?"

"That's what I'm told."

She frowned. "I mean, I could use some variety up here, but that's a shame. He's always seemed so nice."

He did seem . . . nice.

My conscience pricked. I shouldn't have said anything. Technically, I didn't have a confidentiality agreement with Trista, but I didn't need to get in the habit of hearsay. Why had I said anything?

Because you remember being an exposed nerve like that child and wanted her to redirect her emotions somewhere else, pretty much anywhere else.

I shrugged, not able to say something about how looks could be deceiving. Instead, I told the truth. "I shouldn't have said anything. And really, the music is no problem. I only hear it in the bathroom for some reason. She seems like a good kid."

April's shoulders lowered with relief. "Thank you for saying that. I've been so busy trying to make sure my youngest is getting the support he needs, I sometimes forget Addie isn't as self-sufficient as she would like for me to believe."

"What's happening with your youngest?"

"Oh, don't get me started. A school board member has canceled the after-school tutoring program that's been helping him catch up."

"The one for this district?"

"Yeah." She was about to say something else when a young boy, about ten, appeared at the door.

"Mom? I cleaned my room. Can I have the Wi-Fi password now?"

"You can't *have* it, but I'll come type it in for you." April gave me a weak smile and a little wave before returning to her apartment.

I had the oddest urge to offer something to her. She was so bedraggled, kinda like my mother had been back when we were a family. Single parenting had become so hard for my mom then that she'd passed me off to Nana.

But I had no idea what to do for April to make her life easier. Surely, her kids were too old to need babysitting. She didn't appear to need a petty personal assistant. Maybe the best thing I could do would be to leave her alone?

Once again downstairs, I paused outside Malone's door. Technically, I had no reason to ask him about cats and kittens if Addie's info was correct, but . . .

I knocked anyway.

After much fumbling and more time than was strictly necessary for opening a door, Malone appeared wearing those damned aviators. Did he wear them to bed?

"Change your mind about pizza?" he asked.

"No." My stomach growled. I'd had a granola bar after serving papers but had forgotten to eat anything more substantial. "Maybe."

He stepped back and gestured for me to enter his apartment.

"But that's not why I came by."

"Oh?"

I started to ask my standard cat questions, but he hadn't taken off his sunglasses. Inside. So instead I asked, "Your future so bright you gotta wear shades?"

He frowned, and I regretted my nosiness. Maybe there was a reason why he wore dark glasses. An eye injury, maybe. Why was it so important that I see his eyes anyway?

Because that adage about how eyes are a window to the soul held a great deal of truth. Being able to look into someone's eyes was part of how I gauged their truthfulness. Did they make eye contact? Maintain it? Look at the floor instead? Look from right to left?

"Forgive me," I said. "It's none of my business."

"Well," he said with a sigh. "If I want you to share . . . pizza with me, then I suppose I should take off my glasses."

"Only if you want to," I said, pulling out my phone. "What do you like? Plain cheese? Everything but the kitchen sink? A mighty meaty?"

That last one came out in a husky voice, and I willed my ears not to turn red. I was here to ask questions about a kitten. And apparently to get pizza. Not to make double entendres.

When I dared to look up, he was trying hard not to laugh.

"My safe word is 'anchovies.'" I waited a beat. "Anchovies."

He laughed out loud and took off his sunglasses, but he looked away from me. "Stark, you are a breath of fresh air. I'll give you my pizza order if you promise not to freak out."

"Freak out about what? You're obviously not a pirate. Otherwise, you'd have a patch."

He slowly turned to face me, and his eyes—one light blue and the other dark brown—met mine.

"Amazing." I sucked in a breath, mesmerized and, truth be told, not quite sure where to look. Not that long ago, I'd been flippant about signs from the universe, and here was a big one. The little hairs on the back of my neck stood up, and I told them to lie right back down because this was all a coincidence. Nothing more.

He arched an eyebrow—the one over his blue eye, to be exact.

"Seriously," I said. "Why would you hide your eyes? They're beautiful."

His shoulders sagged with relief. "Order that pizza, and maybe I'll tell you a story."

"Mighty meaty?" I asked, this time with quadruple entendre.

He grinned. "Why not?"

Oh, I could think of a few reasons not to get pizza with Malone. One, he was married. Two, he was married. Three, I really liked him, but he was married.

That said, if I knew more about him, then I might be more successful in future attempts to earn the rest of that $3,000.

I tapped on my phone. "While I'm ordering, let me ask the question I actually came to ask you."

"Which is?"

"Have you seen any kittens or a mother cat around the neighborhood?"

"No," he said with a frown. "Should I have?"

"Just wondering because I found a kitten on my patio."

"Cool!"

"I'm glad you feel that way. Would you like a kitten?"

He hesitated. "I'm going to steal one of your phrases and say 'yes, but no.' I don't think I'm going to be here long enough to get a pet."

It was on the tip of my tongue to ask if he planned to run off with his side chick, but I didn't want to tip my hand. Earlier, Mrs. Q had mentioned bringing her signature casserole to him, so I wasn't out of the petty game yet.

Malone, however, was proving tricky. I needed this fact-finding mission so I could formulate plans J, K, and L.

So what if I'd felt a pang of disappointment when he said he wasn't sticking around? No one ever did, and it would be best for me to get Malone out of this apartment complex before my hormones made me do something stupid.

Havisham had literally upped the ante with her bet; I didn't have the spare fifty dollars for a romp with Malone. Bless her for adding another incentive for doing the right thing.

Then again, if *I* were the one to end up playing the ten-minute version of "All Too Well" back-to-back-to-back, then that might provide logical consequences for Addie.

And for me.

Nope. You're not going to fall for it. This is strictly a fact-finding mission, Stella.

Chapter 12

"Hey, why don't we take this over to your place?"

I studied him and searched my gut once again. It told me he might've been a charming cheater, but he didn't mean me harm. If I'd thought he did, then I never would've stepped into his apartment. Even so, it never hurt to do a second gut check.

Also, I had a Taser hidden in the drawer of the coffee table. For reasons.

"Why my place?" I'd already decided my place was fine, but being a contrarian was fun.

"One, I don't have a table."

I looked around, and he sure didn't. "Odd."

"Stark, I'm not here for a long time; I'm here for a good time. Scratch that. I'm just here. Speaking of scratches, you have a kitten, and I would like to meet it."

"Fair. She's adorable. Maybe you'll decide you want to keep her after all."

"Unlikely," he said. "Also, I have a bottle of wine, but I don't have a corkscrew."

"What kind of operation are you running over here?"

"A very temporary one. Do you want the wine or not?"

"What kind?"

"Malbec."

Of course he had a Malbec, my favorite. "Yes, please."

The first thing Malone did upon entering my apartment was scoop up my kitten as though he'd never seen a kitten before. The second was to study the framed puzzle piece on the wall.

"Uh . . . Stark?"

"Yes?" I asked from the kitchen, where I was searching for the corkscrew.

"Why do you have a single puzzle piece on the wall?"

Looking at the tiny piece surrounded by a thick navy mat made me smile. "Wouldn't you like to know?"

"Yes. That's why I asked." He scratched underneath the kitten's chin, and she looked up at him with devotion.

"After you tell me your story, maybe I'll tell you one of mine."

Later, we sat at my small but sturdy Ikea table, full of pizza and warmly toasty from our wine. The kitten lay nestled in the crook of Malone's arm, sleeping without a care in the world.

"You promised me a story, I believe."

He sighed. "That I did."

He frowned at my puzzle piece, the only relief to unrelenting beige walls, but I could tell he was gathering his thoughts rather than crafting a lie. It felt as though he were deciding how much to share.

Feeling's mutual, Malone.

"Remember when you told me you'd just got out of a long relationship?" he finally asked.

"Yeah."

"Same."

I had a million questions, but the moment felt delicate. One misstep, and I might not learn more about Malone, and I wanted—nay, needed—to hear his side of the story.

For professional reasons, clearly.

He took a deep breath and then turned his unique eyes on me. "One day, out of nowhere, she told me she couldn't be with me anymore. Said she couldn't stand to look at my mismatched eyes."

Bile surged up my throat. How could Trista say such a thing to him!

Maybe my bullshit detector was irrevocably broken after all.

Maybe I was wrong about Trista, and she'd lied to me about the side chick. Now she wanted me to torment this man because his beautifully unique eyes didn't "match"?

Anger took up all the space in my brain, to the point that I almost missed what he said next: "So she gave me back the engagement ring. Said she didn't want to risk having children who had different-colored eyes."

Wait. The side chick was the long-term relationship?

And just like that I was firmly Team Trista again, but my thoughts swirled.

He looked at me expectantly.

"Malone, that's horrible."

He shrugged. "Better to find out before children were involved."

As if he didn't have children in his *marriage*.

Now I wanted to smack him.

But he also radiated hurt. He gently stroked the kitten's head, and I couldn't handle the cognitive dissonance of it all. Someone wasn't telling the truth, because neither Malone nor his actions matched Trista's description.

"What about you, Stark? Before you tell me about the puzzle piece, what about your relationship? Who did you kick to the curb?"

"Cute how you think I was the one doing the kicking."

His eyes traveled down my body, then met my gaze again. "What kind of idiot would dump a woman like you?"

His warm words were a balm to my wounded soul. Best I could tell, he meant them.

Unless, of course, he had sociopathic tendencies and was very much the asshole Trista had described. Thing was . . . I wanted to believe him.

Tears pricked, but I used the stare-at-the-ceiling-and-blink trick to keep them at bay.

"Hey, you don't have to tell me if you don't want to," he said.

I shook away any thoughts that would distract me from focusing on Malone. His reactions to my story would tell me a lot, so why not tell him?

Instead of telling my story, though, I found myself saying, "I don't even understand what you see in me."

He poured a little more wine for each of us. "You're kidding, right?"

"No," I said with a laugh. "I'm honestly not."

"I mean, sure, you're beautiful with curves for days, but you're also witty. You're philanthropic—"

I snorted.

"—very ladylike—"

Which made me snort again.

"—and I've always had a thing for brunettes. Beautiful smile, and the first day I met you, you were wearing that leather jacket over a tank top and looked like you'd just walked out of a rock video. Stunningly cool."

That's right. I *had* been wearing my leather jacket. Technically it had been a bit warm for that, but I'd almost left it at Nana's house. Wearing it was far easier than packing it by that point.

"Most of all, though," he said as he pointed to the framed puzzle piece, "you're intriguing."

"Now that's an adjective no one has ever used to describe me."

He shrugged. "Then they weren't looking hard enough."

"Maybe I should keep my story to myself. I'd hate to give up 'intriguing' within five minutes of having it used as a descriptor."

"Oh, I doubt that'll be a problem."

I hesitated. If I told him my origin story—i.e., how and why I'd taken that puzzle piece from Aunt Edna—would he catch on to my ultimate plans for him?

I needn't have worried. Once I got to the part about crawling around on the floor while pretending to look for the missing piece, he laughed out loud, startling the kitten. "Who knew you were such a vigilante for justice?"

Oh, Malone, you have no idea.

Just as I settled in, pleased with myself for making him laugh, he turned serious eyes on me. "But what about the idiot who dumped you?"

That night still felt too raw, an incident I hadn't fully processed because I didn't believe in processing anything. Memories and emotions went into the vault. No good ever came of sharing the darkest, most painful things, Nana had taught me that.

Something about Malone's sympathetic gaze had me mentally undoing the combination to that emotional safe. Maybe it was the contrast between his eyes or how gently he held the kitten. Maybe my emotional vault was full of hurts and threatening to burst. Maybe I was tired from hauling it around.

After a shaky breath, I told him the story I hadn't yet told anyone except Havisham and Salcedo. Even then, I gave them only snippets. "One night I came home from a stakeout with a bottle of champagne. My ex had bet me I couldn't serve papers on this guy, but I did. He'd—the ex, that is—been distant as of late, so I thought it would be nice to reconnect with a little celebration."

All those old feelings welled up. The dopamine hit that had come from puzzling out where my target was, serving the papers, the witty comeback in Spanish, the urge to drink champagne and make love . . .

"So I got home after midnight. Didn't turn on the lights because I wanted it to be a surprise. Stripped down to my birthday suit and slid into bed to surprise him . . ."

Malone's eyes dilated ever so slightly. His jaw worked with the effort it took not to interject. His gaze suggested he would've loved to have been in that bed waiting for me. At this point, I wished I could go back in time and put him there instead. Maybe trace that tattoo on his bicep—

"And?"

His question jarred me back to reality.

Focus, Stella.

"And when I slid into bed, there was another woman in my place. Literally. At first, I thought Ken was sleeping in the middle of the bed again. I reached for him. Just as the scent of vanilla suggested my mistake, my hand found a naked breast."

He winced.

"A younger, perkier breast on a younger, more svelte woman who had the audacity to not only be sleeping with my partner but also be doing so on my side of the bed."

"That's . . ."

"The sort of thing that only happens in books?" I swallowed more wine than I should've, but as raw as the memory still felt, I felt lighter for the confession.

"I was going to go with 'horrific.' 'Unfair.' 'Rage inducing.'"

"And mortifying."

"I don't see why *you* should be embarrassed."

"It's bad enough to have your longtime boyfriend cheat on you, but the true mortification comes from having ever trusted him in the first place. Even worse, we worked together. I put so much effort into the business and our home, and I don't have a share in any of it because I never officially married him. To top it all off, we financed the car in his name because my credit was so bad, and now he's being a jackass about signing the title over to me. I feel so . . . stupid."

"You aren't stupid. He's an asshole," Malone practically sputtered. "I have half a mind to *persuade* him to be more reasonable. With my fists."

"Only if you let me at the idiot who said those ridiculous things about your eyes."

He looked down, and I was sorry I'd brought it up.

The next few seconds stretched like an eon, but his hearty exhale told me he'd come to some kind of decision, one that blessedly brought his eyes up to meet mine. He held out his free hand, the one not attached to the arm that was still serving as a kitten bed. "How about if I run across your ex, then I get to punch him. If you run across my ex, you can punch her."

"Deal." I took his hand, then inclined my head toward the puzzle piece on the wall. "But I don't punch. What I do will be far worse."

His eyes widened. "I'm going to add 'terrifying' to my list of adjectives for you. I can't tell if I'm frightened or aroused or . . . yes."

I couldn't help but give him my scariest smile. "I use my powers for good. Mostly."

"Aroused. Definitely aroused. Are you sure we can't add some benefits to this pizza situation?"

I could've taken the kitten from the cradle of his arm and escorted him to my bedroom. Fun would've been had by all, but would I still love me tomorrow?

I sighed deeply. "Honestly? There's a part of me that would love to take you up on that offer, but . . ."

"But what?"

But you are married to another woman, a woman who has hired me to use my special set of skills to bring karma to your front door.

"One, I made a promise to myself. Two, we're both on the rebound. Three—by your own admission—you're leaving soon."

And are married.

"True," he said. "But we could work things out while being friends. With benefits."

I laughed out loud. "You are awfully persistent for someone who wouldn't let me see his eyes for days."

He gave me a sheepish grin. "Full disclosure: My eyes hadn't bothered me in years. After a particularly rough day of third grade, my grandmother spun me a story about how my eyes were magic. That gave me enough confidence to get through school. I must have been having a moment of insecurity after what Selena said. I'd seen you twice with the shades on, and I liked you so much I didn't want to ruin things."

"And how were we going to get the 'benefits' portion of the evening? What exactly was your plan?"

"Shock and awe you with my sexual prowess? By the time you saw my eyes, it would be too late. You'd be hooked."

That part I could, quite unfortunately, believe. "So, you were going to make love to me with your sunglasses on?"

He laughed. "When you say it like that, it sounds absurd."

"Because it is! They're beautiful eyes. Maybe they should've been part of your campaign from the outset."

He studied me. "Nah. I don't think it would've done me any good. You're a woman who knows what she wants, and I, unfortunately, am not it. The only benefit with the pizza will be kitten cuddles."

Sweet Christmas, what was it about a man who could so gracefully take no for an answer that made me want to jump his bones?

In order to keep from acting on that impulse, I lifted my glass in a toast. "To kitten cuddles."

He sighed. "To kitten cuddles. Sadly, I think I've got it worse for you now than before."

"Oh?"

"I'm definitely more intrigued than I was before."

I put on my best *Mona Lisa* smile. "Flattery will get you nowhere, Malone."

"That's a crying shame, Stark."

Chapter 13

Monday morning found me in Trista's well-appointed living room. Her former neighbor had contracted me for an act of pettiness. Usually, I dealt only in photos or videos, but when Trista mentioned that the target lived across the street from her, I suggested a front-row seat might be better.

Or maybe I wanted to show off a little for Trista before showing her the pictures and video of a less-than-miserable Malone. It rankled to have not been able to devise some karmic misery for him, but he had yet to experience Mrs. Q's casserole. I had that going for me.

For now, however, it was all about taking care of Denise, Trista's neighbor. She sat on the edge of an upholstered chair, wringing a napkin and looking older than her fifty-two years. Dark shadows sat under her eyes, and frown lines creased her brow and bracketed her mouth. She, too, was a new member of the Jilted-for-a-Younger-Woman Club.

"And you're sure he'll look at the front yard as he's leaving?" she asked.

"Pretty sure he'll notice," I said as I took in the yard across the street. A large banner in the middle of a sea of plastic flamingos read **Sixty is the new forty**. I had to pat myself on the back for doubling down on the flamingos. Sure, sixty would've sufficed. Maybe sixty-two to be strictly accurate, but there was just something about a hundred and twenty plastic flamingos that really added a je ne sais quoi to the whole situation.

"You'd be surprised at what he doesn't notice," Denise muttered. She'd begun to shred the napkin rather than simply twist it.

"Patience, Denise," I said. "Neither your husband nor his housemate leave the house before eight."

"Oh, look! She's leaving first today," Trista said as a silver Mercedes exited the garage at exactly seven thirty. The car rolled down the driveway and into the street but then jerked to a stop in front of the house.

Denise made a strangled sound, then covered her mouth, her eyes wide. If she scooted any more to the edge of her chair, she would land on the floor.

"Let's see how observant she is," I said.

Sure enough, she put the Mercedes in park and walked out into the yard, staring at the banner. She picked her way around the flamingos and approached the front door, where she rang the doorbell, hugged herself, and then rang again.

And again.

Mr. Dobbs finally appeared.

Trista, Denise, and I walked to the window to better see the angry gesticulating between the two.

"I should've popped some popcorn," Trista said.

Denise couldn't have stopped smiling if she'd tried. Her eyes danced, and her wrinkles had smoothed out. Now she looked younger than her fifty-two years. "It's far better than I'd imagined."

Her soon-to-be ex-husband was alternately waving wildly and making a pleading expression. His paramour shifted back on one leg, her arms crossed over her chest.

"And now for phase two," I said, hitting send on a text message.

The girlfriend didn't move, so I sent another. And another.

He continued talking, and finally she stood up straight and reached for her back pocket. The first text I'd sent simply said, He's sixty-two and, no, the divorce isn't final yet. The second said, He hasn't even filed. The third: Real talk? You can do better.

How had I found her cell phone number? I would love to say I'd used social engineering, a special private detective's database, or even some kind of hack, but no. Once I knew her name, I found her cell through LinkedIn.

Mr. Dobbs took a step toward her. She took a step back. His anger devolved into abject pleading—at least, if body language was any indicator. She, however, wasn't having any of it.

As she got back into her car and drove off, I sent a text to a different number. Mr. Dobbs stood in the middle of his driveway, arms akimbo. Finally, he walked over and kicked a flamingo, but it bounced back and hit his shin. He hopped on his good foot, and I could almost make out the four-letter words despite the street, yard, and window between us.

"And now for the pièce de résistance," I said, as he bent to tear flamingos out of the yard.

Both Trista and Denise looked to me. I pointed outside to a woman walking her dog. She approached the Dobbs house with brisk steps, her corgi struggling to keep up.

"Is that . . . ?" asked Denise.

"Oh yes." Trista laughed out loud, but the sound was closer to a bark. Probably because it'd been a while since she'd laughed.

We all looked out the window to the woman in question, who happened to be the vice president of the homeowners' association. At the edge of the lawn across the street, she stopped and pulled out her phone to take a picture. Mr. Dobbs was ripping up flamingos, often bringing up chunks of sod with them. His angry voice echoed off the house where we sat, but we couldn't make out the words.

Then he froze.

Once she'd taken a picture of the proceedings with her phone, she approached. Her corgi waddled over to a flamingo and hiked his leg to pee on it.

Dobbs's arms now flailed once again, his face practically purple. Finally, the woman flipped him off and went back to walking her dog.

Denise chuckled. Then giggled, then threw her head back and roared with laughter.

I couldn't help but smile at her unbridled joy.

Trista's smile now reached all the way to her eyes. I was grinning so wide that my cheeks hurt.

"I think this calls for mimosas," Trista said. "And then I'd love to know how you crafted this particular piece of karma."

As we sipped, I explained how some digging on Facebook and Nextdoor had revealed an argument between Dobbs and the woman in question, a woman who had once taken to both platforms to protest the $300 fee he'd had the HOA levy on her when she put up dinosaur lawn decorations to celebrate her son's coming home from the hospital after a grueling week of treatment.

Best I could tell from the social media exchanges, she'd lost the fight and paid the bill.

Her story might've been the reason I'd insisted on the full 120 flamingos.

And if you looked really closely, one little T. rex in their midst.

An hour later, Denise was still sporadically giggling when she handed me the rest of the payment. "Oh, this is the best money I've ever spent. Thank you."

"I have to say it was an absolute pleasure."

"Good. You know, I have another friend who might need your services."

"Send her my way," I said.

"I can't wait to see what you've done for me," Trista said.

"About that . . ."

She frowned but waited for Denise to leave before turning to ask, "Is there a problem?"

"He's not acting the way you described."

"Come on, let's have some champagne. Now that Denise is gone, no need to bother with the orange juice."

We reconvened around an antique café table in the breakfast room, and I outlined my idea about having him awakened at the butt crack of dawn to work for Habitat for Humanity.

"Oh, that's genius," she said. "He hates getting up one second earlier than he has to."

"Honestly, I expected him to cuss the volunteers out and then slam the door in their faces, but he didn't."

"Even better. He doesn't know a flathead screwdriver from a Phillips."

My unease heightened. Either Trista's glee was genuine, or she should be nominated for an Academy Award. This woman had been wronged, and she desperately needed to see her husband's comeuppance. I proceeded with caution. "I thought that, too, at first. But take a look at these pictures I took from my car."

Trista frowned at pictures of a smiling Malone. You could practically hear him whistling as he worked. Through the picture. "Is he smiling? Are those sweatpants he's wearing?"

"Yes and yes."

She leaned back and stared at the ceiling, blinking furiously again. She then looked forward but closed her eyes and took a series of even breaths. "Maybe the problem was me all along?" she said in a small voice.

"No, no," I said. "Here, just look at the video and tell me what you see. We'll get him yet. Don't you worry."

She sighed deeply but took my phone to study the first video. I looked away, but the memory of a shirtless Malone leaning against the doorjamb remained burned in my brain.

I heard the bang of the door on the video, and then Trista made a choking noise. "That's not my husband."

Chapter 14

Relief coursed through my system, sheer relief that I wasn't attracted to my client's husband. Only then did curiosity join the party, I'm ashamed to say.

"Then who is he?" I asked.

"I don't know." Trista sat back in her chair, her mouth an angry slash. "You're the private investigator. You tell me."

Oh, this wasn't good. I could refund her money, but I needed everything I'd made so far to get my student loans back on track. Time to shift into conciliation mode.

"Here's what I know: He's living where you said he would be. The first time I saw him, he wore a tailored suit, aviators, and drove a silver Lexus. The mailbox says 'Malone.' I even asked him point-blank if he was Blake Malone, and he said yes."

But he'd flinched.

Just a momentary hesitation when I'd said the full name, and then he had quickly said he preferred Malone.

"So someone who looks like your husband, answers to your husband's name, and drives your husband's car lives in an apartment owned by the family business. Why? And who is it?"

When Trista didn't answer, I looked over. She'd blanched, her eyes now wide.

"Trista?"

"What?"

"Any idea who this guy is?"

"Maybe." She sucked in a breath but didn't let it go.

I looked at her expectantly.

"Blake has a cousin. I've never met him, but I've seen pictures. The two do look eerily similar—especially from a distance."

"Wait. Does Blake have heterochromia?"

"What?"

"One eye is light blue, but the other is a dark brown."

"No. His eyes are both brown."

Further proof I hadn't been flirting shamelessly with a married man. "What about the cousin?"

She stood and began to pace. "I don't know. I told you I've never met him."

"It doesn't matter. If the man across the breezeway isn't your husband, then the next task is to find him."

"No."

"No?"

"I don't know." Her voice came out as a whisper. "I need to call my lawyer."

"I can help you find—"

"No, no."

I took a deep breath. "Then I'll refund your money."

"Just keep what I've already paid you," she said. "But if you wouldn't mind showing yourself to the door, there's a lot I have to do before the children get home."

"Can I help?"

Already on her feet, she shook her head.

I had been dismissed. Only now I had more questions than before.

My first stop was a petty project. One of my clients knew that her neighbor was stealing her packages off her porch. With a little help from the kitten, I had a package that would hopefully make them swear off porch piracy.

I walked to my client's door with a brisk efficiency and put down a box, one that my client already knew not to open. Then I took a picture, both as proof I'd done my part and as an Amazon delivery person might do. Since my client didn't have a doorbell cam, the next step would be to repeat the process until the porch piracy ceased.

When I got back into my car, my mind returned to my newest quandary: Who was that mysterious man with the mismatched eyes?

I could definitely try some new searches, but why not go straight to the source if I wanted to know who was impersonating my quarry?

Former quarry.

Once I arrived home, I knocked on Malone's door. He wasn't there. Neither was the Lexus.

If Finnegan's were open, I'd go ask Havisham and Salcedo their opinions on the whole mess, but it wasn't even noon. Calling or texting Havisham would be a very bad idea because she would either be waking up or busy running errands.

As for Salcedo? I couldn't be completely sure she wasn't in class.

Instead, I spent the rest of the day on paralegal homework and jury research for Attorney Lawless. The kitten took a nap in my lap most of that time. We were playing with the laser pointer when I heard Malone's voice in the breezeway.

I'd already opened the door before I realized my folly: Mrs. Q had brought down the casserole.

"Stella!" she said. "I was just telling Mr. Malone here that this was *your* idea."

Ho boy.

"Very thoughtful of you," Malone said. I couldn't see his eyes behind the aviators, but I knew they were dancing. "If you don't mind sharing your apartment, we could all eat together."

"Of course," I said, hoping my smile hadn't faltered at the thought of the bland, underspiced casserole of waxy vegetables and soggy Tater Tots.

Karma had found me, and it was hardly fair. How was I supposed to know I had been attempting petty revenge on the wrong person?

More importantly, how was I supposed to ask Malone who he really was with Mrs. Q around?

"Come on in," I said.

Mrs. Q entered carrying the casserole. How she'd managed to get down the steps with her hands full, I was afraid to ask.

"I'll be right over as soon as I change clothes," Malone said.

"Oh, is this your kitten?" Mrs. Q asked once she'd put the dish down on the table.

"Yep."

"What's his name?"

"It's a she, and she doesn't have a name yet."

Because she's not going to be my cat for very long. Naming animals meant keeping animals, even I knew that.

Note to self: Look up shelter hours for tomorrow.

I took three of my four plates from the cabinet in the kitchen and prayed I had enough clean silverware. "Want a cat, Mrs. Q? She'd be good company for you."

"No, dear. She'll probably outlive me, and that's not fair to her. No, you keep her. She'll be good company for *you.*"

Well played.

At this rate I was going to name the cat Hot Potato because no one wanted to keep her.

"Honey, I'm home," Malone sang as he entered the door I'd left unlocked for him.

My heart squeezed. All those years with Ken, and he'd never once made that joke.

Stop it, Stella. This man is not who he says he is.

But at least he wasn't a cheater.

That you know of.

To quell the arguments in my head, I took a bag of salad from the fridge and opened it with a bit too much force. Romaine shot up and then rained down like confetti.

"It's okay—we don't need a salad," Mrs. Q said. "There are vegetables in the casserole."

"Good point," I said as I picked up the lettuce that had flown all over the little kitchen. "I thought I'd be semi-fancy, but the universe had other plans."

"Hey, let me help you with that," Malone said as he bent to pick up lettuce from the floor. "Besides, I brought a bottle of wine. That can be our fancy."

"Thanks, Malone," I said. As his last name met my tongue, I remembered that I didn't know for sure he was a Malone. Probably? Maybe? A preliminary search between homework and jury research had shown that Blake Malone did, indeed, have a cousin of approximately the same age. More research showed that Blake's father and the cousin's father were twins, which might've explained why they looked so much alike.

The cousin even lived in California, which would explain why Malone had said he didn't plan to be here long. Oddly, I couldn't find a picture of the cousin anywhere, and if I couldn't find a picture of someone on Pedro Pascal's internet? That person worked very hard to make sure they couldn't be found.

Also, even if I'd found a picture, that wouldn't explain why he'd answered to Blake. I itched to know the answer to that question, but something told me not to have the discussion in front of Mrs. Q. He wouldn't be as forthcoming with her involved.

"Silverware?" he asked as he washed his hands.

I pointed toward the top drawer, then opened a cabinet and reached for stemless wineglasses. My kitchen was so tiny, Malone and I backed into each other. He grinned, but I must have been looking at him too speculatively because his smile faded and he mouthed, "What?"

I mouthed "Later" in response.

Soon we were seated at the table, and Malone poured wine for each of us. Mrs. Q ladled out casserole. Sadly. I would've definitely taken a smaller portion than what she gave me.

"Before we eat, how about a toast to neighbors?" Malone lifted his glass, and Mrs. Q and I did the same. He lifted the glass with his left hand. *So, a southpaw. Interesting.*

"To neighbors," he said.

"To neighbors!" we responded before clinking glasses.

My pulse thrummed in anticipation of what would happen when he took the first bite. He might not have been the man who claimed casseroles were cheating, but I had a healthy enough respect for schadenfreude that I couldn't wait to see his reaction.

It felt like forever before he took his first bite. It was all I could do to act casual and not stare at his fork on its way to his mouth.

"This is really delicious!"

My eyes snapped to his face, trying to gauge his expression. He might not be Blake Malone, but he was still a marvelous liar.

Mrs. Q preened. "I'm so glad you like it."

In confusion, I looked down at the uneaten gelatinous scoop on my plate. Had the casserole changed? Had I fallen into an alternate dimension where Blake Malone was nice and Mrs. Q's casserole was tasty?

I took a bite.

Nope.

Still bland. Veggies still waxy. Tots still soggy.

I forced my lips into a smile because the creator of my torture was watching me. "Delightful as always, Mrs. Q."

Now who's a lying liar who lies, Stella?

We ate in silence for a minute or so before Malone snapped his fingers. "Mrs. Quattlebaum, I hope you don't mind if I add some hot sauce. I totally forgot. My doctor said that it can help keep my blood pressure lower. Oh, and it adds antioxidants and revs up your metabolism, too. I hate to ask, but doctor's orders, you know?"

With that sheepish grin, the man could get away with anything.

"I had no idea," Mrs. Q said. "If it can do all that, then I would like to try some, too."

Stunned, I watched as Malone left the apartment and returned with a trio of hot sauces. No table, but he kept more than one kind of hot sauce?

While I was pondering that conundrum, he explained the properties of each sauce as well as possible health benefits but was sure not to oversell, saying that hot sauce was only one part of a healthy diet. Mrs. Q interjected from time to time with an "I declare" or a "What do you know?" but she was riveted to the discussion. Then she added a tiny drop to her casserole.

She held the fork away from her mouth for two seconds before taking a bite. At the pop of flavor, she closed her eyes with a satisfied "Mmmm."

I'd been outmaneuvered again. Thank goodness Little Miss Petty's reputation was no longer on the line. Unfortunately, her heart was in danger of once again falling for a most unsuitable man.

When Mrs. Q looked down at her plate, he winked at me.

My heart fluttered.

I was a goner.

Chapter 15

The rest of supper passed in a surreal blur. Malone, who might not actually be Malone, charmed Mrs. Q. I had to admit the hot sauce did wonders for the casserole, as did the pitch-perfect screw-top sauvignon blanc Malone had brought over.

I was beginning to wonder if he was an android designed to lull women into a false sense of security. Hot sauce to salvage a bland meal, the perfect white wine already chilled—who was this man? If I hadn't already known he wasn't Blake I-don't-like-casseroles-or-talking-to-women-over-thirty-five Malone, then I would've figured it out by this meal alone.

Meanwhile, Mrs. Q was certainly enjoying herself.

"Oh, you," she said with a giggle as she listed to one side.

Huh. Her one glass of wine must've hit her hard, because her cheeks were rosy, too.

"Almost forgot. I also brought chocolate. Truffles, anyone?"

He had brought wine and chocolate. Definitely an android—designed by a woman, at that.

The universe was sorely tempting me, and now I didn't have the marriage thing as a barrier. The most galling part of all was that Salcedo, a mere babe in the woods, had been right, while I had been wrong. I could hang my hat on two things: One, the fact that he was lying about his identity. Two, that I couldn't afford to pay Havisham fifty bucks.

Even worse, my intuition suggested he had a really good reason for pretending to be someone he wasn't.

Probably because my intuition would like to get laid.

"I never turn down chocolate," Mrs. Q said, jarring me back to the present. My foot tapped underneath the table as a way to soften my impatience about the fact she was still with us. I had questions that needed to be answered. Wasn't it almost time for freaking *Wheel of Fortune*?

"Sometimes," Malone said, as he chose one with a caramel center, "the brain needs sugar to function."

"Truer words were never spoken." I selected a dark-chocolate truffle, and we each savored our mini desserts.

"What is it that you do, Mr. Malone?" Mrs. Q asked. "I hate that I've been living upstairs this whole time but don't know anything about you. I used to know all the neighbors."

"Just call me Malone," he said. "Mr. Malone is my father."

Mrs. Q collapsed into giggles disproportionate to the scale of the joke. Malone held up the bottle to top off her glass, but she put a sinewy hand over it and shook her head. He angled the bottle toward me, and I nodded to indicate he could pour away.

"As for what I do? That's classified, and if I told you, I'm afraid I'd have to kill you." He softened the sentence with a lopsided smile, and I had to mentally tip my hat at his deft use of humor to evade the question.

He wouldn't be so lucky with me once I got him alone.

I was about to lay the groundwork for my inquisition, the threat to my life notwithstanding, when Mrs. Q's expression changed abruptly. She belched, then put a hand over her mouth.

"Goodness, Stella, darling, could you help me upstairs? The room is spinning."

"Absolutely." I frowned. She couldn't be feeling well if she'd just asked for help.

"Are you okay, Mrs. Q?" asked Malone, his brow furrowed with concern. I loved that he'd picked up her nickname just from listening to me address her.

"I'm doing a little too well," she said, her words ever so slightly slurred. "This has been so much fun, and I hope you won't hold it against me that I'm such a lightweight. I'm afraid being old and taking eleventy billion medications means you become a party pooper."

"Not at all," Malone said. "It'll give me a chance to do the dishes."

And he does dishes. Of course he does dishes. The universe hates me.

With me to steady her, Mrs. Q climbed the steps quicker than her usual pace, but it was still a slow-motion struggle. Once we reached the top of the stairs, it took her three tries to get the key in the lock because she kept swaying. The whole experience reminded me of college. I'd often been the "responsible one" who got her friends home and safely tucked into bed.

Once we were finally inside, Mrs. Q said, "Oh, Stella, I'm so sorry I harshed your mella . . . er, mellow." She giggled at her own rhyme. "I know better than to have a glass of wine. Bad enough with some of my medication, but I must've forgotten to eat lunch today and—"

She belched loudly.

I tensed, ready to race her to the bathroom, but she leaned back into the couch, where she'd plopped, and looked relieved rather than green. At least I wouldn't have to hold her hair since she kept it cut short?

"Would you like for me to help you to bed?" I asked.

"That would be lovely," she said with a slur as I helped her to her feet. "And then I'm going to need you to grab a stack of Bibles from the bookshelf over there and swear upon them that you won't tell my children that their mother got inebriated. Especially not on one glass of wine. And you can't tell them I skipped lunch, either. I didn't do it on purpose. Sometimes the days run into each other. Hours run into each other. It's dreadfully dull being old and alone, Stella."

By the time she finished this cautionary tale, we'd reached her bedroom at the end of the hall.

"But you," she said, while trying to point at me but actually pointing more toward the closet behind me. "You should go back down there and kiss that nice young man. Wine, chocolate, and he's doing the dishes? He's a handsome one. And funny. That's a keeper if I've ever seen one."

"So it would seem," I said with a sigh.

She frowned at my lack of enthusiasm. "What's wrong with you young women today?"

"I'm not sure I want another relationship so soon, Mrs. Q."

She grimaced as I sat her on the edge of the bed, still swaying while I tried to remove her shoes. I wasn't surprised to find she was wearing knee-high stockings with her slip-on sneakers. Where did one even buy knee-highs these days? And didn't they defeat the purpose of having shoes you could step into?

"Bah. No one is ever ready for a relationship." She tilted her head, considering. "No one's ever ready for one to end, either."

"My last boyfriend was definitely ready to end ours," I said.

She blew a raspberry at me and fell on her side so hard I was afraid she might wake up with a bruise. At least she'd fallen on her bed? "Everyone needs relationships. You're right to be choosy, but you're going to have to put yourself out there eventually. In the meantime, surround yourself with good friends."

I thought of Havisham and Salcedo. "That's sound advice."

"You're damn right it is! If I haven't figured some things out by now, then I'm never going to. I should've had more girlfriends . . . friend girls . . . oh, you know what I mean. Harold was so jealous of anyone who took my attention away from him. Then what friends I had started moving away, but we didn't have money for me to take trips to see them. And people didn't do that anyway, not like today's young people, gallivanting all over creation at the drop of a hat. It wasn't like that . . ."

She kept talking, her eyes closed, and I let her chatter while I went to the kitchen to get a glass of water for her. She didn't notice that I'd left, much less that I'd returned.

"By the time I started looking up my old friends on Facebook, half of them had had the audacity to die on me. You have no idea how weird it is to have people you know dropping like flies. In your mind, you still see them as they were in their thirties, or maybe even as teenagers. It's . . . well, it's disconcerting, Stella. When the philosophers say life is short, they aren't lying."

How I understood all this, I'll never know, because the slurring became progressively worse. I scrutinized Mrs. Q for any signs of a stroke, but no, she moved one hand and then the other, both sides of her face animated as she spoke.

"Maybe not philosophers. Aren't they the ones who said God was dead?"

"That was only Nietzsche."

She scoffed. "I'd love to hear from him now, see what he thinks. I bet he's had a nice long chat with the God he thought was dead. But anyway, what I'm trying to say is not to waste time like I did. Wasted it with Harold. Wasted it with my children. One minute they were bugging the snot out of me for sugary cereals or cheaply made toys, and the next thing I knew, they'd moved out and were too busy to call. All very 'Cat's in the Cradle,' you know."

She paused for a breath, and I bit my tongue to keep from giving a "Well, actually . . ." response about how Nietzsche only meant that the role of religion in the Western world had declined. She didn't care. She wouldn't remember it. Sometimes it did a person good to have something to be indignant about.

"Oh, the room is spinning, but it's not so bad. Kinda fun. Like the Tilt-A-Whirl. Feels like that time I let Harold talk me into three Old-Fashioneds. Whew, I was younger then."

I had almost sneaked out of the room when she said, "Oh, Harold. That man could curl my toes."

I backed up another step. Definitely didn't want to know more about Harold's toe-curling skills.

"I put a glass of water for you on the nightstand, Mrs. Q. Need anything else?"

"No, dear. I'm good. Now you go downstairs and make hay while the sun is still shining."

"I think I'll leave my field fallow, Mrs. Q."

She blew another raspberry but then sat up suddenly. Or tried to.

I rushed over to make sure she stayed in her bed, and she grabbed my hand.

"Stella, darling, there's a book on the shelf by the door. I want you to read it."

So help me, if she tried to get me to read *Men Are from Mars, Women Are from Venus*, I would leave this apartment and never come back. I had been nine or ten years old when Mom brought home that drivel. Even so, I braced myself for her eventual answer. "What book is that, Mrs. Q?"

"*Daring Greatly* by Brené Brown."

"Okay, I'll pick it up," I said.

She squeezed my hand, then held on when I moved to let go. "Promise you'll read it."

"I will," I said, confident she would never remember her drunken epiphany.

She released my hand and lay back on her bed. I tiptoed down the hall and to the door. Sure enough, I found a dog-eared copy of the book on the shelf by the door. A casual page flip revealed sentences she'd highlighted and notes in the margin. Despite my cynical tendencies, I was touched she would lend me a book she obviously esteemed so highly.

Down the steps I went, thinking about how Mrs. Q really needed to live in a place without stairs and also how much of my life I'd already wasted on Ken. I shoved those second thoughts away because there wasn't anything I could do about that now.

When I entered my apartment, the entire kitchen had been tidied and the dishwasher hummed. Malone sat on my love seat, reading one of my Nora Roberts books with the kitten in his lap. He looked awfully at home for someone who swore he was only in town temporarily.

When he looked up, I said, "Person who is not Blake Malone, we need to talk."

Chapter 16

His smile disappeared, but he recovered quickly. "Oh, no good has ever come from that sentence. And here I was hoping you'd decided to discuss the benefits package."

"Nope. I want to know why you're living in Blake Malone's apartment and answering to his name," I said as I tossed Mrs. Q's book on the small table by my door.

He froze, and the kitten looked up at him expectantly. "Who says I'm not Blake Malone?"

"His wife."

He relaxed, absently scratching between the kitten's ears. "Well, I suppose she would know."

One of a private investigator's best tools, one I've had to cultivate in spite of my nature, is patience. Often, if one waits, the other person will fill the silence with just the information you were looking for.

After two excruciatingly long minutes, it became clear Malone was not one of those people.

I took one of the dinette chairs and turned it around so I could straddle the chair and lean my arms on the back while I stared at him. Intently.

He had reopened the Nora Roberts. Without looking up, he said, "That strategy isn't going to work."

"Stubbornness," "pettiness," and "spite" were all ugly words often used to describe women who were merely persistent; I had been blessed with all three.

"Seriously, I couldn't tell you if I wanted to," he said.

Waiting made me itch from the inside out, but I maintained my position and exuded a calm demeanor that was the very antithesis of how I really felt.

He had yet to turn a page, and the book was one of my favorites, *Midnight Bayou*, so I knew he was only pretending to read.

With a sigh of exasperation, he closed the book and met my gaze. "Look, it's complicated."

"Then simplify it for me, Artist Formerly Known as Malone."

"I am Malone."

"Well, you're not Blake."

"Thank God!" he said with so much feeling that my kitten looked up at him in disgust and then scampered off to find a seat that wouldn't move so much or make loud noises.

I pounced. "So you know him. I'm guessing you're the mysterious California cousin."

"Yes," he said through gritted teeth. "I am his cousin. Unfortunately."

One theory confirmed. "And you don't like him, but you're pretending to be him?"

He sighed. "It's complicated."

"So you say, but this isn't a Facebook post, so you're going to have to do better than that, Malone. Why are you pretending to be your cousin?"

"I'm *not.* I'm just not disabusing anyone of the notion that I'm him. When I said I couldn't tell Mrs. Q about the job I'm doing, that wasn't a lie per se."

"Well, I'm not Mrs. Q. Call me old-fashioned, but if you're willing to share your body, then I think you should also be willing to share your secrets."

He looked down to where the kitten had returned to sit at his feet because she couldn't resist him any more than I could. She gazed up at him with blinking adoration. She might follow him home whether he wanted her to or not. After what felt like an eternity, he muttered, "I knew you were going to be trouble."

"What did you say?"

His eyes met mine. "I knew it would be trouble to have a private investigator living across the breezeway from me."

"So you looked me up?"

"Of course I looked you up. I researched everyone in this apartment complex." He pressed his lips together before he could say more, but he'd already given up valuable information with that one sentence: Whatever he did for a living was very similar to what I did, because the first thing I had done before moving in was take a look at who my neighbors would be. Informally, of course.

"Are you a private investigator?"

"Not exactly."

"What do you mean 'not exactly'? Either you are or you aren't. Which is it?"

After a pause, he said, "That casserole sure was atrocious."

"Hot sauce was genius, by the way."

"Thanks."

"Also, you're not changing the subject that easily."

He took in a deep breath and expelled it while setting his shoulders. "I've already told you more than I should have. I can't tell you anything else. I *won't* tell you anything else."

My eyebrow arched.

Much like the Mounties, I always got my man.

"I'm sworn to secrecy. You couldn't even torture it out of me." The corners of his mouth twitched.

"Who said anything about torture? How about a little quid pro quo."

He leaned forward. "I'm listening."

"Maybe I put benefits back on the table . . ."

"I think that's extortion."

"No money will change hands. Besides, this isn't a spy movie. The stakes are relatively small, but I don't like loose ends. Blake Malone is a loose end, and I have a feeling his wife will be calling me sooner or later asking for help. I also think you know where he is."

"Honestly, I don't. Wish I did."

"I think we need to make this conversation more intimate." Slowly, I rose from my chair. "May I sit in your lap, Malone?"

"Please." The word came out choked.

I slid into his lap and then placed a hand on his face and felt his jaw tense. I rubbed my thumb lightly over his bottom lip. "There. That's better for an intimate conversation like this, isn't it?"

"Uh-huh." His hands clamped down on the sofa cushion.

I chuckled. "What? Now you don't want to touch me?"

"Oh, I want to touch you very badly, but I'm not going to participate in my own honey trap."

"Fine by me." I framed his handsome face with both hands. My breath hitched. This was a bad idea, a very bad idea.

But now it was also about the principle of the thing: Malone had information I needed, and I aimed to have it.

In the back of my mind, I also wanted to prove to myself that I still had what it took to beguile a man. Soft Hands had called me a saggy-ass bitch with such disdain. Months earlier, Ken had said I was getting too old to play the honeypot, but . . . what did he know? I was almost forty—not dead.

Slowly, I moved in for the kiss, gratified by Malone's quick breaths. At the moment he surrendered and leaned in to kiss me, I turned my head so his lips grazed the corner of my mouth. He graced me with a gratifying groan. I kissed along his jawline until I whispered in his ear, "In all seriousness, I will stop if you want me to. Despite the fact you were the one to first mention benefits, I'm going to need some enthusiastic consent to continue."

"Oh, I'm on board with the kissing," he said, his voice rumbling through me. "But you're not getting any answers out of me."

I sat back to gaze into his eyes. "Either way, I'll have fun trying."

"You were wrong," he said. "This *is* torture."

I wrapped my arms around his neck and began to move in for the kiss. "For you, maybe."

His lips parted ever so slightly.

The minute my lips met his, electricity shot through my each and every nerve. We sat like that for seconds that felt like hours, long enough for me to breathe in his distinctive scent beneath the vanilla bourbon and spice cologne. I groaned in spite of myself, and he deepened the kiss, his hands leaving the cushions to pull me closer.

I should've been asking him questions, but I wasn't done tasting him, feeling him, reveling in his reaction to me. His beard rasped against my face, but I didn't care. His thumb twitched respectfully on my rib cage just under my bra band, and an impatience for more burbled through me.

Sabbatical, Stella!

I broke up our kiss. "What's your job?"

He kissed a spot behind my ear. "I can't tell you."

"I don't believe it's *that* classified."

"No, it's so unsexy, you'll kick me out immediately."

"Try me."

"Forensic accountant."

I rewarded him—and myself—with another kiss. When I finally came up for air this time, I asked, "Why are you pretending to be Blake Malone?"

Gently placing me on the sofa beside him, he sighed. "And here I was hoping you were kissing me for me."

"I am, but I also want information. It's called multitasking, Malone."

He studied me. "I'll tell you everything I can if you'll accept the benefit package."

My turn to hesitate. Oh, I had no problem kissing him, but I couldn't date him.

It wouldn't be dating, *now would it?*

"You drive a hard bargain, Malone."

"Not really," he said. "Seems to me it's win-win. You get your answers . . . I get you . . . Fun will be had by all . . ."

"Malone—"

"Going once!"

"Seriously—"

"Going twice . . ."

"Okay, okay. Friends with benefits." I extended my hand.

"Stark, don't you think that this sort of arrangement should be sealed with a kiss?"

I waited for him to advance on me, but instead he pointed to his mouth to signify I should make the first move.

Ah, so it was going to be like that, was it?

I considered, taking my time to look into his eyes, gauging the difference between chilly blue and warm brown. Slowly, exquisitely, I leaned in to give him the lightest, chastest of kisses before asking in a low whisper, "What's your first name?"

He groaned. "Can't we leave some mystique to this relationship?"

"Nope."

"My first name is Tiberius. My father is a huge *Star Trek* fan."

That answered why he preferred to go by Malone. Middle school must've been hell with a name like that. I gave him a long, tender kiss for his past pain and suffering.

When we came up for air this time, he said, "Woman, I will give you my Social Security number, date of birth, and mother's maiden name if you will get naked with me right now."

With information like that, I could find out anything and everything I'd ever wanted to know about him, and he knew it. My old friend, confidence, warmed me from the inside out. I couldn't have quit grinning if I'd tried.

Slowly, I stood, knowing that anticipation was the key to all good things in life. I took the hem of my shirt and raised it ever so slightly, looking at him expectantly.

"January twenty-fifth, nineteen eighty-one."

Over my head went my shirt, to reveal a lacy concoction of a bra. My subconscious had known I would eventually cave to Malone's appeal. I loved that about my subconscious.

"Mother's maiden name: Franklin."

With a languid grace I had learned from a former client who was an exotic dancer, I maintained eye contact while unhooking my bra in the back and then holding my arm over my boobs so the straps fell but the cups remained.

"This is happening." Malone pinched himself. "This is really happening."

I arched a brow.

"Okay, okay. Five four six—"

Someone banged on my apartment door.

Chapter 17

Malone and I froze.

"We're going to ignore that," I whispered.

"Great idea," he whispered back. "Where were we?"

"Your Social Security number."

"Right, right. Five four six—"

"Stella, open up now. I know you're in there."

I flinched at the sound of that voice. The Douchecanoe had found me once again.

"The ex?" Malone asked, one eye fire and the other ice.

I nodded, and he jumped up from the couch. I was gratified to see the tent in his pants. Too old to be a honeypot, my not-so-decrepit ass!

But my joy was short-lived as I pieced together the gravity of the situation in light of our previous handshake agreement. "Malone, don't!"

"Just a talk, man to man," he said, even though the set of his jaw suggested otherwise.

As I scrambled to hook my bra and throw my shirt back on, several things happened all at once: Malone opened the door. Ken took one step in. Malone punched him. Ken fell backward into the breezeway. Malone slammed the door before turning to me. "Wait. Why is your shirt back on? You're not getting the rest of my social until you are as naked as the day you were born."

"I can't believe you just . . ."

"We shook on it, Stark. I take my obligations very seriously."

My God, that's so hot.

A rage-filled roar came from the other side of the door. "Open up now or I'm calling the police!"

"Now you've done it," I said as I walked to the door, trying not to look at the bulge in his pants.

I opened the door but blocked entry. "What do you want?"

Ken worked his jaw back and forth, and my emotions fluctuated between giddiness that Malone had socked him and disappointment he hadn't busted Ken's nose.

"I need the flash drive that's also a voice recorder."

"I don't have it."

"You have to have it," he said. "I can't find it anywhere."

I leaned back and crossed my arms over my chest. "My days of finding things for you are over. If you've lost it, then *you* put it in the wrong place. I took nothing that wasn't mine."

"Except the car."

"The car is mine. I've made all the payments."

He didn't argue with me for once.

And he wasn't wearing his wedding ring.

"You're looking good, Stel," he said in his cajoling tone. Was there already trouble in paradise? Was he really hitting on me after getting punched in the face? He had to be some kind of confidence incubus. He'd taken all mine, and now he had a surplus he didn't deserve.

I said nothing, a trick I'd learned, quite ironically, from him.

"Already got a new boyfriend?"

Malone now stood behind me, and I was glad for his presence, especially when he grabbed the kitten before she could run out the door.

"And a cat?"

If I continued to stare at him and blink, he would eventually spill his real reason for being there, this I knew.

"Listen, things haven't worked out with Eloise. It was all a big mistake. It's time for you to come home."

Still I stared. Sly sentence construction was doing a lot of work for Ken. *Things* didn't work out. *It* was a mistake. Not that *he* had made a mistake, and because he wasn't admitting his mistake, then there was no need for forgiveness. How convenient for him!

"No thank you. I'm good," I said as I started to close the door.

He caught the door with his shoe. "Why don't you come out here so we can talk without an audience?"

"No."

"Stella, be reasonable," he wheedled.

"Get your foot out of the way before I slam this door on it," I said. "And don't bother coming back. I didn't give you my address for a reason."

"Jeez, you don't have to be a bitch about it."

Once again, Malone moved with the stealth and speed of a cheetah. Before I could formulate a reply, he'd pressed the kitten into my arms and brushed past me to take Ken by his collar and shove him against the opposite wall.

"I'm going to use small words in short sentences so you can understand," he said. "'No' means 'no.' The lady said to leave. Don't come back. Insult her again, and you will regret it."

"Whoa, calm down, big fella," Ken wheezed. I was familiar with his "just one of the guys" routine, but I didn't think it was going to work as well as he hoped. "Really got you by the balls, doesn't she? I mean, it's a sweet piece of ass, but she's still a—"

Malone's fist connected with Ken's nose, proving that wishes sometimes came true. Ken cried out in pain and fell to the ground.

As much as I liked to consider myself a liberated, independent woman, I had to admit I took great joy in having someone defend me.

"Know what? You need to go home and thank your lucky stars for the years you were privileged enough to live with this lady," Malone said. "Because memories are all you're getting."

"Can I at least get a towel and some ice?" asked Ken from behind his blood-soaked hand.

"No," Malone and I said in unison.

"You're still not getting the title to the car," he said, struggling to get to his feet.

"Whatever," I muttered, my spirits deflated.

Ten minutes later, the mood had been effectively killed. Why? Because I knew cuts on the hand from punches to the nose or mouth could cause gnarly bacterial infections. The minute I had seen the cut on Malone's fist, I'd dragged him to the bathroom and commenced first aid.

Sexy nurse, I was not. More like Nurse Ratched.

"Stark, believe it or not, this isn't the first time I've punched someone," he protested.

"Well, it was very sweet of you, but please don't do it again. My father once—"

I stopped.

"Your father what?"

I took a deep breath. "One of my few memories of my father is when he punched a guy in a bar fight. His hand got severely infected, and we had to take him to the emergency room. They ended up keeping him in the hospital for almost a week with an antibiotic IV drip."

"That must've been awful."

And that's not even the half of it.

"Yeah, well, if you knew him, then you'd know that was a very logical consequence for him." My own bitterness startled me, but it shouldn't have. Discussing my father always seemed to bring that emotion out of me.

Malone studied me, wise enough to say nothing.

"Thank you, though," I said.

"It was my pleasure."

"I mean, I can defend myself, you know."

"Oh, I know. I saw the video where you did that impressive leg sweep," Malone said.

I looked away, my cheeks warm.

"Hey, Stark."

I forced myself to meet his gaze.

"Just because you *can* defend yourself doesn't mean you have to," he said. "At least, not all the time."

His good hand cupped my cheek, and I leaned into his warm touch.

I bit my lip, considering a return to where we'd left off. After all, I had only the first three digits of his social. I didn't need them, but I hated to leave things unfinished.

Unfortunately, my phone wouldn't stop buzzing. Satisfied that I'd cleaned up Malone's cuts as best I could, I washed my hands, then checked my phone. Havisham was having a flying duck fit because I had clients to see.

Of course, she'd understand if I told her what Malone and I were up to.

But now that the heat of the moment had cooled, I wasn't sure I wanted to go down that road.

A coward? Maybe.

"I gotta go," I said with a deep sigh. "Mulligan on cashing in my benefits?"

His eyes were flashing, smoldering, or both. "I'm gonna hold you to it."

I followed him, intending to leave as he did. He paused at the tiny table by the door where I'd placed Mrs. Q's copy of *Daring Greatly*. "This is a really good book."

My insides froze. What was it I'd so blithely said about how my perfect dude wouldn't be afraid to read a self-help book?

"Mrs. Q suggested I read it."

He paused in the breezeway while I locked my apartment door.

"Thanks again," I said, suddenly feeling shy.

"There's nothing to thank me for," he said. "You just let me know when you're ready for that mulligan."

Chapter 18

After meeting with a few new clients and closing down Finnegan's, we went to the Waffle House, of course. We were engaged in one of my projects: sewing shut the flaps of several pairs of men's underwear.

"You did wash these, right?" Salcedo asked, her mouth pursed in a look of disgust.

"Twice. In hot water," I said. "Also, the quicker you stitch, the sooner we get this project done."

"This is disgusting. Some other man's underwear." Salcedo stopped sewing long enough to gape at Havisham, whose stitches were quick and precise. She was sewing three flaps to my one. "How do you do that?"

"I had to take home ec," Havisham said.

"What?"

"Home economics. Sew, clean, make sure you serve vegetables with meat."

"I probably should've had that class," the youngest among us said. "Mom had me taking four sciences, four maths, AP this and AP that. Now I struggle to sew on a button."

"Probably could've used that class myself," I said as I picked up the last of the underwear.

"Maybe if I'd taken more classes in math and science, I wouldn't still be working at a bar," Havisham said.

"Y'all using up two of my tables and now you're sewing on men's drawers, but you don't have any boyfriends," Betty said as she took the dishes from the booth behind me. "Y'all are some odd ducks."

"Well, we couldn't very well do this project at the table where we ate," I said. "Might get food on these freshly laundered briefs."

"Whatever," she said. "Y'all are weird."

I paused. Being called weird by a Waffle House waitress had to be a whole new level of strange. I didn't want to imagine some of the things Betty had seen.

But Betty also reminded me of our previous late-night conversation. "Salcedo, at the risk of failing your Bechdel Test, I need to get both of your opinions on something."

"What?" Salcedo asked at the same time Havisham said, "Shoot."

"So, you know how I was doing a job for Trista Malone?"

"The trophy wife who drinks cougar juice?" asked Havisham.

"Eh, yeah. Pretty sure there's a lot more to her than that, but that's a succinct description for now."

At this point I had to catch Salcedo up on everything that had happened, because she'd been busy with final exams and a couple of presentations. She listened intently. "So, the guy who you thought was her husband is not, in fact, her husband?"

"Yep."

"And you're attracted to him?"

"Almost did the deed right there in the living room with the cat watching."

"Stark. Too much detail," Havisham said with a snort.

"Or not enough," Salcedo countered.

"But then he punched out Ken, and I was worried about fight bite—"

"Worried about what?" asked Salcedo.

This necessitated a discussion of how nasty the human mouth was, proximity of the nose thereto, bacteria, gross hand infections, and so on.

"So you think he's hot?" asked Havisham, bringing the conversation to more pleasant topics.

"Understatement of the century."

"And he's not a cheater?"

"Doesn't appear to be."

She tilted her head to consider me, and her sum conclusion seemed to be that I was off my rocker. "Then where's the problem?"

"He's going back to California, so we're talking friends with benefits."

And pizza.

Heavens, just the thought of him made me smile.

Havisham snapped in front of my face to bring me back to reality. "And?"

"I think she's afraid she'll catch feelings," said Salcedo.

"Catch what? How does one catch feelings?" asked Havisham.

While Salcedo translated current slang into Boomer, I looked out the Waffle House window.

Correction: I attempted to look out the window, but the air-conditioning had to have been set at sixty, while the outside was a balmy eighty-five, so condensation prevented me from actually seeing out.

"But that's not the weirdest part," I said to no one in particular.

"What?" asked Havisham and Salcedo in unison.

"Remember how we were joking around about the universe?"

"I wasn't joking," muttered Havisham. Salcedo shot her a dirty look.

"Here's the kicker: He has one brown eye and one blue eye."

Salcedo's jaw dropped, and she laughed.

"And he mentioned that he's read this self-help book that the lady upstairs gave me."

"What book?" asked Havisham. Based on the straight line of her mouth, she wasn't as ready to buy into signs from the universe.

"*Daring Greatly* by Brené Brown."

"Oh, you should totally read that," Salcedo enthused.

"But what are the odds, right?"

"Eh, you have several other criteria he hasn't met, and I have yet to meet my cowboy billionaire philanthropist."

"You're right. It's all ridiculous," I said.

"Come on, what can it hurt?" Salcedo asked.

"I should just be alone."

"No one needs to stay alone forever. It goes against Maslow's Hierarchy of Needs." Salcedo tossed her last pair of underwear into the pile.

"I swear you are making some of this shit up," Havisham said.

"Ugh, no. It was in my psychology class."

"I do remember that one," I said.

Havisham said nothing. Silence hung among us long enough that I could hear Betty and Jasper squabbling about whose turn it was to clean the bathrooms. We all knew Betty was going to win the argument and leave the task to Jasper, but I couldn't grudge him his part in their evening entertainment.

"Havisham?"

She took a deep, ragged breath. "Listen, Stark. A month ago, maybe even a week ago, I would've agreed with you, but living alone isn't all it's cracked up to be."

"Fine. I'll keep the cat."

"Oh, I definitely think you need to keep the cat, but maybe be open to something more?"

"First of all, it hasn't been a year. Second, he told me he's leaving. If *he* were open to something more, don't you think he would've mentioned that? Third, I'm not entirely sure who he is beyond having the first name Tiberius and not being Blake."

"At least he hasn't promised you more than he's going to deliver?" Salcedo said in a small voice.

"Y'all aren't all that helpful," I said.

"Au contraire. We are helpful indeed. Where's the tally on the car fund?"

I checked the Notes app on my phone. "Well, I'm not getting the other fifteen hundred from Trista, but I have almost four thousand down with another three thousand to go. In . . . eleven days. And that's the other reason I can't sleep with him. I can't afford to pay Havisham fifty dollars."

She and Salcedo laughed. Salcedo looked up, the very devil in her eyes. "I'll spot you the fifty dollars if you'll spill the tea after you do the deed."

"It's the principle of the thing, Salcedo."

"Three thousand dollars is doable, Stark," Havisham said. "If I have to beat the bushes to find more patrons for you, I will, but let's see if we can avoid any other underwear-related jobs."

Once back at the Bel Air Apartments, I looked at Malone's windows. Dark. I considered knocking on his door. Didn't. Instead, I picked up Mrs. Q's book and had a seat on the couch. My kitten soon followed.

Mrs. Q had had the audacity to circle a chapter heading about how people can't go it alone. All her notes and highlights were for herself, but I felt reproached nonetheless. I rolled my eyes and kept reading. Eventually, I came across the chapter in which a man tells Brown that men suffer from shame, too. Even worse, according to this man, women couldn't handle it if a man expressed raw emotion despite saying that's what they wanted.

A lump formed in my throat as I thought about . . . my father. Did shame explain why he'd done the things he had? Or hadn't done the things he didn't do, as the case might be.

Nope. Putting those memories right back in the vault where they belonged.

Shame didn't excuse some of the things he'd said to me.

Unfortunately, being a child didn't absolve me from my part in the drama, either.

My kitten jumped into my lap and settled in the middle of my book like the world's cutest, fluffiest, most misshapen bookmark.

"It's very difficult to read through you," I said.

She purred.

"I suppose you want to be petted?"

If there had been a subtitle for our situation, it would've said "purring intensifies."

"How am I supposed to learn about embracing vulnerability and shame if there's a cat in the middle of my book?"

She rolled over on her back, baring her belly and blinking slowly at me.

That little, fuzzy belly called to me. I wanted desperately to feel her fur, but would she close her claws over my hand and bite me to form the world's cutest bear trap?

She arched her back and exposed more belly.

"Oh, so you're going to *show* me how to be vulnerable, huh?"

My only answer was more purring and tiny air biscuits. Tentatively, gently, I reached down to rub her belly, and it was as soft as I'd imagined. She did close her paws around me, but no claws.

"Look at you, my little queen of vulnerability. I'm gonna call you Brené Brown."

Wait. My queen? I was not going to keep this cat, much less elevate her to royal status.

I couldn't even finish the thought still believing it was true.

It was too late.

I'd named her. We were bound together for the duration, so there was no need to call the cat shelter.

At the mere thought of taking my sweet Brené Brown to a shelter, my heart hurt. I couldn't, and I wouldn't.

Unaware of my inner turmoil, she yawned before sliding out of my book and curling up to sleep on my lap. Trapped, I had no choice but to continue reading her namesake's book.

While I was brushing my teeth before bed, I got the phone call from Trista that I'd been half expecting. She didn't even bother with hello. "Did you mean it when you said you could find my husband?"

"Yes. Finding people who don't want to be found is one of the things I do," I said cautiously.

"Money's back on the table if you can find him in the next month and serve him with divorce papers."

"You're on," I said.

"I just want this all to be over," she said.

"Then I'll do my best to make it sooner rather than later."

We made arrangements for me to meet her the next morning.

Chapter 19

We met for coffee after she got the kids to school. I almost didn't recognize her at first. She wore her hair in a ponytail, had on no makeup, and wore yoga pants.

I sure hoped she'd started early on her plans to eat what she wanted and do what she liked, because it looked like she was going through it.

"How about I'll get the coffee?" I asked as she sat down beside me.

"Sure," she said, her eyes still distant, as though her mind were on something far away.

"What would you like?"

"Skinny cappuccino with—no. I'd like an iced white chocolate mocha."

"Coming up," I said. Nutritionists might disagree, but I felt it was important for Trista's long-term mental health that she do what she wanted to do. There'd be time to go back to skinny cappuccinos later, if she wanted to.

I brought over a double-chocolate muffin, too. She reached for it, jerked her hand back as if she'd been scalded, then delicately pinched off a little piece.

"You had them warm it up." Between the smile and the color in her cheeks, she looked like a new woman.

"It's the little things in life," I said.

Once again, I waited. Patience wasn't one of my better virtues, but I'd learned to fake it until I made it.

Finally, she spoke. "Can you really help me find my husband?"

"Before I was a fairy godmother of vengeance, I was a private detective, so yes. I should be able to help you find him."

"I can't afford to pay you right now," she said. "But I will find a way, even if I have to ask my parents to loan me the money, which I do not want to do."

"I'm going to guess Blake disappeared with a chunk of change?"

"All our investment accounts," she said with a sigh. "Most of the checking account. All our savings."

It wasn't even my money, but I still felt a punch to the gut. It was the injustice of it all, really. It never ceased to amaze me how shitty some people could be. The day I got used to it, I should probably go into another line of business. "I'm sorry. That's just . . ."

"Shitty?"

"Exactly the word I was thinking. Let's start at the beginning and go over the last time you saw him and what you do know."

I grilled her mercilessly, and she took it with the same stoic grace she probably showed her gynecologist during a pelvic exam.

"I need to serve him with papers as soon as possible so I can stop the hemorrhaging from our funds," she said, her brow furrowed. "He probably doesn't realize I know the extent of what he's done because he never shared financial information with me. I asked questions, yes, and the cagier he got, the more determined I became to do my own investigating. Fortunately, I have an account that *he* doesn't know about."

I arched an eyebrow. Good on Trista!

"I have no intention of hiding it, but a couple of years ago, I had a nightmare that he'd left us high and dry. I wanted to have something just in case."

"And 'just in case' has arrived," I murmured.

Unfortunately, Trista had no idea where her husband might be. He'd never admitted to having another girlfriend, but she suspected. She'd already checked the vacation home in Florida. A different private investigator had told her that he was hiding out at Bel Air Apartments, and she hadn't wanted to spook him while she was working things out with her lawyers. Then I brought her the video of my Malone.

After I left the Monday of the Flocking, she'd looked for Blake everywhere she could think of. She'd called him, only to hear the prerecorded apology about how his number was no longer in service. In short, she was desperate.

I reached across the table to grab her hand. "He can't hide forever."

I, however, could hide like a champ.

I may or may not have gone on a long surveillance trip. My official reasoning was that Attorney Lawless had called with a job, and I needed money. My unofficial reasoning? I was ticked with Malone.

Here we were ready to do the deed, and then he ghosted me.

Sure, sure. I was the one who'd left him on Monday night, but I was coming back. Surely he knew that. I got back late Monday night / early Tuesday morning, but he was gone before I woke up. I waited for him the rest of the day Tuesday. Nothing. When I got up early on Wednesday only to see his car wasn't there, I decided I'd wasted enough time mooning over him.

When Attorney Lawless called, I took the job.

Either Malone was wrapped up in business and would get back to me, or he'd already left for California. His leaving was a foregone conclusion, so there was no need for me to wait around the apartment and mope for him—especially not when I could make a cool hundred and fifty an hour working for Attorney Lawless.

So I hired Addie to take care of Brené Brown—the kitten, not the author, professor, podcaster, and shame researcher—and I loaded up the Corolla to go to scenic rural Alabama. Was it my first choice for a vacation? Absolutely not.

But then again, I wasn't on vacation.

Even worse? It required camping.

I could tolerate being stuck in a motor vehicle for hours on end better than your average person. As an only child, I'd learned to amuse myself at a very young age. No brothers and sisters for me. Three elementary schools in six years, so I didn't have the same attachment to my peers as many friends my age. My mother was often gone. Nana was exhausted, and Aunt Edna was, well, a battle-ax.

So, while on stakeout, I remembered the lessons of my youth. I sang songs, listened to audiobooks, dictated fan fiction, debated with myself. Whatever it took.

But camping?

I supposed the bathroom question was a bit easier with camping, since I could usually pop a squat without taking my eyes off my target, but it was still fraught with the possibility of bugbites or thorns or bears. I also had to slather on Skin So Soft to keep the mosquitoes away and keep vinegar and water on hand to get rid of the ants because camping meant sleeping on the ground. Thus I didn't do much sleeping. And the worst part was no campfire, which meant no s'mores. You can't have smoke and a fire when you're hiding out in the bushes. Especially not when you're in a wildlife-management area to avoid trespassing but technically it's not camping season, so you'd have to play dumb if caught.

Or, even worse, pretend to have a fondness for birdwatching in general and the red-cockaded woodpecker in particular.

TL;DR: I hate camping.

While sitting in the woods on the side of a mountain in Alabama, I attempted to ascertain whether a mother had transported her kids over state lines in violation of a custody agreement. Normally, I would've also done some research for my other cases, but reception was nonexistent rather than spotty.

In fact, I thought I might lobby Attorney Lawless for a bonus for this particular job because I was surrounded by poison ivy. To date, I'd been one of those lucky individuals who didn't seem to be allergic to the vine, but if I ended up in a bathtub full of oatmeal followed by a liberal dousing of calamine, I would demand recompense.

Sadly, this wasn't the first time I'd found myself surveilling a dilapidated trailer in the hinterlands between Cedartown, Georgia, and Piedmont, Alabama. It was very much as I'd suspected: A number of people were coming and going—quite a few for a spot in the middle of nowhere. They also weren't staying very long. I could only conclude that our client's wife was shacking up with a drug dealer of some sort, probably meth.

Eventually, the mother emerged from the dingy trailer I'd been surveilling with her two children in tow. I snapped pictures that included the mailbox. It wouldn't be hard to pinpoint the exact location. Was it mere miles over the Georgia-Alabama state line? Yes. Did that still count as transporting children over state lines without the other parent's permission? Also yes. Did those children need to stay as far away from that trailer before it blew to high heaven? Most emphatic yes yet.

As I drove back to Marietta, I had to concede, however grudgingly, that at least my mother had never taken me to a meth lab. Skip's owner hadn't been a bad guy. He might've been a good stepdad. All these years I'd been resentful of how she'd left me at Nana's house, but looking through a telephoto lens at the shell-shocked expressions of children leaving a dilapidated trailer had left me with a new appreciation for the serenity of Nana's house. Aunt Edna wasn't the menace of my childhood she had once been.

Maybe my mother had been doing the best she could. After all, she was little more than a child herself when she had me.

But she'd said some things to me, things she couldn't erase by sending me articles about not fearing my fortieth birthday. Maybe she had feared *her* fortieth birthday, but I didn't fear mine.

Currently didn't feel too great about it, but I didn't fear it. One would probably have to have access to all one's emotions to fear something, and according to Brené Brown—the author, not the cat—I'd put up all kinds of emotional shields.

But remembering my self-help book reminded me that Malone had read it, and that brought up the interesting idea that the universe could be trying to tell me something about him.

If I stuck my fingers in my ears and sang "la la la" loudly enough, would the universe hush?

Or you could give Malone a chance since he's nothing like Ken or your father.

And how exactly did I know that? I'd known Ken for almost twenty years, and he'd managed to pull the rug out from under me. As for my father, he changed after marrying Mom. People changed all the time, so even if Malone were perfect right now, there were no guarantees he wouldn't become a person I didn't like.

A mosquito bit me, and I'd never been happier to be attacked by one of the bloodsuckers because at least it interrupted my thoughts.

Chapter 20

Friday afternoon I came back to the apartment complex after completing two other surveillance jobs, serving three sets of papers, and thoroughly avoiding Malone while I ruminated on our arrangement.

On the one hand, I'd already agreed. Instinct told me fun would indeed be had by all if I joined Malone for some hot monkey sex. On the other hand, best not to start something with Malone that he had no intention of finishing. I wished I could say I could be casual, but it didn't seem to be in my nature.

You could try casual. Other people seem to do just fine with one-night stands.

I was still arguing with myself as I walked up to the apartment building. Malone's patio door was open, as was his apartment door. My heart sank to the asphalt between my toes. Was he moving out already? Had I missed my chance?

A quick peek into his apartment showed Malone looking at his phone while swatting away bugs. It was an infestation of some kind. One of the bugs in question flew past me with a flutter of wings. Another landed on my arm.

A ladybug.

"Uh, Malone?"

"Not now, Houdini. I have a situation," he said without looking up.

The Houdini part stung, but that sting was quickly replaced with irritation. "Seems to me like the pot is calling the kettle black. And maybe if I had your number, I could've texted you to say I was on a job. Or, I don't know, you could've texted me, Criss Angel."

"Well, you couldn't leave fast enough on Monday night, so I took the opportunity to get some work in."

"What do you think I was doing?"

"Listen, Stark. I have a bit of a situation here, so can we schedule this argument for later?"

"Fine. Anything I can do to help?"

"I don't know. Are you an entomologist?" he asked.

"Huh?"

"A person who studies bugs."

I didn't care for this sarcastic Malone, although I had to admit I'd be irritated, too, if I had an infestation in my apartment.

When he swatted another bug away, I noticed he still had a bandage on his left hand. That made me feel terrible all over again. The man had punched someone on my behalf, and what had I done? Ghosted him.

"Listen," I said. "I'm sorry to have disappeared on you like that. I had work to do, but I should've left my phone number with you at least."

"That I could find if I wanted to," he said while frowning at his phone.

True. In my first round of investigating all Malones—but mostly Blake—I'd confirmed that my Malone worked as a forensic accountant for a cybersecurity company. No doubt he had his ways of finding out anything he wanted to know.

"You just wanted me to *give* you my number."

"Correct."

His tone might've been nonchalant, but I'd definitely wounded him. Even worse? He looked positively delicious. I'd never understood the hullabaloo about gray sweatpants until that very moment.

"Come on, Malone. Let me help you with this"—I waved my hand around—"situation, and then we can talk this over."

"Sure," he said, his voice still flat. "You're a PI. Tell me who sent that package."

As I reached for the box he'd pointed to, three or four ladybugs dive-bombed my face as if they were in *Top Gun* and buzzing my tower.

If you'd asked me before today whether I thought ladybugs were a problem, I would've said no. I would've said they were cute. Turned out a swarm of them was disconcerting.

I finally picked up the box that sat on Malone's recliner and felt inside gently. Nothing there. Even the outside didn't give a return address. Beside the box, however, was a note: "If you don't like Taylor Swift, then you deserve to be bugged by some ladies."

I laughed. I wasn't the only petty person in this apartment complex.

Malone shot me a dirty look. "It's not funny."

I swallowed any possible retorts. One, I didn't want to accidentally swallow a ladybug. Two, the whole situation was comedy gold, but Malone would need some time to come to that realization.

Ladybugs kept landing on his shirt, undercutting both his stern expression and his uber masculine hands-on-hips stance. One landed on his nose, but he kept his commitment to scowling at me.

Respect.

I drew my phone from my pocket and snapped a picture.

"Hey!"

"C'mon, Malone. You've gotta admit it's at least a little bit funny," I said while holding my thumb and forefinger close together. "They're ladybugs, not roaches or snakes or . . . deviant chinchillas."

The corners of his mouth twitched.

I almost had him.

"Could be ferrets or alligators or"—here I paused to genuinely shudder—"rats."

"Did you do this?"

"No."

But I may or may not have put the wheels in motion.

I was still weighing whether I wanted to admit my culpability when someone at the door cleared their throat dramatically. Addie, arms crossed over her chest in a sassy pose, skewered Malone with a stare and said "Look what you made me do" before flouncing upstairs.

"What was that all about?" Malone asked.

I pressed my lips together in the hopes of not laughing. Oh, I was not the true Little Miss Petty of Bel Air Apartments. All I could say to that was what she herself might: *Slay, queen, slay.*

After a few minutes of research, which consisted of alternately scrolling down my phone and gently swatting the bugs that insisted on flying around my face, I finally asked, "Do you have a vacuum?"

"No."

Of course he didn't have a vacuum. The man didn't have a kitchen table. Probably slept on a mattress on the floor like a frat boy who'd used his furniture allowance to buy beer.

"Do you have one?"

"Of course not. That was Ken's vacuum cleaner. I told myself I'd buy one when I moved in, but I've had other pressing concerns."

"What about Mrs. Q?"

I checked my watch. "We have four minutes before *Wheel of Fortune* or else we'll have to wait until after it's over."

"I'm going." Malone raced out the door but then popped back into the doorway. "Is there a special kind of vacuum cleaner that we need?"

"One that's easy to empty," I said. "Oh, and see if either she or April has a spray bottle."

"Spray bottle?"

"Ladybugs don't like the smell of peppermint, and I happen to have some essential oil."

"Essential oil? Huh. Maybe then a massage?"

"The day's not over," I said. That got him in motion.

Vacuuming up the bugs and then taking them outside to release them was a laborious process. It took several trips. So many trips. On what we hoped to be the last one, Malone nudged me. "You know why ladybugs are the most observant insects, right?"

"No, why?"

"They're always . . . spot on."

I groaned. "How long have you been—and I use this word loosely—refining that joke?"

"Since the second trip outside," he said with a grin.

"You're incorrigible, Malone. Please tell me you don't have any other puns."

"I can neither confirm nor deny that I have more puns."

Once the bulk of the invaders had been escorted out, I mixed water and peppermint essential oil in one of the sprayers and went to town while Malone returned the vacuum cleaner. Once I'd carefully sprayed around the entrances, windows, and doors, I took the opportunity to do a little snooping.

If the apartment was kept for entertaining visiting guests, then Malone Construction needed to add more amenities to the entertaining spaces. A bare minimum of linens in the bathroom, almost no dishes in the kitchen, no table, one recliner, an older-model television—that's all I could find.

The master bedroom was equally sparse, but I was gratified to see an honest-to-goodness bed frame. It looked new, and the lack of box springs also suggested the mattress was a newer edition. Malone, for his part, was fastidious other than a pair of socks that had missed the hamper.

In the second bedroom, I flipped on the light switch to see a massive computer setup. Multiple towers, three monitors, external hard drives, and equipment I didn't even recognize, along with an ergonomic chair.

But then I saw something that made me gasp.

The writing was on the wall. Literally. Someone, presumably Malone, had written directly on two of the walls—a long series of dollar amounts and digits that looked like account numbers. Numbers ran almost from ceiling to floor. Sticky notes littered the closet doors along the third wall.

Holy shit.

Was he okay?

I turned off the lights and slipped out of the bedroom just in time to nonchalantly spray the hall as Malone entered the apartment.

Nothing to see here.

But on the inside? I was very chalant.

And Malone thought *I* was intriguing?

He closed the apartment door behind him. “Are we bug-free yet?”

“I think we’re down to the last of the stragglers,” I said as I plopped into his recliner.

Act normal, Stella. Act normal.

He paused by the chair. “I would say Grandpa needs to add more furniture to the place, but he’s getting rid of the apartment at the end of the year.”

Another reminder that Malone’s stay was only temporary. “Oh?”

“Yeah. I recommended it. Suggested he get rid of the company car program, too.”

“I bet you’re popular with all his employees,” I said.

“Not really. No one likes the bearer of bad news, but it’s better to cut perks than workers, and things like apartments and cars can easily be abused.”

Trista had mentioned that she and Blake had “visited” this apartment when they were dating, but how many guests could a construction company have coming through that they needed to permanently lease an apartment? The whole idea seemed like a relic from an earlier time, but my earlier research had confirmed that the apartment lease was in the name of Malone Construction.

As I shook off such thoughts, he turned to me. “Bet you didn’t have pest control on your bingo card today.”

“Malone, I never have pest control on my bingo card.”

“Oh, then what *do* you have on your card for the day?” His tone was light. His lips curved into a smile, but his eyes? Shrewd. Calculating.

Reminded me a bit of myself.

"Oh, a little of this, a little of that," I said.

"Pizza?"

"Maybe."

"Other fringe benefits?"

"Maybe. Depends on why *you* ghosted *me*."

He scowled. "I got called into work early Tuesday morning. It was an all-hands-on-deck sort of situation."

It shouldn't have been this hard to pick up where we'd left off, but I'd had time to think, time to wonder if I would be doing the right thing by hooking up with Malone. I didn't know how to get back to where we'd been.

"What about you, Stark?"

"I got a job doing surveillance. It involved camping."

"Fun!"

"Not fun. No campfire."

"Bummer."

We stared at each other while I grappled for a way to broach the subject of what I'd seen earlier.

Just ask him.

But how was I supposed to phrase that question? Maybe all forensic accountants wrote on the walls. Hadn't I seen that in a movie?

"Come on, Stark. What's . . . bugging you?"

I snort-giggled. "I may have peeked in your guest room, and I'm a little concerned."

"Huh?"

"The numbers, Malone. And the sticky notes. At least there wasn't a murder board with red yarn crisscrossing it?"

"Oh, that. Uh, forensic accountant stuff. I told you, it'd make you want to run."

That he had. I considered. "You told me I'd want to run because it was unsexy, not because I would worry you'd gone all *Beautiful Mind* on me."

He laughed out loud. "They're just numbers. Usually, I do my analysis on my computer, but sometimes I like to step back and look at the whole picture. I figured if it worked for *The Accountant*, then it was at least worth a try."

"The accountant?"

"Ben Affleck movie about a—never mind."

Ah. That was the movie where I'd seen something similar. Come to think of it, I'd found Ben Affleck hot in that. Maybe I had a type.

"Do you have Blake Malone's personal accounts on that wall, too?"

He frowned. "I have to plead the Fifth."

"His wife called me, as I'd suspected she eventually would. He's cleaned out several of their joint accounts."

"Interesting," he said. "But not unexpected."

We studied each other. Unfortunately for me, Malone didn't mind silence. I was the one itching to fill the void. "He stole from Malone Construction, too, didn't he?"

"Of all the amendments, my favorite is the fifth."

"Are you pretending to be Blake Malone as a part of your investigation into missing money?"

"As the great philosopher Dave Chappelle once sang . . . fifth."

"Could you help Trista find the money that he took from her?"

"Fifth."

"Do you know where he is?"

Just when I thought he was going to refer to his favorite amendment again, he simply said, "No."

"But you're one of the good guys?"

"I thought we were supposed to be naked for this interrogation."

My stomach growled.

"Ah, I have to feed you first, I see."

"That and I'd like a shower because I smell like a candy cane."

"No problem. I love Christmas."

"It's June."

"It's always Christmas in my heart, Stark," he said with a grin. "How about I order a pizza and meet you at your place in thirty?"

Chapter 21

Malone, whose wet hair indicated he'd also taken a shower, showed up in exactly thirty-one minutes with a bottle of wine and a box of fancy pizza from a place on the square. My subconscious had once again suggested matching underwear.

Not that Malone could see it just yet.

"You must've showered in two minutes flat to have accomplished all of this," I said.

"Ah, but that's the miracle of DoorDash—especially when you offer an excellent tip with the promise of even more upon a speedy delivery."

Good tipper, too. Dammit. Why did he have to live in California, and why had I not met him at least ten years earlier?

"How's your hand?" I asked as I opened the wine and poured a glass for each of us.

"Fine," he said. "That thing with your dad really messed you up, huh?"

"You could've simplified that sentence to 'your dad messed you up,' and you would've been even more accurate."

He angled his wineglass to study its contents, then turned his eyes on me. "You're not messed up, Stark. Not any more than the rest of us."

"But I don't even get to punch your ex like you punched mine," I said before sinking my teeth into the most delicious pizza ever. On focaccia bread, maybe? I was ruined for future delivery. "Not that I thought you actually would."

"I do what I say I'll do," he said. "But funny you should mention my ex. I have a proposition for you."

This had best not be a ménage à trois situation. I regretted ever putting that out in the universe.

"Another one?"

"Well, my grandfather has this gala event each summer and I have to go. My ex will probably be there."

"Ah, so you'd like to make her jealous? I can do that."

"The truth is I hate going by myself because it's dreadfully dull and pretentious. Making her jealous would, however, be an excellent bonus. It's such a production, and we all have to go and bend the knee to Grandpa or else he threatens to write us out of his will."

I took the last bite of pizza and turned my attention back to the wine. "He'd do that?"

"In a heartbeat. Pettiest person I've ever met."

I stiffened in spite of myself. He'd said "pettiest" with such disgust. What if he found out about my side hustle?

Fortunately, Malone didn't seem to notice my reaction, a rarity, but I could tell his mind was elsewhere as he described how the gala was supposed to be a charity event but really functioned as a way for his grandfather to show off to his colleagues.

That's when it hit me: Blake might be there, too. If he were in any way interested in an inheritance, then he would be. After emptying several personal accounts and skimming from the family business, one would think Blake would be satisfied. For some people, however, enough was never enough.

"Yoo-hoo, Earth to Stella. Are you willing to be my plus-one?"

"I don't know. When is it?" I asked, as if a part of me hadn't already cleared my calendar for him.

"Next Tuesday."

I whistled at the short turnaround. "Dress?"

"I mean, I'd wear one if I were you. As much as I'm hoping to see you naked shortly, I don't want to share with other people."

"Cute. Is the event casual, Sunday, formal? What are we talking here?"

He scowled. "I have to wear a tux. What's that?"

"Formal. Very formal," I said.

His expression changed. "And that means expensive, doesn't it? Forget I asked. I'll suffer alone."

"Free meal?"

"Of course. Open bar, too."

"I'm never mad at an open bar, Malone. I'm in."

"Even though you'll have to dress up?" His face scrunched most adorably. I could tell he hated getting dressed up just as much as his cousin purportedly loved primping.

"Don't worry. My nana has a bridal and formalwear shop. She'll do layaway for me." I winked.

"But still—"

"No, Malone. It's been decided. I have to keep my end of the bargain and do something worse to your ex than throwing a punch."

"You really don't—"

"Malone?" Feeling fussy—or needing to do something with my hands—I put leftover pizza in storage bags and cleared the table of all but the wine bottle and our glasses.

"Yes?"

"Accept the help."

"Yes, ma'am."

My fingers tapped on the tabletop. It was now or never. "So."

"So?"

Why was this so awkward? It wasn't the pizza. We'd had pizza last time, and I hadn't been thinking about my breath then.

Once I sat back down at the table, I took another sip of wine. Maybe the alcohol would neutralize any garlicky breath problems. "It feels weird to slide into the benefits portion of the evening without any questions to ask you."

"Kinky, Stark."

"Oh, you know what I mean!"

"Ask me some questions, then. My safe word is 'banana pepper.'"

"Now who's being kinky?"

"Don't kink shame, Miss Anchovies," he said.

"Fine. What," I asked in the same tone of voice as the character from *Monty Python and the Holy Grail*, "is your favorite color?"

"Whatever color your bra is."

"So, purple. That's interesting."

"I love purple," he said. "I must look at all things that are purple. It's a rule."

"A rule you just made up. How about you start the stripping this time?"

He slid his chair back from the table and placed Brené Brown on the floor so quickly, the poor kitten was confused. Possibly dizzy.

Then he stood and whipped off his shirt. It was my turn to look a little dizzy. I stood and rounded the table to stand in front of him, finally tracing the words that ran around his bicep. I read aloud, "Things are only impossible until . . ."

"They're not," Malone finished.

I sucked in a breath. "That's beautiful. Who said it?"

He sighed. "I'm trying to get laid here, Stark."

My eyes locked with his. "I've had daydreams about tracing that tattoo. With my tongue."

"Jean-Luc Picard."

Despite my best efforts, the corners of my lips threatened to twitch upward. His father wasn't the only Trekkie in the family.

"I answered your question," he said as he crossed his arms. "I now need to see your bra. Because it is purple."

I took off my black T-shirt to reveal a royal-purple satin bra.

"Ooh, front hook." He reached for the clasp, and I smacked his hand.

"You take off yours . . . I'll take off mine."

His sweatpants pooled on the floor so quickly, I wasn't sure what to do with myself. Another point in favor of sweatpants. And Adidas slides, since he'd stepped right out of those before pantsing himself. My eyes locked in on his boxers, once again tented.

"Your turn, Stark," he said.

I forced my eyes back up to his and kicked off my wedge flip-flops before unbuttoning my denim shorts and unzipping them slowly. One hip shimmy, and they were on the floor.

Malone swallowed hard. "Is that a thong?"

I did a slow three-sixty.

"Yep, that's a thong," he said. "And that is a stellar ass."

He took a step toward me, and I sucked in a breath. The next thing I knew, he'd picked me up and plopped me on my kitchen table. He stood between my legs, pulling me toward him so our bodies met where we were most sensitive. I only had time to gasp before his lips met mine. My legs wrapped around him of their own accord, and the end result was a delicious friction courtesy of his erection.

Cool air hit my breasts. A light buzzing sound made me look around for ladybugs.

That sound had to be in my head.

No, definitely my apartment.

"Malone, stop," I said, shuddering as he freed my hair from its messy bun and turned his attention to my breasts.

He paused.

Just as I thought I might have imagined the whole thing after all, the buzzing began again.

"It's my phone," he said. "And I don't want to talk to anyone right now. Not a soul."

Our lips and tongues met again, our hands frantically exploring each other's bodies.

The buzzing resumed.

We ignored it.

More buzzing returned.

"Anchovies," I said with a deep sigh. "At least make sure it's not an emergency."

Letting loose with a creative series of curse words, he squatted and fished through the tangle of his sweatpants until he freed his phone. One look at the person who'd been calling him—and texting him, from the looks of it—and his face drained of all color.

After adding a few more colorful words to his repertoire, he looked up at me, then at the phone, then back at me, his expression one of agony.

"You have to take it, don't you?" I asked, now feeling awkward with my legs dangling.

"I don't want to," he said as he stood.

"But you have to."

"What I want to do is push that thong to the side and bury myself in you, but I'll be damned if the first time I have sex with you is a hit-and-run," he said as he shoved his legs into his pants. "You touch yourself and think fond thoughts of me because I will be back. I can't guarantee it's tonight because a catastrophe of epic proportions has just happened on the work front, but . . . it will happen. I promise you that."

He pulled me close for a rough and hungry kiss, gave a groan of frustration, and then practically ran out the door. I heard his apartment door open and close, open and close before the Lexus started and departed with a squeal of tires.

Just call me Little All Undressed Up with No Place to Go.

Normally, I didn't like being told what to do, but Malone's suggestion had some merit.

Chapter 22

The worst part about Malone's departure was the conversation it forced me to have with myself.

He's abandoned you.

No, he hadn't abandoned me. He'd gotten an emergency call for work, similar to my situation the first time around. Truth be told, I'd had less reason to leave him than he'd had to leave me. Probably. Hard to know since I didn't know the particulars.

Well, he'll be done with you the minute he actually has sex with you. That's what men do.

If that were the case, he would've done just as he pleased with no concern about how things went for me. He had walked away with a raging boner because he cared enough to want the experience to be good for me too.

Mind you, the idea of his sliding my thong to the side and—

Cold shower, Stella. You need a cold shower.

The shower ended up being hot; I ended up thinking those fond thoughts.

Afterward, sleep came more easily to me than I would've anticipated, but I still jerked awake every few hours and looked outside for his car. By seven, I groggily decided I'd better get something productive done since my final project for my Legal Research class was due on Monday.

I worked on that project, then did background checks on potential teachers for a private school. Working that job along with another added four hundred or so more dollars to the tally.

I'd moved on to looking through my assorted databases for any hint to Blake Malone's whereabouts when I finally heard someone out in the breezeway.

I jumped up so quickly that the cat yelped. I opened the door and sagged with relief at the sight of him.

"Malone!"

When he turned around, he was on his phone, his eyes inscrutable behind the aviators.

But something seemed . . . off.

"I can't talk now," he said before turning back to his door.

He's already done with you.

My brain told my inner child to have a seat and then brought some reason to my would-be pity party.

Slightly different aviators. Black suit, not navy. Ridiculously expensive shoes. Hair hanging over the collar of his suit in an odd way. His beard was more neatly trimmed than the day before. A glint of sunlight dancing on a watch worth more than my car.

He wasn't my Malone.

Based on the resemblance and the fact that he had a key to the apartment, I could only surmise I'd found the elusive Blake.

I texted Trista first, wishing I had the papers in hand because I'd serve him then and there. Unfortunately for me, I needed to get those from her lawyer's office, and I hadn't done so because I'd been busy avoiding Malone, then even busier not avoiding Malone. Either way you looked at this situation, I needed to get my act together.

If I had a GPS tracking device, I'd be sorely tempted to put it on whatever vehicle he was driving, illegal or not.

Brené Brown gamboled along beside me as I paced, unsure of whether I should break up whatever was going on in the apartment across the way. Was he doing something to Malone's computer setup? Was he desperate enough to hurt me if I tried to stop him?

Even worse, I didn't have Malone's phone number. I'd been about sixty seconds away from knowing him biblically, but I couldn't text or call him.

Well, you can.

With the information I had, I could learn a lot about Malone, including that pesky Social Security number I didn't really need. I hadn't researched him because I didn't have "permissible purpose."

But surely he would want to know about this?

I was in the process of pulling up Malone's number when I heard the apartment door slam.

I'd missed the opportunity to stop Blake.

If I were smooth, I'd have plants on my patio that I could pretend to water while actually checking to see which vehicle Blake got into.

Note to self: Get a fern. Those things always need misting.

Screw it.

I went outside anyway. What did I care if Blake thought I was nosy? For all he knew I was looking for his cousin, and I was eventually getting paid to be nosy about him.

He zipped through the parking lot in a Hyundai Sonata, and I studied the license plate, chanting it until I got back into the apartment and could write it down before plugging it into one of my databases.

"Dammit." Vehicle registration showed the vehicle belonged to one of the umpteen rental car agencies at the Atlanta airport. I turned my attention to my Malone and typed in his information.

He had more than one phone number.

Of course he did.

After trial and error and leaving messages with who knew whom, I called each number enough times that Malone eventually picked up. "Who is this?"

"Malone, it's me."

"Stark?"

"Yeah, listen. Your cousin was just here in a black Hyundai Sonata, license plate Delta Charlie Foxtrot eighty-seven fourteen, rented through Hertz at the Atlanta airport."

"Did he take anything?"

"I don't know. I was debating whether or not to break in, but he left before I decided. He was in and out. Appeared to have a key."

More creative cursing. "Wait. You can break into my apartment?"

"In multiple ways. Do you have a rod in the slider of your patio door?"

"Noooo."

"Oh, good. That's the easiest."

Five minutes later, I'd hopped the barrier to Malone's patio and used a flathead screwdriver to pop open his patio door. Once inside, I made a beeline for the spare bedroom.

"He's taken the tower," I said.

Malone cursed. "Did he take any hard drives?"

"What hard drives? I don't see any."

"That answers that question. I guess you'd better check my bedroom, too," Malone was saying when I saw the walls.

At my gasp, the first thing Malone said was, "Are you okay, Stark?"

Ink and pencil streaked down the walls. It looked as though Blake had started with the bottle of peppermint essential oil and water that I'd left behind but then decided that wasn't fast enough. I could deduce, based on the puddles on the floor and an empty pot, that Blake had repeatedly filled the pot with water and then thrown its contents at the wall.

And at the closet. The sticky notes now lay on the ground in mushy piles.

"He erased all your work," I said.

"He what?"

"He threw water on the walls. It's all gone."

As much as I hated math, my heart ached for Malone. Countless hours had gone into whatever the hell he was doing with all those numbers.

Malone sighed. "And that's why I usually keep everything on my computer. Cloud backup. Encryption."

"So you have a backup?"

He snorted. "Don't you worry, Stark. I have backups for my backups. I even have pictures of the walls, so that's not as big a loss as you think. I won't be reinventing the wheel."

"Backups for your backups, huh?"

"Yep."

"That's sexy," I said, my voice finding a new lower register.

"You got a thing for nerds, huh?" he answered with a lower voice of his own.

"Just one in particular."

He groaned. "You are absolutely killing me, because I can't come home to finish what we started. It's a shitshow."

"I figured," I said with a sigh. "Anything else you need me to look for?"

"In my bedroom . . ." he started.

I walked out of the guest room and into the main bedroom.

"Okay."

"In the closet . . ."

"Yeah?"

"There's a shoebox on the upper shelf—"

"There are a lot of shoeboxes on the upper shelf. I think you have more shoes than I do."

"Doubt it. Look for one that has 'Jarvis' on the bottom right corner."

I eyed the twelve boxes until I found the pair with the appropriate style name. "Got it."

"Take that box with you and keep it safe, will ya?"

"Only for you, Malone. Anything else?"

"No. Wait. Didn't you install one of those doorbell cameras?"

"Sure did." I bit my lip to keep from adding that I'd done so specifically to get pictures of him.

"Fabulous. Do you have any footage of Blake breaking in?"

"Probably." Which was thanks to setting up the camera to capture Malone's door in the first place, but he didn't need to know that. "But it doesn't *look* like breaking in."

"Doesn't matter. Please save it. I promise I'll make it worth your while."

His words sent a shiver down my back. "Anything else?"

"Keep thinking fondly of me," he said, his voice rough. "Because I could be gone a few hours or a few days. Either way, I know I'll be back in time for the benefit on June twenty-seventh, so find something pretty to wear, please and thank you."

"I can do that. Underwear optional, of course."

He groaned.

"Why don't *you* think fondly of *me*, Malone, just like I thought fondly of you earlier."

He made a strangled noise on the other end of the line, and I hung up before he could answer.

Chapter 23

Once I'd put Malone's patio door back to rights, I returned to my apartment with the shoebox.

Should I open it?

He hadn't said I *couldn't*. That said, curiosity did things to the cat that Brené Brown's cute little ears were too young to hear.

But of course I was going to open it.

Inside I saw . . . shoes. Specifically, a part of faux-leather pull-on loafers that were so cheap, I could see the glue on the soles. I was about to put the lid on the box in disgust when something shiny caught my eye. Inside each shoe were a couple of thumb drives.

I grinned.

Backups for your backups really was sexy. Gotta love a man who was prepared. Even better? A man who knew his opponent well enough to know he wouldn't look in a box of cheap, unfashionable men's shoes.

I replaced the USB drives and put the shoebox in a safe place, then returned to my laptop.

It was past time to do a deeper dive on Blake Malone. Tracers, my favorite search engine, didn't show any additional residences, but it did indicate that the Florida home's property taxes were delinquent. Only one vehicle, the SUV that Trista drove, but I already knew the Lexus was being leased to Malone Construction, as was the apartment across the hall.

No arrests. Not even a traffic violation, other than a speeding ticket three years ago.

He had had only three employers of record: a movie theater when he was a teenager, a sandwich shop in his college years, and then Malone Construction. Nepotism at its finest, I supposed.

The Malone Construction website said he was on personal leave, though, so it seemed nepotism stretched only so far.

I turned my attention to my Malone.

Tiberius James Malone, born on January 25, 1981, in Santa Rosa, California.

He leased an apartment in California and drove an older-model Mustang convertible. His mother's maiden name really was Franklin. She had been married to Malone's father for almost forty years.

My heart leaped with hope, then thudded with the remembrance that our situation was temporary. More importantly, I was not supposed to jump from one long-term relationship to another for a variety of reasons.

I needed to get out there and do things for myself, so I would do Malone at his earliest convenience. I would not, as Salcedo suggested, catch feelings, either. We were two consenting adults. He had already shown concern for my welfare, and I was going to enjoy the arrangement he had offered me without thinking of anything more.

I didn't need anything more.

I didn't *want* anything more.

Relationships only led to heartache. Sexy times led to orgasms.

Besides, based on the years I'd wasted on Ken, the longer the relationship, the fewer the sexy times, so better to *not* have a forty-year marriage.

Keep telling yourself that, Stella. Keep making those rationalizations to cover up for the fact you've always wondered if things would've been different if either your nana or your mother had stayed married. Keep telling yourself that marriage isn't important since—

Nope. Not going there. Not doing it. Absolutely not.

Focus.

Other than having way too many phone numbers for my liking, Tiberius James Malone was squeaky clean. No arrests, convictions, bankruptcies, speeding tickets. No mortgage. He voted frequently—yay for civic duty—and appeared to have at least partial ownership in the company where he worked, Chateau Cybersecurity.

And that was that.

Trista called just as I was trying to decide which frozen meal I wanted for lunch. "Is he still there?"

"Afraid not," I said as I watched my entrée whirl around in the microwave. "I got his license plate, but it was a rental."

"And you're sure it wasn't the cousin?"

"Positive." I almost told Trista that I knew the cousin very well, but that felt like the sort of information that should be on a need-to-know basis. Trista didn't need to know even a tenth of the things I knew about Malone. Not about his tattoo and certainly not about his carnal promises.

I shuddered.

"How did he look?"

Delicious. Fit, but not so cut he would be cranky from lack of carbs—

She's talking about Blake, Stella. "Uh, pretty pleased with himself."

She sighed. "No. Like, what was he wearing?"

I bit back any sarcastic remarks about how the Bel Air Apartments weren't exactly the Met Gala. Instead, I detailed what Blake was wearing, down to his expensive shoes and watch.

"What about his hair?"

"Uh, hanging over his collar. Didn't seem to fit with the rest of his vibe."

Trista let out a whoop.

"Uh, am I missing something?" I wanted to ask if she was having some kind of health emergency, but I was professional enough to keep that to myself.

"No, no. I'm fine. But I have an idea of where you can find him."

"Oh?"

"Every four weeks he goes to Salon Blaise. The only person, and I do mean the *only* person, who can cut his hair to his specifications is Fabiano."

"Surely he wouldn't see that barber if he's trying to keep a low profile."

She laughed, but the sound held no humor. "Fabiano is more than a barber. He's a stylist!"

I rolled my eyes but said nothing. My last haircut had come from CheapClips, and there would be no trims for me in the near future.

"If his hair is over the collar, you might be able to catch him at Salon Blaise. In fact, go ahead and mark your calendar. We have sixty days to serve the papers, and if you don't catch him this time, then you can try again in another four weeks. Mama did always say to have a plan B."

Her accent slipped a bit on the last sentence. Slowly but surely, Trista was reverting to her natural state. She'd shed the posh affectation of her accent almost as quickly as she'd traded in couture for yoga pants.

"Your mama is wise," I said, making a note to look up Salon Blaise and Fabiano. "Trista, *that* was very helpful. I'm headed over to your attorney first thing on Monday to get those papers."

She sighed. "I'm going to make an awful confession."

"I'm not a priest, but I'll try to absolve you anyway," I said, my mind already racing to how easy it would be to get information out of the famous Fabiano.

"I was a terrible snob the day that I met you."

"Oh? I didn't think so."

She snorted in response.

"No, really. I mean, it was obvious you had more money than I do, but that, I can assure you, is a low bar to clear." Maybe she'd been a little pretentious, but it wasn't my job to judge anyone for that. While working with Ken, I'd learned that pretentious people had no problem spending money. That said, working-class folks—especially older ones—often had even more money and were more likely to pay the first bill that came their way. Basically, it paid to treat everyone with respect. That was my philosophy.

Trista sighed. "I knew you were a private investigator and that you did process serving, but I chose to go with . . . someone else to serve papers on Blake. When it became clear he wasn't going to be able to do it, I called you."

"Let me guess: It wasn't going to be as easy as he had hoped, so he decided he didn't want to do it."

"Something like that."

"And he probably wouldn't have taken you seriously about the haircut thing."

"Oh, definitely not. It still could be nothing."

"Hey, don't second-guess yourself."

"Thanks for that," she said softly, showing she'd picked up what I was putting down: to trust her instincts on things both big and small.

I almost steam-burned myself removing the plastic film from a less-than-appetizing chicken marinara situation. "I'm trusting your instincts. If you think of any other oddities like the haircut thing, you text me. Any time of day or night. Let me know before you forget about whatever it is that came to mind. The last guy I served papers on loved this one bar. Ken—that's my ex—made fun of me for waiting outside his house every night for *weeks*. But I somehow knew this guy was going to cave and head for his favorite place eventually. On day fifty-nine at ten p.m., probably thinking he was in the clear because who would serve papers on him in a bar that late at night, he sneaked out of his house. I got him."

She made a sound that could've been a sob or a laugh or something in between. "I hate to sound like Princess Leia, but I think you're my only hope."

"Hardly. You'll make it. But if there's one thing I can promise you, it's this: I'm stubborn as hell."

Later that night I went to Finnegan's to meet other clients. I'd managed to save up a little over $5,000. With six days and a few jobs to go, I just might make it. I'd have enough to make rent, cover my annual car registration, and get straight on my student loans.

As for then getting the title to the car, I would figure something out. Maybe Ken would inspire me to new heights of pettiness.

But I needed to think quickly because I had to have that title in my name in order to renew my car's registration, which was due on my birthday. Dadgum birthday tax. Who the heck wanted to get an emissions test and pay a lump sum for their birthday?

About that time, Malone texted me. It was simply a pizza emoji along with the one for prayer hands.

"What are you thinking about with that grin on your face?" asked Havisham.

"Nothing."

"Bullshit."

Now that my client meetings were over, I'd taken my usual seat at the bar, so I knew no one was behind me. No one sat beside me, either, so I was confident I could tell Havisham in a soft voice, "If you must know, I'm close to getting my jollies with my hot neighbor."

"Good for you, Stark! I have a bead on a playmate myself," Havisham said. "Corner booth in the cowboy hat."

I looked over. "A cowboy hat? Really. Is he into philanthropy and also a billionaire?"

Havisham waggled her eyebrows. "More into misanthropy. I like 'em bad."

Eh, whatever. He looked like a poor woman's George Clooney, which was to say Havisham could do a lot worse.

She bustled to the other side of the bar, and Salcedo slumped into the seat beside me.

"Hey, kid. What have you been up to?" I asked.

"Went on a quick vacay with the fam. What did I miss?"

"Well, I helped a woman leave six cricket noisemakers behind in the apartment she was being forced to vacate. Hilarity ensued."

"Oh, I hate I missed that. Anything else?"

"I had a compass sent to a dude who said he was dumping his girlfriend because he needed to find himself."

She giggled.

"What about you?" I turned my wineglass sideways. This Malbec wasn't as good as the one Malone had brought me.

Probably because it was Malone who'd brought it.

"The whole vacation thing was a bait and switch. They're moving to New Jersey, so we spent some time at Cape May and the rest of the time looking at houses."

"I gather from your scowl that you weren't a fan of that idea."

"No. But they want me to move up there with them."

"Do you want to move to New Jersey?"

"No."

"Then don't," I said with a shrug.

Her mouth fell open with shock. Such an idea had never occurred to her. After a few seconds of analysis, she sighed and said with resignation, "You're obviously not my mother's daughter."

"True." It was on the tip of my tongue to say something sarcastic about how it must've been nice to have a mother who wanted you around, but I didn't.

Personal growth? Maybe.

Oblivious to the huge strides I'd just made, Salcedo said, "I know she was only sixteen when she had me, but I think it's pretty unhealthy how close she wants to keep me."

Havisham slid a cider in front of her. "What's going on down here?"

"Salcedo's mom wants her to move with the family to New Jersey."

"You're nineteen, aren't you?" Havisham asked. "You can decide."

Before Salcedo could respond, the bartender was off again. It was busy even for a Saturday.

"Easy for her to say." Salcedo muttered before chewing on her bottom lip like it was an Olympic sport. Her eyes were glassy.

"Hey," I said. "My mom was sixteen when she had me, too, but you won't find her anywhere around."

"Really?"

"Yeah. Nana raised me. It's a good thing your mom wants you around, but you do get to choose what you want to do."

"It's not that simple," she said. "I'm still living at home. If they leave, then I'll have to get a full-time job and shift to night classes. But if I transfer to someplace up north, then I'll get behind because you know not all my credits are going to transfer."

"If you decide to stay, you could live with me."

Where had those words come from? I didn't want to live with someone else. It was one thing to canoodle with Malone, but he was going to leave eventually and had his own place in the meantime. On the day I loaded up the car to move my things from Nana's house to the apartment, I vowed to myself that I wouldn't share my next home with just anyone. Heck, Ken had basically kicked me out but then had come poking around asking me where something was.

Eh, that had been an excuse.

Maybe.

When we were together, I had spent a great deal of my time looking for things he couldn't find, which I found pretty ironic considering he was a private *investigator*.

"Are you sure?" Salcedo asked. She'd picked up on the swirl of emotions that had come after my offer.

"Yeah," I said, feeling the confidence even as I said it. "I have an extra bedroom. It's not padded, though, so you'll have to keep yourself out of trouble until your twentieth birthday."

Salcedo grinned. "I'm going to think about it, but thank you for the offer. Look at you being vulnerable after reading the book!"

"What?"

"Oh, come on, Stark. You're not as tough as you want the world to believe. First, you told me something about your past even though you clearly didn't want to. Then you opened up your home to me even though you've been burned in the past. It's very kind of you."

"Well, look at that. I really am growing as a person," I said. "By the way, I named the cat Brené Brown."

"Of course you did."

Chapter 24

"Brené Brown Dammit Quit!"

Upon hearing her first and middle names, she quit scratching the back corner of the love seat. I could see where Jim Davis got the idea for some of his *Garfield* cartoons. Now the picture of innocence, she started licking her paw to wash her face.

"Uh-huh. I saw it. You're not as slick as you think you are."

She gave me her cutest look and did the slow blinks that the internet told me meant "I love you" in cat.

"Yes, yes. I love you, too. And I'll get you a scratching post, but . . . we may have a roommate one of these days, so you're going to have to learn to behave."

She rounded the love seat, jumped up to the cushion, and curled into a ball. No concern of hers if I wanted to add a roommate.

My phone buzzed.

"Could be her right now," I said as I checked my phone.

Malone.

"Stark, I've got good news and bad news."

At the sound of his voice, my pulse was off to the races. "Bad news first."

"I'm not going to be back until the gala."

"Booooo. What's the good news?"

"Work seems to be under control. Finally."

"Excellent. Do that forensic accounting voodoo that you do so well."

"You really have no idea what I do, do you?"

"Only the vaguest of notions. I mean, I know about accounting, but I keep thinking you're some kind of number medical examiner performing nerd autopsies."

He laughed. "I miss you."

"You miss my purple bra."

"Well, yes, but I miss you. I miss whatever perfume it is you wear—"

"J'adore."

"I miss your smile, your sense of humor, and the fact you know how to do terrifying things like break into my apartment."

"That's the tip of the iceberg, Malone. I have all sorts of talents you haven't even discovered yet."

He took in a ragged breath. "Can you show me sometime?"

"Sure. If you're a very good boy."

"Promise?"

"Promise." I smiled in a way I hadn't since my teen years.

"And we can have a Finnegan, when I get back?"

His response startled me. How did he know about Havisham's bar? "What?"

"A Finnegan, a mulligan for a mulligan."

"I'm sure you're speaking English, but once again your words don't make sense to me."

He chuckled. "It's a golf term."

"Oh, I don't play that game."

"If you were Lucius Malone's grandchild, you would, but basically it's a do-over for a do-over."

"Third time's a charm?"

"One can hope. Bottom line: I don't care if the apartment building is collapsing around us, the next time I kiss you, I fully intend to make love to you. Thoroughly."

I shivered. "How thoroughly is 'thoroughly'?"

"I'm going to ruin you for other men."

And then you're going to leave me.

I shook that thought away. No, he and I were going to enter a short-term, mutually beneficial relationship. "And how do you know I'm not going to ruin *you*?"

"Oh, Stark. I'm counting on it."

That Sunday night, it was time to start a new module in my online paralegal education. I'd turned in my last project, so Legal Research, Part One, was in my rearview mirror, as were such scintillating topics as law office management, estate planning/probate, criminal law, and family law.

Probably best not to mix those last two. Unless I wanted to be a consigliere, which might require a course entitled Criminal Family Law.

All in all, I'd already taken seven of the thirteen courses I needed for my paralegal certificate and was on pace to complete the program at the end of the year—thanks to adding an extra course here and there.

My next two courses would be Civil Litigation, Part One—who knew civil litigation was so vast that it needed two parts?—and Tort Law. Sadly, tort law appeared to have nothing to do with tortes.

What had I learned from these past few months? I still preferred letters and words to numbers, and it was just as well I had never gone to law school. I found the subject of law intriguing, but I liked keeping my own hours and not having to go to an office each day.

In an odd sort of way, I suppose I owed Ken a thank-you note for sending me down a different path, a career path I liked a whole heckuva lot better than I would've liked working in an office and/or trotting off to court, which was, sadly, more boring than television and movies would have you believe. Far better to have the flexibility of doing both private investigation and paralegal work from home than to be a buttoned-up lawyer.

But no thank-you note for the Douchecanoe.

As Little Miss Petty, I had a lot of better options for him, and as soon as I figured out how, I just might become my own best client. In the meantime, however, I needed a fancy dress for this gala.

I knew just the place to get one.

"Stella Bella Mortadella!" my nana said as I walked through the door of Shindigs and Soirées, her boutique shop that specialized in weddings and other formal events. As of late, she'd been doing brisk business in quinceañeras, partially thanks to some work I'd done for a bilingual lawyer down in Buckhead. Her added success probably explained her excitement to see me as well as the extra few seconds of her hug.

"It shouldn't take needing something for you to come see your grandmother," she chided, just as I'd expected she would.

"I know, I know. It's been . . . a lot."

"That Ken. I never liked him," she said.

"You've made that abundantly clear over the years," I said. "Would it help if I said you were right and I was wrong?"

Her brow furrowed. "It doesn't *help*, but . . . I'm not mad at the acknowledgment that your nana does know a thing or two—especially since you had me open up the shop just for you."

"Thanks, Nana."

She shrugged. "That's what grandmothers do. Or what they try to do if only their prickly granddaughters will let them."

I took in her earnest brown eyes and sleek navy sheath dress. She colored her hair to an ashy blond and kept it just long enough to graze her shoulders. She'd be seventy-four in September, but she said she wasn't ready to retire just yet.

"I'll try to do better at asking my nana for favors. Do you have anything suitable for a gala?"

"Which one?"

"The Malone Gala."

She gave a low whistle. "I've never managed to snag an invite to that one, but I should have something. I can't promise anything from a major designer, though."

"I don't need a major designer."

She tilted her head to one side. "No, but I need *you* to look good if *I* want to attract the attention of everyone there, now don't I?"

Always both thinking ahead and thinking of her bottom line, that was my nana.

She led the way from the front hallway down to a room that had probably once been a dining room for some wealthy Marietta family. The hardwood floors creaked under my feet in a familiar way.

The formalwear market had changed many times over the years, but Nana's storefront had changed very little. She now owned rather than rented the Queen Anne house a few blocks off the square, but it still sported buttercream-colored walls, all the original fireplaces, a rainbow of gowns on the bottom floor with a bridal boutique upstairs, and the lingering scent of mulberry potpourri.

"Okay, summer gala. Over at the fancy Hilton, I'm guessing?"

"You know it." I touched a satiny skirt. Nana smacked my hand as she must've done a hundred times before. "A girl gets Cheeto dust on one dress, and she's never allowed to touch any of them ever again?"

"Correct," Nana said. "Besides, you don't know what looks good on you."

I sighed dramatically. "Fine. Since I'm expecting to get the friends and family discount, you can pick out my fancy dress. I promise that I'm only seventy-five percent sure I won't wear Converse with it."

Nana pointed at a chair by the fireplace. "You have a seat right there, and I'll pick out a few things that could work."

She didn't ask for my size; she didn't have to. Fortunately for me, she didn't overstock sizes six and under to the neglect of the larger ones. She told me once that she'd learned long ago that the zeroes and twos often ended up on the clearance rack, so no need to overdo it.

As I watched her efficiently swan about the room, pausing occasionally to put a dress on the rack by my chair, I thought, not for the first time, that she and Havisham would probably get along swimmingly. My only hesitation in introducing them? I didn't need them to join forces.

Then again, if they were running the world, it might be a better situation for all of us. Since they couldn't apply themselves to world domination, however, they'd probably focus on me, and I didn't need that.

After flitting around the room and even down the hall, she had accumulated five dresses for me to try. She then gently touched my cheek, turning my face from one side to the other. "No makeup. Good girl."

As if I would risk a tirade on the scourge of foundation stains on her nice dresses. No thank you.

"Hop in there and let me see how that first one looks on you."

I took a floor-length sour-apple-green sheath into a small room beside the fireplace where I'd been sitting. The small space had once been a pantry of sorts, but Nana had converted it into a dressing room.

The dress slid down my skin as though it had been molded to my shape. There was just one problem. "Nana, how am I supposed to wear a bra with this?"

Her turn to sigh.

We sighed a lot when we were together, but the overall number of sighs had decreased exponentially since I turned twenty.

"I forgot about your bazombas, but I guess you could wear one of those adhesive bras. Come out here and let me see."

I took another look at the strappy back of the dress in the mirror before returning to Nana.

Her brow furrowed. Her lips pursed as though holding pins that weren't there as she studied the dress. She stepped back and twirled her finger. I slowly spun.

"No. Try the electric blue."

I took that dress in, then removed the green one before placing it back on its hanger.

The blue was a shorter sheath. No worries about a bra with it, thanks to its conservative neckline, wide straps, and closed back.

Done deal, so far as I was concerned, but Nana said, "Too conservative."

"C'mon, Nana. Isn't 'conservative' exactly what I need for that crowd?"

She shook her head. "I think it'll be the purple."

Purple.

The color reminded me of Malone, and the memory of Malone caused my pulse to quicken.

I turned around so she could unzip me and took the purple dress with me into the dressing room.

"Purple" didn't really do the dress justice. It was a luscious almost-eggplant color with gauzy layers of fabric. Low cut, but it had wide straps. Full skirt, but it cinched around the waist and had a daring slit.

And pockets.

"This is the one, Nana," I said.

"Come here and let me be the judge of that."

I turned to the right and then to the left, watching the fabric swish with my hands in my pockets. The girls—or my bazombas as my nana liked to call them—were out and proud. "No need."

"Stella Angelina Stark, let me see."

Swallowing a sigh, I stepped outside, and her brow smoothed. She nodded. "Yes, the purple."

"Like I said—"

"Turn! Perfect, and I shouldn't have to hem it more than an inch."

"Nana, it's fashionable to drag the ground. And I'm going to wear my Converse anyway."

"Not with that slit, you aren't. Get your stuff and come over to the mirror where we do alterations. I have a pair of shoes that will work with that dress."

My lip extended in a pout, but I followed her and did what she said. After all, she was the expert in formalwear. She brought me a pair of strappy wedge sandals, and I loved her for remembering I could do a wedge but not a heel. Then she had me stand on the platform for what felt like an hour but couldn't have been fifteen minutes as she pinned, stepped back, then stepped forward and pinned again.

"Oh, I forgot to mention I need it for Tuesday night."

"Always the last minute with you, isn't it?"

"I didn't get the invitation until Friday." I put my hands in the pockets of the dress.

"Stop that! It messes with the length. You can play with your pockets on Tuesday."

I put my hands over my head. Nana indulged in our love language: sighing. "Put your hands at your sides, please."

I did as I was told, and she added one more pin before declaring the dress ready for hemming. While I was in the makeshift dressing room, she asked, "And how did you get an invitation? Surely no *gentleman* would wait until the last minute."

It was on the tip of my tongue to tell her Malone was no gentleman, but Nana didn't need to know about our plans. Besides, he was a gentleman in all the ways that counted.

And who the heck ever said I was a lady?

In the end I settled for, "I haven't known the gentleman that long."

"Interesting," she said as I exited, carefully handing the dress over to her.

"If you must know, he's the grandson of Lucius Malone."

One of her eyebrows practically kissed the ceiling. "Oh. Well then. If you marry him, you'll be back in here a lot. Those Malones have more money than they can count."

I bit my lip to keep from reminding Nana that I had no intention of marrying anyone ever. It was an old argument, one I was still inclined to agree with, but it wasn't worth having that argument with someone who made a living from weddings.

Even if she didn't believe in happily ever after herself.

"Would you like for me to see if I can get you a ticket?" I asked her.

Now her eyes twinkled. "If you get me a ticket, I won't say a word if you wear Converse under that dress. I'll even adjust the hem so you can."

"You're on," I said. "Wait. Does that mean I have to put the dress back on so you can change where the hem's going?"

"Yep."

Chapter 25

The first thing I did on Monday morning was visit Trista's attorney. The second? Head over to Salon Blaise.

Unfortunately for me, Salon Blaise was in East Cobb.

While I technically grew up in what should've been neutral territory, Marietta, West Cobb was a little more my aesthetic.

In high school, we had to read *The Great Gatsby*, and when our teacher talked about how East Egg represented old money and West Egg represented new, I thought to myself, "Well, the more things change, the more they stay the same."

Obviously, both Fitzgerald and my English teacher were making gross generalizations, but I didn't feel comfortable in East Cobb. Heck, half the time I didn't feel comfortable in West Cobb. New money? I usually had *no* money.

All this to say, it made perfect sense that Blake would select a salon east of the Big Chicken.

The upshot was that I would be near the Trader Joe's, where I planned to stock up on snacks, cheap international wines, and other assorted goodies. Why West Cobb couldn't have a Trader Joe's, I'd never know.

While Salon Blaise didn't look like much on the outside, due to being in a strip mall, the inside was opulent enough. Pencil-thin stylists, both men and women, were dressed in black and looked like Parisian fashion-house refugees. Only two were male, so that narrowed down the odds of which was Fabiano.

While making an appointment for myself that I had every intention of canceling, I considered how best to approach Fabiano.

If Blake was smart, he tipped well, something that would inspire loyalty on the stylist's part. Unlikely that I could talk my way into inspecting the appointment software—how I missed the days when appointments were in books. Humans were easy to distract, so books left on counters were easy prey.

Equally unlikely that I had enough cash to bribe Fabiano. My best bet might be to observe. If Trista was right, then it was likely Blake would come in for a haircut this week. While it would be a pain to surveil for a week or more, it could be done.

I smiled my thanks and stepped outside to survey the parking lot for the best places to sit unobtrusively—preferably in the shade, although that appeared unlikely.

I'd need to rent a car. Nothing good would come of sitting in the same car in the same parking lot for a week. It wouldn't be camping, but there would be other logistical considerations and—

Malone?

My heart leaped at the sight of a tall, handsome man in aviators. But then I clocked the name-brand polo and crisp khaki shorts on the man exiting the Land Rover. My Malone would never.

Nope.

Blake.

Well, well, well.

I'd have to look up the patron saint of private investigators and light a candle tonight because fate had seen fit to bring my quarry to me.

I took the papers from my purse, glad I'd chosen to carry the large bag, since I usually went without a purse. Experience had taught me long ago to be prepared. I forced myself to walk at a good pace but not so fast that I *looked* like I was in a hurry. Blake put the keys in his pocket as he cast a careful look around the parking lot. His eyes traveled right over me. No apprehension, not even a flicker of recognition from when we'd briefly met in the apartment breezeway.

Seemed I was invisible to him, too.

I stepped forward, blocking his path.

"Hi, excuse me," I said in my most I'm-just-a-silly-woman-nothing-to-fear-here voice, "could you help me find the Trader Joe's? I must've missed my turn."

Oh, you know women drivers, my tone said. As if I didn't already have a plan for navigating that tricky parking lot because a girl's gotta have her dark chocolate–covered almonds.

Blake's whole demeanor relaxed. "Turn right out of the parking lot, and it'll be on your left."

"Thank you," I said. "Could you hold this while I take a look on my phone to see how I got turned around?"

Irritation turned the corners of his mouth down, but he took the papers. No wedding band, but his left ring finger still held the white indentation from when he'd once worn one.

I looked up with my brightest smile. "Oh, and by the way, you've been served."

His eyebrows lifted above his glasses. "What?"

My task accomplished, I started walking away briskly, but he called after me: "Wait. You live in Bel Air Apartments. That's where I've seen you before."

I may have flinched, but I kept walking.

"How the hell did you find me?"

Nope. Not going to answer that one, either, but I should tell my Malone.

I took out my phone to text him just as Blake grabbed my shoulder and wheeled me around. "Hey! I'm not taking these. You've got the wrong guy."

"I don't think so."

"No, who do you think I am?"

"Blake Malone."

He gave me a familiar lopsided smile. "No, you have me confused. I'm his cousin, Ty."

"Take off your glasses," I said, my voice back to its default setting: irreverent cynicism/sarcasm.

He hesitated, no doubt due to Ty's heterochromia. I was sure he was hoping against hope I didn't know my neighbor that well. Little did he know just how well I knew his cousin.

Not biblically, but that wasn't for lack of trying.

I could almost sense when he came to the decision—"might as well give it a shot"—and then decided to take off his glasses.

Uncanny.

They said every person had their twin, but the resemblance with my Malone was over the top. At a distance, no one would've been able to tell the difference between the two. Up close? Brown eyes, slightly thinner lips, and a smile that didn't reach all the way to his eyes.

"Nope. You're Blake Malone, and you're hiding for some reason," I said.

"And who are you?"

"Just your friendly neighborhood process server."

"No, you're more than that," he said with a smile as he put his aviators back on. "Let me buy you lunch, see if we can come to an understanding."

Ah, a charm offensive. Such sudden shifts in demeanor always reminded me of Ted Bundy.

"No, thank you. I have errands to run."

"Trader Joe's, right?"

"That was just a ploy to get your attention." I crossed my fingers behind my back. "I shop at Whole Foods."

"I don't know what lies my wife's been telling you, but I'm really a nice guy."

Sure. All the truly nice guys say that. Saying it makes it so.

But I knew how to play the game. One, keep the smile on my face to prevent any unwanted ugliness. Two, keep Trista out of it, but, three, don't tell an outright lie. "Your wife? I work for lawyers. Have a nice day."

With that, I quickly sat down in my Corolla, being sure to lock the door before I fished around in my bag for my keys. In my peripheral vision, I saw Blake take a look at the papers, then pinch the bridge of his nose while looking up at the sky. On his way into the salon, he tossed the papers in a trash can.

Bad move, Bizarro Malone. You're gonna need those papers, and tossing them doesn't mean you haven't been served. They make affidavits for that sort of thing.

More paperwork for me, but . . . I would drown my sorrows in a cheap Côtes du Rhône and some white-cheddar corn puffs.

I took a meandering route through the parking lot, curious about the license plate on the Land Rover Blake had been driving. Probably a rental, but it wouldn't hurt to check it out. Just in case he was watching, I didn't stop to write it down. Instead, I chanted the letter and number configuration to the tune of Outkast's "So Fresh, So Clean" all the way to Trader Joe's.

To say Trista was happy I'd managed to serve her husband with papers would be the understatement of the century. When I called, she squealed so loudly that I feared permanent hearing loss. And in both ears, at that, because I had called on speaker.

Malone, on the other hand, had answered neither phone call nor text by the time I headed back for Bel Air Apartments with a treasure trove of snacks.

My phone rang as I was juggling a bag while unlocking my apartment door. I put the bag down and looked to see who was calling me.

Malone.

"Guess what?" I asked in lieu of "hello."

"I'm afraid to ask, Stark."

"I just served your cousin with divorce papers."

"What?"

I told him everything, including how I'd found his cousin by his need for a specific haircut from a specific stylist. Malone muttered a few choice words before adding, "And here I am wasting my time in freakin' Wyoming."

"Wyoming? You were looking for him, too?"

He said nothing.

"You and that Fifth Amendment, I swear. You know we could be working together. Finding people is one of the things I do."

"I'll take that under advisement."

"You do that. Also, I bet you fifty bucks he goes to your grandpa's function tomorrow."

"No way. He wouldn't be that stupid."

"Aha! He did steal money. But it's not about stupidity," I said. "He thinks he's outsmarted everyone. He even thinks he outsmarted me by dumping those papers in the trash can."

"There's no way. Why would he do that when—" He paused before he said too much. "I could've stayed with you this whole time."

My heart fluttered.

It's just the sex he's after, Stella. Don't take it as anything more.

"We'll be together soon enough," I said. "And we can celebrate, because I'm awfully close to meeting a major goal."

"Which is?"

"Funny, I seem to have developed an affection for the Fifth Amendment . . ."

Malone said nothing. "Does this have something to do with the ex?"

"Fifth."

Malone sighed deeply. "Would you wait for me before you see him about the car title or whatever else you have up your sleeve?"

"You're cute. I can handle myself—you know that. Besides, you've got a lot on your plate."

"I know you *can* handle yourself, but I don't like that guy."

I laughed out loud. "I don't think anyone does except his mother, and having met her, I'd say even that's debatable."

Malone didn't laugh. "I'm serious. I'll be there tomorrow at the latest, later tonight if I can get an earlier flight. No need to see him without some backup."

"Okay, okay. I'll wait for you."

"Promise?"

"Promise."

"And be careful with my cousin, too. I have plenty of reasons not to trust him."

"Such as?"

"For starters—" But then someone in the background called out to Malone, which caused him to sigh. "I'll have to tell you later. Just be careful, Stark."

"Same to you," I said as he rushed through his goodbyes.

He disconnected the call without saying anything about benefits or bras or purple.

Maybe he had an audience.

But he cares enough that he doesn't want you to face the Douchecanoe alone.

Eh, that was Malone. He would've done that for anyone.

Chapter 26

By the time Tuesday evening rolled around, I was ready. Buffed, polished, shaved—you name it. My purple dress fit like a dream and concealed the same purple bra Malone had seen once before. I was even wearing the matching underwear, but I'd given careful consideration to not doing so—it would've been so much fun to see the look on his face if I stuffed it in his pocket.

Despite his accounting adventures, he had finagled a ticket for Nana, so I wore Converse underneath the dress. Not as sexy as the strappy sandals, but so much more comfortable.

And my sneakers were good for pacing, which was what I was doing because it was five thirty-five, and I hadn't heard from or seen Malone since a text the night before.

Brené Brown watched me pace from her perch on top of the love seat, her tiny, fuzzy head tracking my motion as I paced toward the patio door and then back toward the apartment door.

Finally, the doorbell rang.

"You be good," I said to the cat before turning my attention to the door.

Malone walked in, his hair still wet from the shower. "Stark, could you please help me with this torture device?"

"Can't. It goes against my religion to dress you."

He arched an eyebrow, the one over his blue eye. "The sooner you get me dressed, the sooner you can get me undressed."

"Well, when you put it like that," I said as I stepped closer. When I breathed in his vanilla bourbon chai cologne, my fingers fumbled, but I recovered enough to fix his bow tie.

"Not usually a suit kind of guy," he said as I straightened it.

"You look awfully good in a suit, but you also look good in sweats. I'd say you're very versatile in that way, Malone."

"Well, let me take a look at you, then."

I stepped back and curtsied. "It's your favorite color."

He made a sound that wasn't quite a word, more an appreciative grunt of choked admiration.

"And it has pockets!" I said with a twirl.

He laughed. "What is it with women and pockets?"

"Oh, you wouldn't know. You've always got pockets. They even put pockets in some swim trunks, as if that isn't an invitation to accidentally take one's wallet and phone into a pool."

"You're right about—are those tennis shoes?"

I stood up straight, prepared to defend my footwear choice. "They're sparkly. And sparkly means fancy."

I waited for him to complain, but instead he shook his head in amusement before pointing at the puzzle piece on the wall. "See? Intriguing."

By this time, Brené Brown had come to inspect her favorite human. Malone bent and scooped her up.

"Stop it! You're going to get cat hair all over your suit," I said.

"But she's so cute."

"Her name is Brené Brown." I took the kitten from him but held her away from my body as I walked her back to the bathroom. Not only did I not quite trust her to have the run of the apartment while I was gone, but I also had a lint roller in there.

"Come on, Stark," he said a few minutes later, as I attacked his suit with the roller. "I'm the one who has to perform, not you."

I laid a hand along his jaw. "Oh, my sweet summer child. I am your date. You will be judged by me, which is why I almost didn't wear the tennis shoes, but . . . I hate heels."

"No one's gonna be looking at your feet," he said before pointedly directing his gaze to my cleavage. "In fact, let's just skip the whole thing . . ."

"Nope," I said. "We go. You play nice with Gramps. We get free food and free booze. We come home. We get naked. That's the plan."

He winced. "There are so many reasons why I only like the last part of that plan."

"Come on. You can tell me on the way."

As we drove to the Hilton, Malone told me about how he'd flown to the Caymans and then to Wyoming in search of information. He'd come up empty both times.

"Because you were looking for shell companies and had some reason to believe Blake might be in town to create one, dissolve one, or just visit Old Faithful," I said.

"I can't get anything past you, can I?"

"And shell companies are a great way to hide, launder, or embezzle money. Or to avoid paying taxes."

"High marks, Ms. Stark. We'll make a forensic accountant out of you yet."

"No thanks. I took one accounting class so I could handle the books for the PI business, and it's not my ministry. Come to think of it, I can't wait for Ken to come asking me to do the taxes next year. That's going to be a big fat no."

"All that and brains, too."

"Laying it on thick, aren't you?" I said. "I mean, keep it up. Flattery will get you everywhere."

"Oh, keeping it up isn't going to be a problem. Keeping it down until it's time to get it up is going to be the problem."

I couldn't help but grin. "You're incorrigible."

"And you love me for it."

That I do.

Nope. Not even. Uh-huh. No L-word. Time to change the subject. "I still bet you that Blake makes an appearance."

Malone snorted. "He's not that stupid."

"I told you. It's not about being stupid. He tricked you into thinking he was somewhere else. He probably thinks he's destroyed all the evidence you've been collecting, so why not?"

He opened his mouth to speak but then closed it.

"Speaking of, Malone, what do you have on your cousin?"

"I can't tell you, it's—"

"Classified," we said together.

"But who am I going to tell? I've served the papers, but I wish I could help Trista get her hands on some of the money he took from their joint funds."

He stared out at a sea of brake lights. I gave him time to consider. He had plenty because there was a wreck up ahead. Thanks to both the accident and rush-hour traffic, it was going to take us twenty minutes to go five miles. Finally, he said, "There was a security breach a few years back, and Grandpa called my company in to both investigate and shore up security."

"Okay," I said.

"We found the source, a nasty piece of malware, and I strongly suspected Blake was behind it at the time, but I couldn't prove anything."

"And he's somehow used the info from that breach to embezzle money?"

Malone winced. "Yes. So after the malware, he used a SQL injection to—"

"I'm going to stop you right there," I said. "You can go through all your computer jargon, and it will sound like Farsi to me, so to sum up: He hacked his own company and has been benefiting ever since, so they called you in again."

"That's the long and the short of it," Malone had to admit. "I've tracked down two shell companies, countless fraudulent invoices, deliberate misconfigurations—"

"English, Malone. English."

"My cousin did a bunch of shady shit, but I have to connect all the dots and then show my work."

"Better."

"Good. Am I still getting laid tonight?"

"Absolutely. I'm sure you can explain all that to me later tonight in a technical way, and it will be like sweet nothings. For now, though, I'm just trying to get a clear picture of what Blake did."

"That's the problem. Even worse, *someone* distracted me, so I hadn't taken a picture of my wall in a few days. I've got to redo some of the work I'd already done."

"Sorry not sorry?"

"One of my hard drives didn't back up to the cloud, either. It's a mess. Definitely more complicated than usual, which makes me think he's not working alone. He has to have someone else on the inside who's helping him, because while he may not be stupid, he also isn't that bright. For example, I would've skipped the haircut if I were him."

"That's because you're not a raging narcissist."

"True."

A car jumped in front of him. He neither cursed nor gestured nor questioned their parentage. I was impressed. Had I been driving, I would've called that person everything but a child of God. In multiple languages.

"Well, fifty dollars still says he shows up tonight," I said.

"I think you're wrong there, Stark. He wouldn't dare."

"He would. In fact, he will," I said.

"Fine. I'll take that bet," Malone said.

"Now, tell me about the ex. I take my obligations seriously, too."

He groaned. "Must I?"

"I gotta know who I'm figuratively punching."

"Fine. When I came to Atlanta to look into the data breach, I met Grandpa's personal assistant."

"Why do I think this story isn't going to end well?"

"Because you're a smart woman. When I met Selena, I was sure she was the one. We dated long distance for a couple of years, with a lot of flying between Atlanta and California, and I'd proposed. I had even researched opening a branch of my company in Atlanta so we could live here. Then she dumped me."

"So she is *not* a smart woman."

"I don't know about that," he said with a chuckle as we inched through traffic.

"And she's the one who was so hateful about your eyes."

"Yeah," he said with a sigh. "She also said I lacked ambition, was a poor dresser, and was an out-of-shape slob."

"And you want me to smile in her face rather than smack her?"

"Yes."

I practically pulsed with anger. "Wait a minute. Lack ambition? You're the cofounder of Chateau Cybersecurity."

"Someone's done her homework."

"And I can assure you that you are neither a slob nor out of shape," I said, squirming in my seat at the memory of our mostly naked dining room table encounter. Meals hadn't been the same since.

"Ah, well, I may have ramped up my workout game with the hopes of winning her back."

My stomach roiled. "So you invited me to make her jealous enough she would reconsider?"

"Winning her back was the original plan," he said. "But I scrapped it the day I ran into an intriguing woman who was looking for a 'Man in Finance.'"

I felt a stab of something. Wanting? Hoping?

Remember that this is a short-term arrangement. Keep it light.

"Which is funny because I am not looking for a man in finance."

"That's good," he said. "I mean, you did find a man who plays with numbers all day, but . . ."

His voice trailed off as we turned into the hotel's parking lot. The valet, bless him, opened my door before I could say or do anything stupid.

Get it together, Stella.

As much as I hated to admit it, Havisham had to be right. If going this long without sex made me an emotional mess, then I was going to have to find a long-term friend with benefits after Malone left.

After he handed off his keys, he met me on the other side of the car and offered his arm. We entered the hotel, and I almost groaned with pleasure at the wave of air-conditioning that rushed over us.

"You can't make sounds like that until after the party," Malone whispered in my ear.

Okay, so I did groan with pleasure.

"I can make no promises," I said. "My love affair with air-conditioning is well known."

We passed through the lobby and headed down a carpeted hall, eventually coming to the end of a line of formally dressed people.

Great. From automobile traffic to people traffic. Thank goodness I'd worn the Converse.

Malone leaned over to say softly, "You're about to come face-to-face with my ex sooner rather than later."

We inched forward.

Unlike Malone, I couldn't see that far ahead of me. I took a step to the side and craned my neck to see a model-thin woman with tawny skin and long, straight black hair standing at the door with a clipboard. She was the opposite of me in every way: tall, slender, fashionable, reserved.

Stella, it doesn't matter. "Opposite" doesn't mean more or less than.

I could tell myself that, but making Malone's ex jealous felt nigh impossible, so I redirected my attention to finding Blake. He wasn't in line. He could've already been in the ballroom, but I doubted it. He struck me as the kind to run late so all eyes would be on him when he entered—especially since he didn't know about all Malone's backups.

Finally, it was our turn to check in, and I was face-to-face with the woman who'd broken Malone's heart. I put on my best smile, but I couldn't control what my eyes said.

"Selena," Malone said with a nod.

"Ty! So good to see you." She put her clipboard to her side so she could wrap him in a hug.

Apparently, he'd shared his first name with her. Apparently, she'd chosen a nickname rather than calling him Malone. I found that irrationally irritating on his behalf.

Even so, there was no way I would ever be able to make this sleek-haired goddess jealous. What had Malone been thinking?

The goddess turned and extended her hand to me. "I'm so sorry to ignore you. I'm Selena."

"Stella," I said, shaking her hand a tad more forcefully than I had to.

"Nice to meet you, Stella." She turned to Malone and, honest to God, giggled. "Do you only date women with names that begin with *S*?"

"Looks like," said Malone.

"Well, it's good to see you with a plus-one."

He draped an arm around my shoulders. "Amazing how life sometimes plops the perfect person just across the breezeway."

My heart skipped a beat at the word "perfect."

Stop it, Stella. It's part of the act. Now smile. Innocently.

"Yes. Amazing." Her smile stayed in place, but her eyes took on a more calculating gleam. They flicked toward my cleavage. Ha! There was one point—well, two, really—in my favor.

My body, meanwhile, had leaned into Malone like a plant toward the sun.

"Well." Selena cleared her throat in a dainty yet authoritative way. "I've checked you off the guest list, so . . . have fun."

"We will," Malone said, his arm sliding down my shoulders to settle at the small of my back. I shivered with anticipation of our post-party Finnegan.

How little time could we spend here?

Chapter 27

As we entered the ballroom, I rolled my shoulders back and focused on standing up straight. This was, after all, a crowd that took posture and manners very seriously.

Also, since I'd chosen Chucks over high heels, I needed every inch I could get.

All around me, women wore designer dresses, just as Nana had predicted. My dress might not have been as expensive, but it fit me perfectly. Selena wasn't the only impossibly thin woman to gaze with envy at my cleavage. Some of the older ladies barely contained their disdain. I told Nana the electric blue would've been a safer bet for me.

I caught Malone looking at me with hungry eyes. He looked as though he might plop me on one of the tables. I took in a ragged breath at the thought.

Never mind. No regrets.

Finally, Malone settled me at a table toward the front of the ballroom. "Want a drink before I go kiss Grandpa's ring?"

"I'd love one. Something white, please."

As he strode to the bar, I scanned the room. In the corner, Nana chatted with a distinguished older gentleman. She wore the same electric-blue dress I'd tried on, only two sizes smaller.

Well played, Nana.

I had to admit she fit in well with the ladies who lunched.

Finding Blake—so I could get the fifty dollars from Malone I would have to give Havisham later—would be more difficult. Not only were the lights dimmed, but the men all wore tuxedos, an absolute sea of black. This old-money crowd wasn't going to experiment with color or styles like actors at the Oscars.

My Malone returned with a glass of wine for me and a bottle of beer for him. I raised a brow in inquiry.

"Sauvignon blanc," he said.

"As long as you don't serve Mrs. Q's casserole with it."

"Pretty sure it's going to be rubber chicken tonight."

I made a face. "Did you happen to bring any of your medicinal hot sauce?"

He gave me a lopsided smile. "Sorry, but no."

"Alas."

He took a sip of his beer, and I froze as I recognized the label. As casually as I could, I asked, "Malone, what are you drinking?"

"A Blue Moon."

I had not specified to the universe which blue moon I meant. But it couldn't be the beer. What was Malone going to do? Hold the bottle up and let us kiss underneath it as if it were mistletoe?

"Oh boy." His face contorted.

"What?"

"You need to come with me, so sip a bit of that liquid courage."

"Why?"

"Grandpa spotted you and inclined his head. I'm afraid you must be vetted."

My nose wrinkled. "Like a show pony?"

"Something like that."

I took a sip and stood. "Fine. Let's get this over with. I'm happy to help relieve your boredom and to attempt to make Selena jealous, but I didn't sign up to have an old man check my teeth."

"He won't check your teeth."

"Thank God."

"He has people for that."

"Dammit, Malone."

He took my hand and gave it a squeeze; electricity ran up my arm, and happiness spilled over my head and down my body. As we approached a group of people standing at the edge of a dais, the crowd of men parted to make room for us. Each of those men sized me up. I stood straighter, which had the unfortunate—or fortunate, depending on your point of view—effect of pushing my chest forward.

Conversation stopped.

"Grandpa," Malone said as he released my hand with one last reassuring squeeze and then stepped forward to hug his grandfather.

His grandfather's eyes bored through me, and I had a flash of the future. Malone would one day look like this: hair more sandy than gray, eyes crinkling, still trim, still commanding.

But not as scary. No, Malone would always have a twinkle in his eyes.

"This is my date, Stella Stark."

Lucius Malone looked me up and down. He didn't have to check my teeth to make me feel like a show pony. "Stark. Of the Kennesaw Avenue Starks?"

"Uh, more like the McDonald Street Starks?"

He nodded. "And you know this boy is going back to California?"

"He has made that abundantly clear."

"Good. Nice to meet you." He turned back to his cronies, and Malone escorted me to our table once more.

"Malone, I think he just relegated this pony to the glue factory."

"Uh-huh," he replied in such a way I knew he hadn't heard a word I'd said.

"Malone?"

"Oh, sorry." He turned his beautifully mismatched eyes to me. "It doesn't matter what he thinks, but I also won't let anyone take you to the glue factory."

"Great. You look like you just saw a ghost."

Movement across the room caught his attention again. He sighed and took his wallet from his back pocket, flipped through some bills, and handed me a fifty.

My head jerked up, my eyes searching in the direction he'd been looking.

Sure enough, there was Blake Malone, glad-handing and shoulder slapping his way to his grandfather. When he came to us, he stopped, his faux smile fading from his face.

"Ty."

"Blake."

He had almost dismissed me entirely when it clicked for him. "You!"

"Yes?"

"You're the b—one who's conspiring with my wife to take everything I own."

So many things I could've said about logical consequences, not sleeping around on your spouse, not stealing from your own company. I said none of them, which only proved monumental personal growth on my part. Instead, I said, "I was hired to deliver papers. I delivered them."

"You're with *him*?" He said the last word with such disgust that Malone recoiled.

"Yes, quite happily so," I said, putting a hand on my date's chest.

"I *would* have the one process server who'd actually met my cousin," he muttered under his breath before recovering his earlier persona with a ghost of a smile. "No matter."

He jerked his chin upward and moved toward his grandpa.

"Remarkable restraint, Stark," Malone said softly.

"See? I can keep all your secrets," I said.

He started to say something, but a tapping on a microphone stopped him. We sat down at our table, waiting for stragglers to find their way to their assigned seats.

It was time for the show to begin.

An hour later, we'd watched a slideshow about Malone Menagerie, Lucius Malone's literal pet project, while consuming rubbery hotel chicken with equally unappetizing vegetables. While we ate above-average cheesecake and drank questionable coffee, Selena treated us to a recitation of everything Malone Construction had accomplished so far that year, along with sneaking in a not-so-subtle hint that the company was looking to go public.

Aha. If the company wanted to go public, then that would explain a good deal of why Malone was so cagey. Might also explain why he hadn't corrected me when, after our Habitat date, I'd called him Blake.

Habitat date?

Not a date.

But I could see where it might be handy to have my Malone sit in on a Zoom call while others *assumed* he was Blake. That would give the company time to figure out what had gone wrong and to clean up their mess before going public.

Seemed like a scheme Lucius Malone might concoct, but it was also conjecture on my part.

I snapped back to the present when Selena called Lucius to the podium. He pretended to be embarrassed at first but then did an excellent job of pontificating as well as insinuating he had no plans to retire anytime soon.

After dessert, Selena declared the silent auction open and called folks to the sizable dance floor that sat to the side of the dais. Malone excused himself, presumably to visit the little boys' room, and I wandered the edges of the ballroom to ostensibly check out the auction items, which were displayed on white-clothed tables. Each had a sheet of paper and a pen for bids.

Not a single item started at less than $500.

Which hadn't stopped Nana from adding her name in neat cursive to a sheet of paper for a cruise to the Caribbean.

I hugged myself. This was definitely a look-and-don't-touch situation for me.

Blue Ridge Mountain cabin rentals and other vacation packages. Works of art. Jewelry. Autographed sports memorabilia. Rare first editions.

Each and every one was well out of my price range.

I smelled Malone before he spoke. Bourbon, vanilla, spice, and everything nice.

"Wanna dance?" he asked, his voice rumbling through my body.

I whirled around. "Depends. Are we doing the Macarena?"

"Nope."

"Cha Cha Slide?"

"If only."

"The Wobble?"

"In this crowd? That I would pay to see."

We reached the dance floor as the last strains of Kool and the Gang's "Celebration" launched into a slow song. This was both good and bad. My body hummed in anticipation, but our night was far from over.

Also, how were we going to play this? Formal slow dance or lock my hands behind his neck and sway like teens at prom?

Malone put one hand on my waist and took my hand with the other. I put my left hand on his sturdy shoulder. Maybe he was keeping it formal because his body was humming, too.

"You're a good dancer, Stark."

"I took dance lessons when I was younger," I said as the singer crooned about a lady in red.

Then I did a double take as Nana danced past with Lucius Malone. Were they fox-trotting? Bold choice at such a slow tempo.

Malone leaned forward so we were cheek to cheek just as the singer uttered those words. I forgot about Nana or grandfathers, foxtrots or duplicitous cousins.

For a moment it felt as though it really were just him and me.

"You look gorgeous tonight, Stark," he whispered. "But I think I'm going to like that dress even better once it's on the floor."

"You look 007 yummy yourself."

That earned me a chuckle, just as I had hoped it would.

"I think purple is forever my favorite color."

"I'm not sure I'm kitted out well enough to make your ex jealous, though. Faking it until I make it, Malone."

"Stark, your smile is as genuine as your, ahem, assets. And when I went to the restroom just now, she asked if we could catch up sometime soon."

I stiffened in spite of myself. "Oh?"

"I told her I had a lot on my plate right now. Really busy."

Enjoy the moment, Stark.

And so I did, closing my eyes and swaying with a handsome man, enjoying the anticipation of an even better night to come.

"Just so you know, I plan to keep you very busy this evening." His baritone reverberated through my body.

"How soon can we duck out of here?"

Malone held me out at arm's length, his gaze one of hungry admiration. Before he could say anything, though, Selena announced, "And now it's time for our annual foxtrot competition."

"What?"

Malone shrugged. "Weird rich-people stuff. I told you there'd be no Cha Cha Slide around here."

I was about to suggest we leave the floor when Lucius Malone appeared at my elbow. "Mind if I cut in?"

Chapter 28

Malone's smile faded. I could almost feel the tension he held coiled inside. Bless him, he wanted to protect me from potential embarrassment.

But I had mentioned dancing lessons, hadn't I?

"Of course." I bestowed a megawatt smile on Lucius and then winked at a nervous Malone as he backed off the floor, frowning in confusion.

Lucius met my smile with one of his own. Much like Edith Wharton's titular house, it held no mirth, despite promises to the contrary. He was a man on a mission, and that mission appeared to be embarrassing me.

Well, good luck with that, Gramps.

Selena stepped up to the microphone. "Okay, folks, you know the rules. A tap on the shoulder means your foxtrot isn't good enough, so step aside and let the professionals show you how it's done. Good luck beating me and—" She faltered when she saw that Lucius had chosen me as his partner. "Well, good luck beating Mr. Malone and his new partner."

She'd recovered quickly, but now she scowled at me.

So I'd taken her place in more ways than one. A delicious schadenfreude, that.

"Know how to foxtrot, little girl?"

I trained my eyes on Gramps and held my expression neutral. "A little."

The DJ put on a new song, big band. Ah, Frank Sinatra's "The Way You Look Tonight," which happened to be Nana's favorite song for teaching the foxtrot at cotillion classes.

Cotillion classes that she'd made me take more than once because she had to keep an eye on me, and it was easier to do that if I was on the floor with the other students. Also, she never had enough boys, so she taught me how to lead or follow depending on her needs for that day.

I preferred to lead, but Lucius Malone wasn't one to follow, so I gave in to the slow-slow-quick steps, paying attention anytime Lucius wanted to twirl me or promenade. A little zigzag from time to time. A dip. By the time we'd rounded the floor twice, the only couples left were us and Nana and her partner.

She was making him look good, whispering her moves all the while.

Lucius's eyes narrowed as he realized we were down to two. He certainly wasn't telling me his plans, but I adapted easily. His eyes met mine, and I smiled. We had one thing in common: We both wanted to win. I gave him a slight nod, and off we went. Same-foot lunge? I faltered only briefly. Weave, feather-step finish? We did it all.

As the song faded, I saw we were alone. We'd dipped before, but his last dip was deep enough I wished I'd taped everything in place. Blessedly, I remained family friendly.

The crowd around the dance floor applauded. He bowed, and I curtsied.

"Well, well," he said as he led me from the floor, his eyes now crinkling with good humor and admiration. "I see young Ty has found a woman with a few tricks up her sleeve."

Oh, he really had no idea.

"Thank you for the dance, Mr. Malone."

"I think you've earned the right to call me Lucius," he said as he lifted my hand to kiss it. "Now, if you'll excuse me, I'm afraid I've lost a bet and need to settle up."

My eyes cut to Nana, and I knew she'd originated that bet, thanks to her smug smile.

"Hold up, Grandpa."

Blake placed a hand on his grandfather's arm, but Lucius carefully took his arm back. I sat in the nearest seat, pretending to scan the ballroom for Malone while eavesdropping on their edge-of-the-dance-floor conversation. *I* wouldn't have chosen that spot for a serious conversation, but I could pick out only 60 percent of what they were saying, so it wasn't the worst idea.

Gramps told Blake he had nothing else to say to him. Blake said several things I couldn't quite understand, probably because smarm required a lower tone of voice.

When Lucius snapped his fingers, I sat up straighter. Men in black polos and black slacks filtered through the crowd.

Security.

"Tell you what, grandson. You answer all their questions, then you and I can chat," Lucius said before resuming his trek across the dance floor, straight to . . . my nana.

"You ready to blow this Popsicle stand?"

I whirled around to see Malone, his tie already loosened.

"I thought you'd never ask."

When we passed the valet stand, I looked up at Malone. "Where are we going?"

"I thought long and hard—and I do mean hard—about how we can't seem to enjoy ourselves uninterrupted. I decided to book a hotel room."

"Oh."

He stopped. "You don't like that idea?"

"No, that was a good 'oh.'"

He grinned and then grabbed my hand. "Glad you approve."

"Let me just text Addie to see if she can take care of the kitten."

That accomplished, we stepped into the elevator, and he was about to kiss me when another couple joined us. They, too, wore tux and evening gown. They, too, had booked a room for the night, which, based on how the woman was teetering, was probably a good idea.

The woman appeared to be my mother's age, maybe mid-fifties. Her husband—I could see their wedding bands—about the same age. He steadied her elbow as she swayed, then his hand slid to rest on her lower back. She grinned at him over her shoulder, and his small smile twitched.

Despite all my talk of sex and nothing but, some inner part of me twisted, wanting the same long-term bond this couple had. I had no way of knowing empirically that they had been married to each other for a long time, but I'd watched a lot of couples in my time. I'd seen new love, old love, clandestine love, and plain ol' lust. I would've bet the fifty I'd just won that this couple was one of the lucky ones, the kind of couple who got together and stayed together, the kind of couple who understood what they had found in each other, and appreciation of that rare bond kept them together through the ups and downs of marriage vows.

If anyone could ever give me a guarantee that I'd have that kind of love with another person, I would've taken it, but I'd seen too many marriages splintered. At this point staying together *without* a piece of paper seemed daring enough, and I hadn't managed that.

Well, I had. My partner had not.

The man whispered something in the woman's ear, and she laughed out loud. The brash sound echoed off the elevator walls, but she didn't seem to care in the least that she had an audience. No one other than him mattered, and it was clear to see that nothing but her mattered to him.

My eyes met Malone's; his were once again fire and ice.

They got off the elevator on the floor before ours.

Before the door closed completely, Malone pulled me in for a long, searching kiss.

The elevator lurched to a stop, but he took his lips from mine only when the doors opened. Down the hall we went, my hand in his, but I had to take two steps for every one of his, so I was glad for the sneakers. Once we reached the door to a suite at the end of the hall, he held the key to the sensor, and we were in.

I reached for him, but he said, "Hold up."

Something akin to dread threatened to bring my meal back up. Surely, he wasn't going to call it all off now.

"Where's your phone?" he asked with all the sternness of a nineteenth-century schoolmaster.

"My phone?"

"Yep."

He brandished his and then made a production of holding the buttons to power it down before swiping with a flourish to turn it off.

I took my phone from my pocket and did the same.

Then my back was against the wall, and Malone's lips were on mine.

He kissed along my cheek. "No cats. No neighbors. No exes. No cousins. No phone calls."

I took in a ragged breath. We were going to do this. There was no way out this time.

And I didn't want one.

"Wait."

"Wait what?"

"Condoms?"

He looked at me as if I'd lost my mind. "Woman, I am a planner. I was running late to pick you up because I checked into this hotel room *before* I drove over to get you. I dipped up here earlier to make sure everything was in place."

I looked beyond him to see electric tealights flickering. Rose petals on the bed. "Oh."

"Is that another good 'oh,' I hope?"

I bit my lip as I nodded, tears pricking my eyes. "No one's ever gone to this much trouble for me."

"More's the pity, Stark," he said as his hand caressed my cheek.

I stood on my tiptoes to kiss him, a slower kiss this time. He backed toward the bed, leading me as he went. He spun me around and sat me on the edge of the bed, then crouched to take one of my shoes. "I considered drinking champagne from one of your shoes, but I think I'll pass, if that's okay with you. Might ruin the glitter."

"And sparkly is fancy," I said, as he unlaced my high-tops and placed them on the floor. He then stood and kicked off his shoes. They went flying in either direction, no heed paid to whether he stretched them out by removing them without unlacing them first.

I stood to help him with his tie as he shrugged out of his jacket. "I feel as though I'm unwrapping a present."

"No, Stark, pretty sure you're the present."

My fingers trembled as I labored to undo the buttons on his vest, then his shirt, then his cuff links—all of which eventually ended up on the floor. "Well, you're an obstacle course, Malone."

"And for once, you aren't," he said, kissing my shoulder as he unzipped my dress.

"We'll see about that."

My dress pooled at my feet.

"Yep. Definitely looks better on the floor," he said.

My eyes traveled to his tattoo. I traced it with my finger, then traced a line down his chest to his belt buckle, causing him to suck in a breath. He put a hand over mine. "I'm a big believer in ladies first."

"Malone, I'm nearly naked already."

"Nearly," he said as he unclasped my bra. "But nearly is not good enough."

My bra hit the floor, and his hands became my new support. I gasped.

"Perfect," he said.

"Nobody's perfect."

"Hush and let me take my fill of you. I skipped dessert for a reason."

I didn't have time to question what he meant by that because he had my hair at the nape of my neck, gently tugging, his mouth on mine. I gave in to the moment, utterly adrift in the feel of him, the taste of him, the very essence of him.

He worshipped my body with a gentle fierceness. Tears again pricked my eyes.

He did, in fact, intend to ruin me for all other men.

Somehow, I'd landed on the bed, and now Malone slid down my body, gathering my thighs over his shoulders, about to do something Ken had done precisely once. I sat up on my elbows. "Malone?"

"Oh, please don't say 'anchovies,'" he said while tracing my calf, an area I'd never considered an erogenous zone until that very minute.

"You want to do this?"

"Most emphatically yes."

And so he did. At the first touch of his tongue, I lost all thought. With seconds, orgasm found me, and I had a new appreciation for the phrase "earth-shattering."

"Stark, you're supposed to make a man work for it," Malone said with a chuckle from where he now stood at the foot of the bed, working with his belt.

Another full-body shudder came over me. "I meant to play it coy, but . . ."

He dropped trou, and I sucked in a breath at the sight of him: broad shoulders, trim waist, sculpted arms and legs, and an impressive erection.

"Two five seven," I said.

"What are you—oh," he said with a grin. "But I don't need your Social Security number."

"Just covering my bases," I said.

Condom now on, he joined me on the bed, kissing me breathless and using his hands to touch and tease me back to the edge. I whispered, "July fourth."

"A firecracker, huh?" He traced the outline of my breast.

"Jefferson. You can steal my identity if you would only—"

He kissed my words away, and then his body joined mine. Time both slowed down and sped up. Amid the wonder of it all, I looked up to see that small muscle in his jaw tighten with the effort to restrain himself. That act of self-denial sent me hurtling once more, and he soon joined me before collapsing at my side.

Still panting, I laid a hand on his cheek before whispering, "You've definitely ruined me."

He turned his face to kiss my hand. "I was about to tell you the same thing."

Chapter 29

By tacit understanding, we didn't joke about pizza or benefits after that. We did, however, make love twice more. I, by some miracle, woke up before Malone the next morning. He slept on his back with his head resting on his right arm, so I could see the tattoo that wrapped around his bicep.

I had traced it with my tongue.

Kinda wanted to do it again.

As he slept, hair mussed, eyelashes longer than any man's had a right to be, a deep longing ballooned inside me, threatening to burst. This was what I'd thought I had with Ken. This was what I wanted.

No, not the sex, although, yes, the sex.

What I wanted was to go through life with someone who so clearly saw who I was but didn't feel the need to change me, someone who not only loved me but—

There's absolutely no indication that Malone loves you.

Maybe I had been so starved for basic consideration and affection that I was confusing that for love. What was it Havisham had said? That the patriarchy was a helluva drug and too many men were getting high on their own stash? Here was a man who went to what felt like an insane amount of trouble for me. Only one in a million would've walked away from me, giving up a quick pleasure for a longer one, on what I now referred to as the Day I Almost Desecrated My Dining Room Table.

So of course he's going back to California. Of course we won't even have the chance to see if this relationship has legs.

He had mentioned researching a move to Atlanta for her, though . . .

But had what happened in his previous relationship soured him on long-distance relationships?

Talk about putting the cart before the horse, Stella. One night of sex does not a relationship make.

No matter what happened from this point forward, I knew one thing: I would rather be a cat lady than put up with another hollow substitute for a fulfilling relationship.

I wasn't going back to Ken, and I wasn't going to waste my time with anyone like him.

"Stark, why are you staring at me so intently?" Malone's voice rumbled through me.

There were many things I could've said. I could've asked where he'd been my whole life. I could've asked him to stay, but my pride chafed at that. No, I'd stick to the terms of our arrangement—i.e., that this was temporary. I finally settled for a cheeky, "One for the road?"

He frowned, but it was only when he thumbed away my tears that I realized I was crying.

"Hey, hey. I didn't hurt you, did I?"

"No, oh no. Far from it," I said, a sob escaping despite my best efforts.

He drew me closer so that my cheek lay on his chest and then kissed the top of my head. "Then I can only conclude someone else has."

I snorted. "Maybe."

"Are you trying to crack a joke in the middle of what is obviously trauma?"

"Maybe."

"You know, I'd hoped for breakfast in bed, maybe that one for the road you mentioned, but I'm afraid we now only have time to cuddle for ten minutes."

"But I'm comfortable where I am, and checkout isn't until eleven," I said, even as a tear slid down my cheek. "Why only ten minutes?"

"Because at that time, I will have to hunt down the person and/or people who hurt you and beat them up."

I laughed through a sob.

What a mess I was.

I slithered on top of him and began to kiss him with a desperation that scared me. It was a desperation full of fear that he would leave, that I would be wrecked, or, even worse, that I wouldn't be wrecked but would be left utterly numb once again. But most of all, it was a fear that I didn't deserve the affection he'd so lavishly bestowed on me.

"Banana pepper."

I froze.

He was done with me already? I rolled off the bed and went to the window to peek at our mountain view at least once. Doing so had the added advantage that Malone couldn't see my tears. For heaven's sake, why did they have to show up right now? I didn't cry when I discovered Ken was sleeping around on me. Or any of the times my mother left. Or even—

Nope. Not going there.

This was all Brené Brown's fault—the author's, not the cat's. Some of that vulnerability I'd been reading about must've rubbed off on me.

I wasn't a fan.

"What is going on in that beautiful head of yours?" he asked.

So much, Malone. So much—and none of it good.

When I didn't answer, he continued, "For the record, I would love to make love to you again, but I have this pesky rule against having sex with women who are crying. Silly, I know."

"Nope. Not silly," I said, trying to get myself together. "You are just so . . ."

"Oh no," he muttered. "This isn't going to be good."

"Wholesome."

"Wholesome?"

I turned around, furiously wiping my tears away. "Yes. Like Captain America. Or Superman."

He sat up and patted the bed beside him. "That sounds like something you say before you let a guy down easy. And here I thought I was pretty filthy last night."

"You were," I said, as flashes of assorted positions and sensations from the night before flitted through my mind. "But you were also so kind, and I . . . am not."

He looked at me as though I were off my rocker. "Of course you are."

"No, oh no."

The damned tears were back.

"Stella Stark, what are you talking about?"

"If you are the hero, then I am the villain. You remember the puzzle piece story I told you, don't you?"

He laughed. "You were a child!"

I took in a deep breath. "Remember when you said your grandfather was petty?"

"Yeah, and?"

"I am Little Miss Petty. I do mean things to people. Sure, in my mind they deserve it, but that doesn't change the fact that I'm doing mean things. The other day I suggested someone bring in a sweater full of cat hair so a mansplainer, who is allergic to cats, I might add, would shut up."

He fought a smile.

"I suggested one person use a dog whistle at night so their neighbor's dog would bark and keep them awake."

"What had the neighbor done, though?"

"Claim that her dog *never* barked while she was at work. In all actuality, the dog barked all day long."

His expression was oddly neutral. "I know I haven't known you *that* long, but I can't see you being petty, much less mean."

So I told him about Salcedo and what I'd done to Tanner.

"You publicly embarrassed a tool and exposed his sexist ways, probably saved Salcedo both heartache and venereal disease, but you're the bad person here?"

"He sure seemed to think so." Then I told Malone about the flamingos.

He snorted. "He had it coming."

Finally, in frustration, I said, "Malone, I tried to get revenge on you."

"What? Why?"

There. There was some anger, finally. Well, irritation, really. I wasn't entirely certain Malone experienced the sort of bone-crushing rage that sometimes took over me.

"The Habitat for Humanity thing? I did that."

He frowned in confusion. "But you went to the worksite and helped. You told me they must've knocked on my door by mistake."

I shook my head. "No mistake. All carefully orchestrated."

"Why?"

"Trista hired me to deliver some comeuppance to Blake, and she told me Blake lived in your apartment—"

"Which he did until a few months ago."

"I figured he—well, you—would cuss them out and then slam the door in their faces."

"You thought Blake would do a Habitat build?" He laughed to the point of his own tears.

"And Habitat didn't deserve to suffer, so I was in my work clothes and ready to go so they wouldn't be short a volunteer."

"So you, a supposedly mean person, took into consideration the feelings of volunteers and made a plan to make up for any damage you might do?"

"Yes, but that's not the point." I threw up my hands in exasperation, but my boobs jiggled, thus undermining the overall effect. "I'm thinking about it now, and I shouldn't have put volunteers into a position where they might be yelled at just to put someone else in an awkward position."

"All's well that ends well, Stark," he said. "I don't think you're going to make a habit of it."

"That's not all. I told Mrs. Q to make one of her awful casseroles for you."

His mouth dropped open. "Now that's diabolical, Stark. What did I ever do to you to deserve that?"

"Nothing! That's what I've been trying to tell you. I'm an awful person. I take money to do petty things to other people."

"Who paid you to make me eat that casserole?"

"Trista."

"So you weren't trying to get revenge on *me*—you were trying to get revenge on *Blake*."

"Yes!"

"You silly, silly woman," he said, his eyes radiating kindness. "You're not mean. You just have a keen sense of justice."

I sat agape. This was what it must have felt like to be truly seen, because Malone kept seeing only the good in my motives. He had easily observed something I only partially knew about myself.

One woman's petty was another's poetic justice.

"Wait a minute," he said with a frown. "Did you mail those ladybugs to me?"

"That was not me," I said.

He laid his head against the wall. "Thank God."

"But it was a seed I planted."

He groaned, and I told him the whole tale of Trista, Addie, and "All Too Well."

"So let me get this straight: You thought a thirteen-year-old girl *might* do something to irritate Blake, only it was really me, and all because he doesn't like Taylor Swift?"

"I mean, when you put it like that, it does sound ridiculous, but I figure you should never underestimate a middle schooler, and lo and behold if she didn't out-petty the original Little Miss Petty. Truly impressive."

He frowned. "I don't know if you should encourage that sort of behavior."

"What happened to my 'keen sense of justice'?"

He sighed and stared me down, but he was struggling to keep from smiling. "I think enlisting a teen in your revenge business could be considered contributing to the delinquency of a minor."

"No, no," I said automatically, "I didn't encourage her to do anything illegal. Besides, you have to admit the deadpan 'look what you made me do' was hilarious."

His expression didn't soften.

"Lay. Dee. Bugs. A thirteen-year-old came up with the idea of mailing you ladybugs and then implemented that plan. Complete with a punny note. There they were, all flying around."

The corners of his mouth twitched in a way I was beginning to love a little too much.

"If it really had been Blake, you would've thought it was hilarious."

"Well, I'm not Blake—thank God—so I tell you what—"

"What?"

"I truly detest insects, but bygones will be bygones as long as you do one thing for me."

"What's that?"

"Tell Addie that you had me confused with someone else and that I like Taylor Swift . . . 'All Too Well.'"

My mouth opened and closed. Had he just made a joke from a Taylor Swift song title? To get me to do something I didn't want to do in the least? Was this what payback felt like?

"But why? What does it matter?"

"First of all, you have impugned my honor. Second, I would hate to see what she might do next."

Make friendship bracelets that shocked? Burn his pictures? Write a song about him? "That's a fair point. I'll do it."

"Today."

"Today?"

"Yes, today."

"Fine. But only if you'll join me in the shower."

"You drive a hard bargain, Stark." His eyes twinkled as he scrubbed one hand over his lightly bearded chin in faux deliberation. "I guess I should take a shower to maintain my wholesome image."

I smacked his arm.

"Or I could be filthy and *then* we could head to the shower."

We almost got distracted a second time while getting dressed, but we had only ten minutes before checkout. I suggested we revisit my table once we returned to the apartments, and that gave us motivation to hurriedly put our formalwear back on.

"Is it a walk of shame, if we're *both* wearing the same clothes we wore yesterday?" I asked as we entered the elevator together, holding hands once more.

"I'm not ashamed of a damn thing," Malone said. "I'm gonna walk out of here with my head held high. Yes, I am carrying a bag of condoms, rose petals, and little electric candle thingies. Yes, I did have sex multiple times with this beautiful woman. This is a walk of pride."

His enthusiasm warmed me from the inside out, although a nasty little voice inside asked, *What if this is all he wanted? Now that he's had sex with you, he'll leave.*

I told that part of me to hush. We already had a date with my dining room table, so those old patterns of thinking were patently false.

The drive back to our apartments was much quicker than the trip to the hotel had been. For one, there was less traffic in the middle of the day. More importantly, however, I'd given Malone incentive to drive faster. At one point he showed irritation at someone driving slowly in front of him. I didn't say anything, but it gave me joy to see him acting as a mere mortal would.

"Oh, I think I forgot something," I said as we pulled into the apartment complex.

"What?" he asked, trying so hard to tamp down his annoyance that something else might delay us.

"My panties," I said with a wicked grin, as I stuffed them in the front pocket of his suit jacket.

"You are going to be the death of—what the hell?"

I looked from him to our building and saw that once again his apartment door was open.

Chapter 30

Once we reached his apartment door, Malone held out an arm to shield me from any potential horrors inside.

Cute that he thought I couldn't handle myself.

But also sweet.

I could feel that the apartment was already empty, though.

Well, almost empty. Lucius Malone sat in the recliner, staring at a television that wasn't turned on.

"Grandpa?"

"Where have you been, Tiberius?" he asked as he rotated the recliner to face us. Before Malone could answer him, he caught sight of me. "Ah. I see where you've been, and what you've been up to. I hope it was worth it."

"Excuse me?"

"She's in league with Blake's wife," he said, before adding under his breath, "Too bad. I *liked* her."

"I'm right here, so you don't have to talk about me in the third person," I said. "And I'm not 'in league' with anyone."

"Grandpa, what are you talking about?"

"I'm talking about how it would be best if you turned yourself in. I know you were behind the money that's missing." The older man looked as though he'd aged ten years overnight.

"Turn myself in? I've been helping you find the money."

The older man shook his head. "Blake showed me the reports. You may not have orchestrated that first cyberattack, but you've been profiting ever since, and you've tried to pin it all on him."

Malone ran a hand through his hair. "I have no idea what you're talking about. Blake's the one who's been siphoning thousands of dollars from Malone Construction through fraudulent invoices and shell companies. I have—"

He paused, and I could see the moment he remembered that Blake had taken most of his equipment and destroyed much of the hard work he'd put into his nerdy number mural. "I *had* the evidence."

"You still do." I tugged on his sleeve. "Remember Jarvis?"

"Oh, I could kiss you," he said as he exhaled with relief. "My backups."

"I'll bring it to you," I said as he turned to face his grandfather.

By the time I came back with the shoebox, he was showing his grandfather the walls in the second bedroom, how Blake had ruined his work.

"Well, at the very least, you're repainting these walls," Lucius said in a gruff voice.

"I will, I promise you, but I need you to believe me. I don't know how he managed to manipulate the information as he did, but I have a feeling it was the SQL injection and—"

He lapsed into his forensic accountant jargon. Computer terminology wasn't entirely foreign to me, but some of the business jargon was. Besides, I couldn't be a help to him with any of that.

Think, Stella, think.

"How do I know you didn't do this yourself to frame Blake?" Lucius asked, jarring me from my thoughts.

"Because . . ." Malone couldn't find the words because he would never do such a thing, but that wasn't necessarily a defense that Lucius would accept.

"I have video of Blake breaking into this apartment," I said, producing my phone.

"Breaking in?" asked Lucius.

"Well, he had a key, but still. He wasn't supposed to be here, and he was skulking about like he knew it," I said as I powered on my phone. Texts and calls came flying at me from Trista. I frowned but swiped those notifications away to find the video I'd saved.

Lucius frowned as he watched. "How am I supposed to know that's Blake instead of Ty here?"

"Well," I said. "See the glint of the sun on the watch?"

"Yes?"

"Come on, Grandpa, you know I don't wear a watch," Malone said as he held up his arm.

"And you can see Blake is wearing his watch on his left wrist. Which wrist would you wear your watch on, Malone?"

"My right."

Because my Malone was a leftie. Not that there was a tan line on either of his wrists to show he was in the habit of wearing a watch.

"Okay," Lucius said, but it didn't sound as though he believed me.

"Also, if you look at the length of the hair here"—I paused the video—"it's longer than Malone's and straighter. I mean, Blake's hair is shorter now because he was getting a haircut when I served divorce papers on him, but—"

Lucius's eyes bugged out. "*You* served him?"

"Sure did," I said with a grin. "Bet he didn't tell you that because then you'd know he had a reason to get back at both me and Trista."

"Huh." Lucius looked from Malone to me and back to Malone. "And you can show me how he made those reports? They look official to me."

"I'll need to go into the office to use the computer since he stole mine, but I can show you almost all of it," Malone said. "Blake managed to erase some of my work, but I make backups periodically and was in the process of restoring the original from the backups. I didn't want to come to you until I had everything in order."

Lucius looked from him to me. "And I guess Ms. Stark here was *helping* you with that?"

Malone gave him a lopsided grin. "Come on, Grandpa, I was hanging with Stella because, well, look at her."

I blushed. It was an unfamiliar sensation.

"Damn good at the foxtrot, too," the older man said. "That's not something you often see in a young woman."

Young? Well, bless his heart.

"I, uh, if you have everything you need, Malone, then I'll excuse myself," I said.

"Thanks, Stark," Malone said. He looked as though he wanted to say something more, but he shook the thoughts away, and I retreated.

I was fumbling with the key to my apartment when his door opened and then closed behind him. I turned to see what he wanted, and he drew me to him for a searing kiss.

"This is not how I anticipated this day would go."

"Me neither," I whispered. Somehow, resting forehead to forehead with him was almost as hot as the kiss had been.

"I'm going to be regrettably busy for the next few days, but I will be back. I will rent a hotel room again if that's what it takes. How do you feel about living on room service?"

"I'd be willing to give it a whirl."

He grinned before kissing me once more and then returning to what was, no doubt, going to be a lot of work.

I closed the door behind me, touching my fingers to my tingling lips.

Snap out of it, Stella. Malone may need your help again. Trista might, too.

Blake had been busy while we were, well, getting busy. But the very idea that Malone could be framed for Blake's nefarious activities? My stomach roiled.

And speaking of Blake, it would probably be wise to see why Trista was calling me. Technically, my work for her was over and done. And if it weren't for the petty business, we probably would've never met.

Usually, Attorney Lawless kept her clients from speaking to me if I was serving papers on a spouse. Legal technicalities and all that.

But performing acts of pettiness was far from normal, and I was beginning to really like Trista, so it would be nice to make sure she was doing okay.

Since her voicemail was full of noise and hysterics, and her texts were riddled with typos, I opted to call rather than try to figure out her message.

Trista didn't greet me with a hello. Instead, I got a "You!"

"Trista, are you okay?" I asked.

"No, I am not okay. There are a bunch of FBI agents tearing up my house looking for computer equipment, and they've made the kids and me sit in the front parlor while they do it."

I wasn't sure what this had to do with me, but I had a feeling it had something to do with Blake. Lucius Malone's words still rang in my ears: "She's in league with Blake's wife."

"Okay, calm down." Even as I said the words, I knew better. Never in the history of ever had anyone calmed down just because someone told them to do so.

"Calm down? *Calm down?*"

"Poor choice of words." Now my own heart hammered against my rib cage. "Have you called your lawyer?"

"I've called every lawyer I know."

In the background, feet stomped, and men murmured. Doors and cabinets opened and closed.

"Did they give you a copy of the search warrant?"

"Yes. It describes my house, which is unsettling, but not as unsettling as how it sounds like people are taking everything that isn't nailed down. I don't understand. *He* is the one who took the money."

"Trista," I said in my most soothing voice, "it's probably best to say nothing. Probably even better if we stop talking, because Blake told Lucius that you and I are working against him."

"What?" She shrieked the question.

"Blake has been backed into a corner, and I'd be willing to bet you that he set all of this in motion as a distraction."

She groaned. "He's going to disappear again, isn't he?"

"Probably, but he has been served. Ma—his cousin has the information the company needs. You sit tight."

"Hey, don't touch that!"

A scuffle on the other end of the line. A dog barked. A child began to cry.

"Trista, listen to me. I can't give you advice, but I'm going to mention, unrelated to anything, that you can google all sorts of wonderful things, from 'What is the capital of Estonia?' to 'What do I do if someone executes a search warrant in my house?' Some posts might mention, I don't know, taking pictures of everything after the fact . . . things like that."

"I don't understand what any of this has to do with me." Her voice came out as a ragged whisper, which suggested she was close to tears.

"You know, the other day, Malone, Ty Malone, that is, was telling me about his favorite amendment."

"Oh, what does that matter?" she snapped at the same time I continued.

"He really loves that Fifth Amendment, let me tell you."

"Ah," she said, pausing. "That is a great amendment."

"I mean, I like the right to assemble and the promise of a speedy trial as much as the next gal, but—"

"I gotta go. An agent has asked me if I have any questions."

She hung up on me. This was just as well because I didn't want her to remember the fourth amendment about no unreasonable searches or seizures. While a court of law had to have decided that it would be reasonable to search Trista's house, I had a feeling she wouldn't agree.

I collapsed on the love seat, and only then did I realize *my* apartment was entirely too quiet.

Where was my kitten?

Adrenaline surged once again, followed by the guilt of leaving her alone. I'd hastily texted Addie when it became clear Malone had plans for me, but had Addie forgotten? Accidentally let Brené Brown out?

All the interior doors were open. Had the kitten gotten into something she shouldn't have? Surely Addie hadn't taken her upstairs.

"Brené Brown, where are you?"

No answer.

I took in a deep breath and checked my phone for any texts from Addie. Relief whooshed through me. She had taken care of the cat.

But she'd also suggested I shorten my kitten's name to initials. Surely the creature wouldn't have adapted to initials in one evening.

"BB?"

She meowed and trotted into the living room.

"Are you being serious with me right now?" I asked the kitten. "I gave you a perfectly good name, and you and the girl upstairs have decided on something else?"

She paused to clean her face, not even making eye contact with me. If ever there were a poster kitten for the concept of "unbothered," it was my tiny calico.

"BB?"

She looked up and meowed, doing the cat shuffle where she readjusted her feet and tail but didn't actually move any closer toward me.

"Fine. You can be BB. It was a really long and serious name for a less-than-serious cat."

She met my eyes and gave me a slow blink before ambling in my direction.

"Oh, are you going to bless me with your presence now?"

She jumped up beside me, making a tiny mew-ish grunt as she landed.

I leaned back against the love seat, hand on my purring kitten. I was exhausted. Malone had kept me very busy the night before, but there'd also been the adrenaline rushes from Lucius Malone's accusations, then Trista's situation, and then the fear I'd lost my cat.

And that was all before I took into consideration the acute disappointment that my dining room table's main function would remain dining.

As for my pesky emotions, I'd successfully locked those back up while in crisis mode, and I had no interest in unpacking them. I did have some assignments due for my online classes, but my body refused to move. I'd get there eventually. Maybe even go to Finnegan's to do my work with a glass of Malbec.

I couldn't help but worry about Malone, but I also knew he could handle himself.

Oh, how that man could handle himself.

As if summoned by my thoughts, my phone buzzed, and I looked down to see a text from him:

No clue when I can get this
straightened out. Police involved.

Just remember your favorite
amendment

This is a mess, Stark

I know

I regret nothing

Me neither

I'll come by when I can

My table is counting on it

Yeah. There were questions about
my pocket square

Sorry not sorry?

Speaking of . . . remember to tell
Addie that any rumor
that I don't like Taylor Swift is all a
. . . Hoax

I Hate It Here

Champagne Problems, Stark

I'm going, I'm going. And
I Bet You Think About Me

I always do, Stark. I always do

Chapter 31

I thought about going upstairs in my purple dress but decided underwear might be in order for this particular visit. I'd left my underwear as Malone's pocket square—no wonder Lucius had given me such a strange look—and I didn't need to further contribute to the delinquency of a minor.

So I was in a T-shirt and shorts when I knocked on April's apartment door. Luckily, Addie answered.

"Just the person I wanted to see," I said with my most winning smile.

It didn't faze the teen in front of me. "You can't come in. Mom ran to the store, and we're not allowed to have anyone in the apartment when she's gone. I wouldn't have opened the door except it was you."

And the fact I owed her twenty dollars couldn't have hurt.

"I won't keep you long. Just wanted to say thank you for looking out for Bren—BB, and to pay you," I said as I took a crisp twenty from my back pocket. "And, ah . . ."

She took the twenty. "Yes?"

"Well, remember when I told you that Mr. Malone didn't like Taylor Swift?"

She leaned against the doorframe, arms across her chest, chin jutted forward. "And?"

"I had him confused with his cousin."

As soon as the words left my lips, I knew she wouldn't believe them. Funny thing about the truth, sometimes the truest things are those people have the hardest time believing.

"It's not nice to lie," she said.

I winced. I never lied without crossing my fingers behind my back. Childish? Yes, but also a good reminder to not lie unless I absolutely had to. "It wasn't a lie so much as . . . 'Vigilante Shit.'"

Her eyes got wide at the reference to a Taylor Swift song. "That's right! Mom said you're a detective."

"I am."

"Still, if he's a nice guy, then I shouldn't have sent the bugs."

"I know, I know. At any rate, Mr. Malone sent me to fess up. He said to tell you . . ." I paused because I felt the groan coming on, and I would just have to swallow it. "He said to tell you that he likes Taylor Swift 'All Too Well.' Anything to the contrary is just a 'Hoax.'"

Her eyes brightened with a level of hero worship that made me wonder if Malone would prefer her antipathy to her adoration. "He said that?"

"Direct quote. I've apologized to him, and I would like to apologize to you. Please forgive me for misleading you. Oh, and please don't unleash any more ladybugs."

Her smile could only be described as impish.

"And please pull the plug on any other little pranks you may have planned. I mean, I don't want you to get in trouble, and please don't tell your mom I said this, but"—I made a big show of looking right and then left—"your ladybug plan was ingenious."

"Really?" Her voice lilted with excitement, but then she remembered all too quickly that she was supposed to be mad at me. Her tone shifted from enthusiastic to sarcastic. "You really think so?"

"Really."

We stared at each other, and I made a solemn vow to never attempt to use a middle schooler to do my dirty work for me ever again. Too unpredictable. Between the roller coaster of puberty and the horrors of middle school, children of that age were not to be trifled with.

Her eyes narrowed. "And what about you, Miss Stella? Do *you* like Taylor Swift?"

"I wouldn't claim to be an expert, but I enjoy her work. I hope there's no 'Bad Blood' between you and me."

Nope. Didn't move the needle.

Song must've been too mainstream.

Think, Stella, think. Taylor Swift songs. You know Taylor Swift songs. If he can do it, then you can, too.

"Uh, 'This Is Me Trying'?"

"And?"

Truly, thirteen-year-olds were the most terrifying creatures on the planet. Were my palms sweating?

Assert your dominance, Stella.

"'No Body, No Crime.'"

She nodded with all the solemnity of a Yalie welcoming someone to the Skull and Bones society. Relief washed over me.

"Maybe I'll send an apology pizza up one day next week," I said as I backed away from the door.

Enthusiasm lit Addie's eyes for the briefest of moments before she adjusted to cool and added loftily, "I think that would officially make us even."

I bit my lip to keep from laughing and waved before turning for the stairs. The apartment door closed as I descended, and I allowed myself a quiet giggle.

Kids, man.

That Addie needed to look into law. Or maybe just go straight to being a fixer.

My phone buzzed.

Meet Salcedo and me at the Waffle House at midnight.

Another summons. With Malone out of pocket, what else did I have to do other than worry about him and finish my homework?

Once again, I was the first person at the Waffle House.

"How's the plantar fasciitis, Betty?"

"Bah. Those stretches you taught me do help, but I think the only thing that's going to cure it is retiring."

"You're probably right," I said at the same time Jasper said, "You're never going to retire. I'm gonna have to cart you out to the dumpster at the end of your shift one night."

"Watch yourself, Beanpole," she said. "I'm not in the mood for your mess tonight."

"Trouble in paradise?" I asked as I slid into my customary booth.

"I'm tired of him," she said.

"I heard that," he called from his station in front of the griddle.

"I meant for you to," she yelled over her shoulder before turning back to me. "Where have you been?"

"Oh, you know . . . paralegal homework, found a kitten, PI stuff . . ." *And getting most deliciously laid but then having multiple existential crises about the whole thing because I apparently suffer from foreboding joy, a thing I learned from Brené Brown, the author, not the cat. Why enjoy things when you could spend your time waiting for the other metaphorical shoe to drop?*

"Huh." Betty stared through me as though she'd read my mind and decided it was a scary place.

"True story." I held up both hands in surrender.

"Worried you'd moved off to Alaska or something since I hadn't seen you."

"C'mon, Betty. I can't come in here every night. I gotta work. Bills to pay and all that."

"Whatever," she said as she hobbled away. "Coffee? Chicken biscuit? Hashbrowns scattered?"

"You know me so well."

Havisham said something to Salcedo as they entered the Waffle House. They each slid into the booth across from me. With a sigh, I took the fifty from my pocket and slapped it on the table in front of Havisham.

Salcedo literally squealed.

Havisham palmed the fifty and smiled, something she didn't do that often. "I'm so proud of you, Stark."

"How was it?" asked Salcedo.

"A lady doesn't kiss and tell."

"One, you aren't a lady," said Havisham. "Two, only gentlemen are bound by that stricture."

"Well," I said, but then the words didn't come to me.

Salcedo clamped a hand on Havisham's arm. "She's blushing! Look at her! She's blushing!"

"I knew you weren't telling me everything," said Betty, who'd appeared by our booth. "What were you really up to?"

"Getting laid," Havisham said.

Betty whooped. "You hear that, Jasper?"

"Hear what?" he called over the sizzle of his griddle.

"Oh, you never mind," she said before taking the rest of our orders. We waited until we had our drinks, napkins, and silverware before returning to the discussion.

"Again I ask you, how was it?" Salcedo practically leaned over the table. At least she could keep her voice down when asking questions, though.

"Both the best and the worst of my life," I said.

"You make no sense, Stark." Havisham took a sip of coffee.

"It was absolutely the best sex of my life, but also the worst because now I am ruined for all other men. Here I agreed to a friends-with-benefits situation, and he's going back to California . . . so I'll just have to enjoy it while I can."

Havisham arched an eyebrow. "And?"

"Did you not hear a word I just said? It's like getting a taste of the best chocolate cake you've ever eaten while knowing you'll never get to have that particular cake ever again."

"Heard it all," she said at the same time Salcedo said, "The contract can be renegotiated. Long distance is a thing. At least until you get tired of us and move to California."

"Y'all make this sound easy."

"Because it could be," said Salcedo with all the optimism of her youth.

"Well, there are other complications," I said.

"Spill," said Havisham. So I told them about how Trista's job had turned into a different task altogether, about how Blake had sneaked into Malone's apartment and was trying to throw us under the bus, about the gala, all of it.

"And I have two—well, make that one day to figure out how I'm going to talk Ken into giving me the title to my car."

"How much do you have?"

"Six thousand five hundred."

Havisham reached into her back pocket. "I thought that might be the case. Here's a loan of five hundred dollars."

"Havisham, you don't have to do that. I can ask my nana."

"If you do, there will be strings attached. Take it from me. I know you'll be good for it."

Mercy, was I crying again?

"You okay?" asked Salcedo as I swiped a tear.

"It's this damn book y'all have me reading," I said. "I keep feeling things."

"Kinda the point," Havisham said at the same time Salcedo patted my hand.

"Well, feelings are gross and inconvenient and painful. I don't like them."

Betty appeared at that moment with plates of food, so Salcedo jerked her hand back before saying, "But if you can't feel the painful emotions, you'll never feel the pleasant ones."

Out of the mouths of babes.

Even so. "What if I prefer being on an even keel?"

Havisham cackled. "We're women. We're never on an even keel. I mean, we should get more credit for functioning in this dysfunctional world while also experiencing fluctuating hormones, but we don't. Take my word for it: It's better to lean in to the roller coaster of life than to hold yourself stiff against the restraints."

"That's profoundly beautiful, Havisham. I still don't want to."

"Riddle me this, Stark: What exactly can you do to prevent bad things from happening to you?"

"Prepare for the worst and stock up on Malbec."

"The first doesn't do you any good, and the second is called 'numbing.'"

"Oh, I know what 'numbing' is, thank you very much," I snapped. "It's in the book. But maybe I *like* numbing."

Salcedo had been watching our discussion, her head going back and forth like she was a spectator at the world's tiniest tennis match. Finally, she spoke. "Why don't you just tell Malone how you feel?"

Havisham and I looked at her and then at each other. We both burst out laughing.

"No thank you," I said. "He suggested a temporary arrangement, and I will honor it."

"What if he feels the same way you do? What if he only suggested something no strings attached because he thought that was all he could get?"

"Then he can tell me."

She sighed in exasperation and turned her attention back to her hashbrown bowl.

"But I may want you to shut down the website," I said.

Both looked up in wonder, but it was Havisham who asked, "Why?"

"It's fun to think I can facilitate karma, but"—I paused, searching for words—"it's not my place. Heck, the original concept of karma suggests that we might not see the results of our actions in this lifetime, that it might be a future one."

"Believe in reincarnation now, Stark?"

"I'm just one mortal on this planet. What do I know about how the universe operates?"

"Whoa," said Salcedo, eyes wide, at the same time Havisham narrowed her eyes and asked, "Are you reading books on philosophy and theology now?"

I sighed. "No, it's just that some of the things I did seem a bit mean in retrospect."

"They had it coming," Havisham said.

"So far as *I* know, but who am I to know?"

We ate in silence for a few minutes before Havisham asked, "What are you going to do, then?"

I shrugged. "As soon as I catch up on my loans, I think I can cobble together a comfortable life between PI work and paralegal work, and that suits me. I like the flexibility of it, and I do like helping people. The only question is how to get the Douchecanoe to sign over my car title."

Salcedo nodded. "If you're sure, then I'll take the site down."

"After I've paid everything off," I said. "No need to jinx it. But thank you for putting it all together. I don't know what I would've done without you."

"Yeah, well, if it weren't for you, I would've lost my virginity to an asshole."

Havisham dropped her fork.

"I know, I know," Salcedo said as she rolled her eyes. "That's outdated terminology, but Stark probably saved me from at least twelve STDs."

Havisham shook her head. "At this point, don't sleep with anyone until you're twenty."

Salcedo arched an eyebrow that said she would do as she pleased, then turned to me. "Anyway . . ."

"Yes."

"We called you here for a few reasons. We missed you. But I also decided to stay here in Georgia. My mother is beside herself, but she understands why I might not want to transfer schools, which is all to ask if your offer still stands."

"Absolutely."

She grinned. "Good, because I may need to start moving in this weekend."

"All right, then," I said.

"Before I forget, did you draw up the plan for my girlfriend whose roommate is driving her batty? That would be another fifty dollars toward your goal."

"I'll get it to you before lunch tomorrow," I said. "But you just give that money to Havisham as part of my repayment."

"Bah, I'm not worried about it," Havisham said with a twinkle in her eye. "You're not the only one getting laid around here."

"The cowboy?"

She nodded.

"Is he also a billionaire philanthropist?"

"Eh, millionaire, and he's definitely a giver in all the areas of life that count."

This made me think of Malone and his "Ladies First" philosophy of life.

"She's blushing again," Salcedo stage-whispered.

"You'll understand soon enough," Havisham said.

Our younger compatriot rolled her eyes. "Please."

Chapter 32

The next evening we learned that my dining room table was the perfect height for sex. Sturdier than the price tag might've suggested. After a frenetic coupling, Malone and I were both coming down. My legs still wound around his waist, my arms around his neck. I wanted to live in this particular moment forever.

"God bless Swedish furniture engineering," I muttered.

His laughter rumbled through me, and he kissed the spot where my neck met my shoulder. "I take it you missed me as much as I missed you."

"I missed you more."

"Unlikely." Even as he said the word, he wandered down the hall to take care of the condom. I sat there, the air now cool on my naked body. I made the mistake of looking down. The harsh apartment lights showed every stretch mark, blemish, roll of fat.

"What are you doing?" Malone asked as he approached.

"Nothing," I said.

He cocked his head to one side. "No, you were frowning. Something's bugging you."

"I think I've peaked."

He grinned. "Yeah, you did."

"No, I don't mean *that.* I mean I've peaked in terms of physical appearance."

He walked closer and wrapped his arms around me. "If that is what you are thinking, then I obviously didn't do my job properly."

"Oh, that's not it. I'm recommending a raise at your next performance review, but—"

He reached underneath me, picking me up so quickly I squealed. "Come on, Malone. I'm too heavy for this!"

"I lift weights so I can carry beautiful women around," he said as he carried me—my legs around his waist, my arms around his neck, and his forearms under my ass—in the direction of my bedroom. Impressive, really.

"I've got to up my cardio," I said. "I'm exhausted on your behalf."

But he showed no signs of exertion as he lightly tossed me on the bed. Then he took my hand and started kissing up my arm.

"What are you doing?"

"I would think that would be obvious," he said as he bent over to trail kisses across my collarbone.

"I'm serious, Malone," I said. "You're over here aging like a fine wine and . . ."

He continued kissing.

"I'll say the salty fish word."

With a deep sigh, he sat back on his heels. "Fine. What is your ridiculous complaint about your sumptuous body?"

"To be honest, I never used to worry about it. I mean, other than the usual concerns that any woman might have. At age twelve or so, the puberty fairy delivers a mental checklist for every girl to study, so there's always been *something* I would like to change—"

"Sacrilege."

"But I didn't really care. This past year, though, has me doubting myself." I looked up at the ceiling. Why was I telling him this?

He lay down beside me. "Let's refute these points quickly because you've done wonders for my refractory period, which is further proof that you are being silly."

"One, Ken told me—"

"That man is a dumbass, and his name should not even be spoken in your presence."

"Fine, the Douchecanoe told me that I was too old to do the honey-trap scenarios."

"The what? Are you out there getting government secrets like a modern Mata Hari or something?"

"No, no. Sometimes a significant other—or a member of their family—would hire me to flirt with someone to see if they were willing to cheat."

"Oh. And what was your success rate? Ninety-seven percent? Because I seem to recall that you had me giving you my Social Security number not that long ago."

"When you put it that way . . ." I rolled over on my side, so we were face-to-face.

He paused, studied me, closing his brown eye slightly more than his blue, almost as though he were looking at me through a microscope or possibly taking aim. "And?"

"This college kid called me a 'saggy-ass bitch,'" I said with a sigh.

"First of all, no. I bet I could bounce a quarter off your ass, and I might like to try that experiment later. Second, what do you care about his opinion?"

"I don't know. So weird to have these thoughts." My eyes met his. "Even weirder to tell you about them. I guess I feel like I can because I know you're going back to California."

Was it my imagination or did he tense when I mentioned California? If so, he quickly recovered. "And here I thought you might feel comfortable telling me these things because we have one of those special pizza-based relationships."

My stomach dropped.

So he wasn't going to deny it. He wasn't going to say he'd like to take our relationship beyond pizza. And if he wasn't going to float that idea out there, then I wasn't going to, either. I'd just admitted to fears about my body, and I sure as hell wasn't going to add being clingy to my list of foibles.

"Stella," he said softly.

I'd been staring at his tattoo while tracing it with my finger, but my eyes immediately met his because he had never addressed me as anything other than Stark. "Yes?"

His hand lay gently on my cheek. "You are the most beautiful woman I've ever seen."

"Malone," I said. I could feel my cheeks growing hotter.

"You know I'm telling you the truth, too, because I've already gotten into your pants."

"Well, that and you'd plead the Fifth before you'd lie."

"Duh. It's my favorite amendment."

I bit my lip to keep from asking him if he would be willing to make our arrangement more permanent. Things would've been so much easier if we did more kissing and less talking. I forced a smile and traced my hand down his body. "How's that refractory period coming along?"

"Terrible, just terrible," he said even as his erection betrayed him. "I think you're going to have to persuade me."

And so I did.

Later, we were eating Chinese takeout when I asked him how work was going.

Malone responded with sad trombone noises.

"You're so articulate," I said.

"I'll have you know"—he held his chopsticks in the air in feigned outrage—"I'm a very cunning linguist."

"Can confirm," I said before pointing my fork at him. I'd given up on chopsticks. "You're also a pro at changing the subject when it comes to your work."

He shrugged. "I don't think there's anything you can do to help. That's all."

"Try me."

"Well, I'd have to know where he is for you to help."

"Aha! But that is the one thing I can help you with. Private investigator, remember?"

"Yeah, but he is seriously off the grid this time. Not just hiding from his wife."

"O ye of little faith. Who told you he would show up at the gala?"

"You did."

"Who served him with papers?"

"You did."

"Who had video footage of him sneaking into your apartment?"

"You did. Because you are as brilliant as you are beautiful, but I also don't want to drag you into this. For now, Grandpa believes me. I've pieced together everything that was erased and everything that was stolen but not backed up, but I'm still missing some pieces of the overall financial puzzle. There's gotta be a shell company I'm missing, one that's hiding really well. Or an employee who doesn't really exist. Something."

"Well, how about you work on that, and I'll work on finding Blake."

"I don't think you'll have much luck, but I'm not going to say no to your help." Malone stabbed his chopsticks into the red-and-white box of lo mein he'd been eating. I'd never seen him with such a sour expression. Not even the ladybugs had provoked him the way Blake Malone did.

"Hey, Malone."

"Yeah?"

"What is it about Blake that really eats at you?"

He stiffened. "Why would you say that?"

"Oh, I don't know. I'm no psychologist, but every time you hear his name, you tense up."

He exhaled and put his box on the coffee table. "That noticeable, huh?"

"Only to someone you're in a special pizza-based relationship with."

He chuckled and studied the ceiling. "Blake Malone is, and has always been, a bully. Our parents thought it would be good for us cousins to spend the summer together, but it was sheer torture for me. I guess Blake enjoyed it, probably in the same way some kids enjoy using magnifying glasses to set ants on fire. I hated it."

"What did he do?"

"Believe it or not, Stark, I was a total nerd."

"No!"

"Yes, I know it's hard to believe that a prime male specimen such as myself, a child with a manly name like Tiberius, would have ever been pale, weak, and bookish, but it's the truth."

"I like bookish," I said.

"Luckily for me."

"So he said mean things?"

"Well, that and sometimes he threw a punch for funsies, but what he really loved to do was to take things away from me. The bigger cookie, the best lawn chair, the prettiest girl. His whole mission in life was to steal from me, no matter how big or small. I soon learned to take nothing I really wanted with me to my grandparents' house because he would steal it."

"Steal it? Aren't your parents all rich? Why would he steal?"

Malone's eyes met mine. "To keep me from having it."

"Do your parents know?"

"They do now, but even if they'd known then, they would've told me to leave anything I wanted to keep at home and to not make waves. My dad isn't into confrontation. He's the younger brother."

"But he and your uncle are twins!"

"Well, that thirty minutes means a lot, Stark. At least that's what I've always been told."

"That's awful." You could say a lot about my mother, but she would—and indeed had—gone full mama bear on both kids and adults who picked on me. Unfortunately for me, my mama bear had a tendency to forage for long stretches of time and thus wasn't always there when I needed defending.

"You gotta understand something about my dad," Malone said. "He's a college philosophy professor in a family full of businessmen. My mom has a chronic illness, and he will do anything—and I do mean anything—to stay in Grandpa's good graces so he can be absolutely sure that he will always have enough money to take care of her. So, in the scheme of things, it doesn't mean a whole lot to him if my spoiled-brat cousin steals my favorite G.I. Joe action figure or my original copy of *The Death of Superman*. Those are things and can be replaced."

"What about your mother?"

"She's really big on turning the other cheek."

"Ah," I said. "So not like me in the least."

"I didn't say that."

"You didn't have to."

We sat in silence for a few minutes more before Malone added, "I could live with all those things. We were just kids, but then he stole my college girlfriend, the first woman I was ever serious about."

"Ouch. Selena?"

"No, no. I didn't meet her until much later. My first girlfriend from back when he went to Stanford."

"Blake Malone went to Stanford?"

Malone laughed. "Not for long. By the end of his freshman year, he'd crashed and burned, but unfortunately for me, he didn't manage to do that *before* he convinced Jada to dump me."

"And now he's stolen money but is trying to pin it on you?"

"Yes!" Malone's response was so loud that BB looked up from where she had been snoozing between us. "Have you ever been in a competition that you didn't want to be in?"

"No, not really."

"Well, from as early as I can remember, my cousin has wanted to 'beat' me. Flag football? I'm going to end up with a bloodied nose from where he 'accidentally' elbows me. Comic books and action figures? If he didn't get it first, then he'll make sure I don't have it. Girlfriends? He's slept with more women, and he *thinks* they were all prettier. The family business? He's gonna be on the board of directors and make sure that my company is hired only on an as-needed basis."

"So he can steal funds."

"Apparently."

"Why didn't you tell me this before?"

"Because it sounds like whining, Stark."

"Not to me, it doesn't," I said softly.

"Well, he's not getting away with this one, because now my business and my reputation are on the line. Material things, I don't care about. In a funny twist, he was the one to teach me how unimportant those things are. And I know now that any woman who wants to be with him isn't right for me. But I've worked really hard to make Chateau Cybersecurity a thriving business, and I have employees who count on me. Moreover, Grandpa and his dad before him worked hard to make Malone Construction a solid business, and my greedy cousin doesn't get to tear that down."

By now he was standing, his chest heaving with the effort of his speech.

"You're hot when you're righteously indignant, Malone."

"He grinds my gears."

"Of course he does," I said. "What he's doing isn't fair. It's not just. It's not right."

"*He* is mean," Malone said. "When you were trying to tell me how mean you are? I kept thinking of him—"

"The other day we sewed together all the holes in all the briefs of a man who'd been cheating on his wife," I said.

"He. Had. It. Coming."

"I set up a website called www.yourkidsgotrobbed.com and then called in a favor from an old client to advertise on an electronic billboard that a certain school board member awarded no-bid contracts to family members for expensive but shoddy school equipment."

"Investigative journalism. A public service, really."

"I may or may not have planted six little noisemakers that sound like crickets in someone's apartment last week. They go off intermittently."

"Stark!"

"I can't be tamed, Malone."

"Fine. Just *try* to use your powers for good. Please?"

"Aye, aye, Cap."

"I'm not Captain America."

"No, but you are a strong contender for 'America's ass.' It's a fine ass, and don't think I haven't noticed."

He gave me a crooked grin. "Are you trying to get laid again, you insatiable minx?"

"Maybe," I said. "Wanna sleep over tonight?"

"Yes." He stood abruptly and tossed me over his shoulder. As we made our way toward the bedroom, BB gave me a look of pure disgust before curling up in a circle with her face toward the couch cushions.

Chapter 33

At two in the morning, a time when I often had epiphanies, it occurred to me that I knew exactly where Blake was and how he'd gained access to parts of the company he shouldn't have had access to.

Somewhere in the midst of his jargon, Malone had mentioned an accomplice.

I might not have known what SQL injections or the Dorminy Meta-Model were, but Malone had, in his own way, given me a very important piece of the puzzle, a piece he was overlooking because, despite all evidence to the contrary, he seemed to believe people were better than they actually were.

Put past and present together, and I was willing to bet Blake had stolen yet another one of Malone's girlfriends. As the administrative assistant of Lucius Malone, Selena probably had access to anything and everything Blake would need to siphon funds from the business.

What a no-brainer for Blake. One, Selena was a very beautiful woman. Two, she had access to the information he needed. Three—the sweetest part of all for him—she'd been Malone's girlfriend.

I ran through my memories of the gala. At no point had I seen Blake and Selena together. Sure, it was a large gathering, but there had been one point where he had seen her and intentionally walked in another direction. I'd thought nothing of it at the time, but what better cover than pretending you don't like each other or don't know each other?

I slid out of bed and scrambled for my phone, but I had forgotten to add the Land Rover's license plate to the notes section of my app once I traveled the short distance between Salon Blaise and Trader Joe's. I'd been high on the victory of serving those papers and focused on white-cheddar goodness. I closed my eyes and willed my brain to play the opening bars of "So Fresh, So Clean."

Along with the tune came the information I sought: XBC2453 and then some tteok bok ki.

Thank you, Big Boi and André 3000!

Also, I was out of my favorite spicy Korean stir-fried rice cakes and the white-cheddar corn puffs once again, so I needed to go back to Trader Joe's.

Focus, Stella!

I tiptoed from the bedroom and into the living room. BB meowed at me, and I held a finger to my lips to shush her. I grabbed my laptop, but she squeezed under my arm and into my lap, so I was holding the laptop away from my body.

"Listen, cat," I whispered. "You can be Stella adjacent, but Mama's gotta work here."

I scooped her up with one hand and placed her beside me so I could hold the laptop closer. My good friend Tracers found the owner of the Land Rover right away—and no one criticized my off-key whisper singing, either.

Who was the owner? One Selena Nance.

Now came the tricky part. Did I tell Malone? Would he believe me, if I did? Obviously, Selena had done a number on him with the mean things she'd said about his eyes, but I'd thought at the time that her rationale made no sense. More likely, she knew she needed to break things off with him and was grasping for a reason.

Heck, if I were her, there's no way I would've ever traded in Tiberius for Blake. No amount of money would be big enough to make me consider it.

But that was beside the point. It was possible that Blake was no longer with Selena either romantically or geographically, so it might be a good idea to stake things out before I told Malone of my suspicions.

He appeared in the hallway, and I snapped my laptop shut.

"You okay, Stark?" he asked with a yawn.

"Yeah, I had a thought. Wanted to look something up before I forgot about it."

"Mmkay," he said as he wandered into the kitchen. Behind me I could hear him open a cabinet and get a glass of water.

Something squeezed inside me at the familiarity of his actions. It was as though I mourned the passing of the moment before it had even finished happening. Malone paused by the love seat and offered his hand.

I took it.

Several hours later I was regretting my decision to attempt surveillance at midday. One, it was hot, and the town house where Selena lived was new enough that there wasn't a tree in sight. Neither shade nor cover for me. Two, I was antsy thinking about another problem. Thanks to the weekend and the holiday on the Fourth, I had only that day and Monday to get my title changed over and my car's registration paid. Technically, I had the entire month of July to get straight with the DMV, but there would be a late fee involved if I didn't get my business handled before my birthday, which was also . . . a holiday.

Oh, how I was tired of late fees.

Great. There'd be another fee for emissions testing, too.

If that wasn't enough to make a person regret having a birthday, I didn't know what was.

Even worse, I had yet to come up with a way to persuade the Douchecanoe to sign the title over to me. Come to think of it, I was probably doing surveillance because the next item on my agenda was getting that title no matter what it took.

Just then the two-car garage on the lower level—did I mention this was a fancy town house?—slowly opened. There was the Land Rover I remembered. It backed out, and I trained my telephoto lens on the driver as the vehicle moved past me.

Selena.

But she was alone.

My heart sank.

I slumped into the driver's seat and yawned. I'd been stuck in my car for well over five hours at this point. I was sweaty, cranky, and dehydrated, *and* I had to pee. How one could both be dehydrated and have a full bladder was one of life's great mysteries, but I seemed to be a champ at threading that particular needle.

Just as I was about to call it a day, the door to the town house opened, and out stepped a man with a trash bag in his hand. From a distance, he looked so much like Malone that my heart gave a stutter.

Then his watch glinted in the sunlight.

I focused the telephoto lens of my camera and took a picture. Then I took a grainier one with my phone. I was about to send the photo to Malone when I hesitated. This was the sort of information he would want in a phone call, wasn't it?

I called but got sent to voicemail, so I tried again.

C'mon, Malone. Pick up, will ya?

"Bula Vinaka, Beachside."

"What?"

"Sorry, Stark. Old joke my dad used to make. What can I do for you today, and please tell me it involves your dining room table?"

"Ah, but it's more what *I* can do for *you*."

"Oh. Even better."

"Remember how you said the only way I could help you would be to find Blake?"

"Yeeessss . . ."

"I've got good news and bad news."

He sucked in a breath. "Bad news first."

"Blake's stolen another girlfriend." When he didn't respond, I added, "The good news is I just saw him at Selena Nance's town house."

Silence.

"Malone?"

"Yeah, I'm here. For a hot minute, I thought you were saying you'd dumped me for my cousin."

I snorted. "Yeah, right."

Wait. Did that mean Malone thought of me as a girlfriend? My heart skipped ahead a minute. *Maybe, just maybe . . .*

"You're serious, Stark?"

"As a heart attack. I can send you a picture I took with my phone. I have a better one on my camera."

"Yeah. Uh, send it when you get a chance."

"Sure."

After disconnecting the call, I looked at my phone. What the heck? The man who had ended the call wasn't the same one who'd answered. For half a second, my spirits had been buoyed by the thought that Malone considered me his girlfriend. Did he still have feelings for Selena? Or maybe the same old feelings of anger toward Blake?

Or maybe he's working. That's it.

Hard to say, but I'd hoped he would've been much happier to get the news. I'd been counting on it, in fact, because my next stop was Chez Douchecanoe.

Chapter 34

I drove to the other side of the Marietta Square, to the cottage I'd once shared with Ken. His car sat in the long gravel driveway to the side of the house, and I felt a mixture of relief—he was there—and revulsion—I didn't want to be.

But my car title wasn't going to find and sign itself, so there I had to be.

I pulled into the driveway right behind him. No easy escapes that way.

As I walked around to the front of the house, I noticed that some of the bricks in the path were uneven. I'd placed those there. I'd also insisted that we paint the house a light peach color that would've been popular in the late eighteen hundreds, when the house had been built. I stepped on the wraparound porch, glad to see the ceiling was still "haint blue."

I turned to a mantra after ringing the doorbell.

Slow inhale: *This is a beautiful home.*

Slow exhale: *I will find another.*

The Douchecanoe opened the door. "Stella! What a surprise."

"May I come in?"

"Sure, sure." He moved aside to make room for me. I walked in, the whiff of dirty dishes hitting me as I crossed the threshold. I fought to keep my expression neutral as he hurried through the small living room, picking up mail and chargers and such so I would have a place to sit.

On the camelback couch that I had picked out after agonizing over color and style for at least six months.

"What brings you here?" he asked hopefully.

"I would like for you to sign over the car title to me so I can make my annual pilgrimage to the tag office," I said.

"I would like an apology."

"And people in hell are partial to ice water. I'm not going to apologize. I had nothing to do with the glitter bomb."

"A likely story."

"Believe what you want, but I'll be sitting here until I get that title."

Brave words, Stella, considering how disgusting it smells in here.

He frowned. "Even if I wanted to give it to you, I couldn't. I don't know where it is."

"Ken," I said. "Let's not make this harder than it has to be."

"I seriously don't know where it is."

My bullshit detector suggested he just might be telling the truth. "Fine. Then I'll look for it."

"Sure, look away." He sat down in his battered recliner, confident I wouldn't be able to find the title. All the better for me if he stayed out of my way.

If I were my car title, where would I be? I asked myself.

I'd probably be upstairs in the office in a pile of mail that Ken hadn't opened because he didn't like to open mail and was used to my handling such things. That would be my first guess. I got up and walked a path upstairs, both familiar and awkward, to the second bedroom. The last time I'd made this trek, I'd been holding a bottle of champagne and shedding clothes as I went.

Don't think about that now, Stella.

I avoided looking at the main bedroom and focused on the smaller bedroom we used for an office.

"What the heck happened up here?" I asked as I surveyed the papers and mail strewn around the office. I immediately regretted it because Ken might come upstairs to answer me.

Blessedly, he didn't respond.

I started sifting through papers, stacking them in piles according to where I would've filed each one. Muscle memory could make a person do the oddest things. I found unpaid bills and bit my tongue to keep from asking him if he knew they were there.

I unearthed tax forms still sealed in their envelopes and could see no evidence that Ken had asked for an extension. For the first time I felt a swell of gratitude that my name wasn't on any of the official documents. If the IRS came calling, they wouldn't be looking for me.

The urge to help him was strong—it was hard to overturn almost twenty years of habit in one afternoon—but no. When I found a receipt he'd printed from the internet for Honeymoon Haven cabins, I said nothing. He'd written "business expense" at the top, but I could tell from the dates that it was his supposed honeymoon with Eloise. The man was always trying to claim something as a business expense that he shouldn't. It was one of our annual fights.

Not my tax return, not my auditors.

After going through all the papers on my desk, I looked behind the upholstered chair that sat beside it. Next, I sifted through the mail on Ken's desk. I checked underneath his chair and even in the trash can. That's when I saw the corner of an envelope that had fallen behind Ken's desk and to the floor.

Eureka!

I opened the envelope, which had been mailed earlier in the spring, and there it was: the title to my Corolla.

After I'd placed it back in the envelope, I tucked it into the back waistband of my jeans and prepared to indulge in some pettiness of the highest order. I gathered the piles of papers one on top of another and then tossed them all in the air over his desk, letting them fall like a wintry mix.

Yep. Pretty much what the room had looked like when I walked in. *If you want me to do your paperwork, then maybe don't sleep around on me.*

I grabbed a pen and hopped down the stairs.

"All right, Kenneth," I said as I approached where he still sat in the living room. "It's time for you to sign this title over to me."

"No."

"Yes."

"Why should I?"

"Because if you don't, I'm going to call the IRS and suggest they audit you."

His eyes widened. "You wouldn't!"

"Oh, but I would. I'm Little Miss Petty, remember? The pettiest person you've ever met."

"How about I sign over the title, but you come back home?"

Was he seriously trying to bargain with me? When he had absolutely nothing that I wanted other than a single piece of paper? A piece of paper that showed he *symbolically* owned something that was truly mine in every meaningful sense of the word.

I took my phone out of my pocket.

"What are you doing?"

"Calling the IRS."

"Fine, fine! I'll do it."

I put my phone away and held the pen out to him. He put the title on the coffee table and added his name in both print and cursive. I'd researched everything that would be necessary for the transfer, and I could handle the rest.

"Thank you. I would say it's been a pleasure doing business with you, but my nana hates it when I lie. Goodbye, Ken. As a good friend likes to say, may you have the life you deserve."

My prize in hand, I had almost escaped when he stepped between me and the door. "Stella, please come home. I'm a mess without you."

His anguished tone made me stop.

Nope. Not going back.

"Quite literally a mess," I said as I gestured to the house around him.

"No, you were right about how I can't make myself any younger by dating younger women."

I said nothing. Hearing a "you were right" should've felt better than it did. Maybe it only counted if it came from someone you loved or, at the very least, respected.

"If we got back together, I could make all your money problems go away."

Earlier I might've been tempted by that possibility for at least a second, but I'd worked hard at legal work, PI work, and acts of pettiness. Thanks to the money earned there as well as Havisham's loan, I no longer needed his help. No, I wanted to get out of this sad house and away from this sad man as quickly as possible. I practically sang, "No thank you."

Each time I tried to get past him, he blocked my exit.

"Er, thank you for helping me with the paperwork upstairs," he said sheepishly. I willed myself not to smile and thus betray exactly how unhelpful I'd been. "Do you think you could help me with the dishes?"

"Absolutely not. Put on your big boy pants and make it happen."

"I don't know how!"

"YouTube is a wondrous place. I bet you can find all the answers there."

He stubbornly stood in front of the door. I could've gone out the back door, but I didn't want to wade through the grass he also hadn't cut. Besides, it was the principle of the thing.

"It's been real. It's not been fun. Time for you to move, or I'll do another leg sweep on you." Bold words I wasn't entirely sure I could back up, but hopefully the threat would do the trick.

Finally, he stepped aside, muttering something about how unreasonable I was being.

"Unreasonable." Add that to "stubborn," "petty," and "spiteful" as adjectives often used to describe women who merely had the audacity to stick up for themselves.

As I was stepping outside, he said, "You're not as smart as you think you are. You sure let Trista play you like a secondhand fiddle."

Chapter 35

"Excuse me?" I said, turning to face him.

"You heard me," he said, now looking really pleased with himself. "I went to high school with her and her friend Jackie, the one who paid you to find a password. A few weeks ago, Trista hired me to do a little job for her. Figured out her husband was staying in the Bel Air Apartments."

"How? Why?"

"Forgot about it until I came back to that stupid bar later that night we argued. I was going to give you a piece of my mind, but you weren't there. Instead, I overheard your little friends thick as thieves talking about some kind of petty business. Really proud of themselves. The young one went out and got these flyers and started taping them up. I saw that bullshit about the patriarchy and karma, and I knew it had to be you. The older one mentioned me calling you petty and just cackled at the idea of it. So I called in a favor with Trista."

So it wasn't as good a business idea as Salcedo had thought? My stomach roiled. My body ran hot and cold at the same time, my face especially warm.

Of course your biggest client was fake, Stella. The whole idea was stupid, and you are a failure at everything you do. Almost forty, and what do you have to show for your life? You should've never let Havisham and Salcedo talk you into something so ridiculous.

Ken laughed. "I wish you could see your face. Little Miss Petty after taking a dose of her own medicine."

Anger clawed its way past . . . shame. Yeah, shame. Maybe a little humiliation. Definitely embarrassment. But naming the feelings took away some of their power, and I could thank Brené Brown—the author, not the cat—for that.

Ken *wanted* me to feel all those things but mostly hoped I'd be humiliated. It was a trick I now recognized, a tool he'd used before to keep me in line.

Rolling back my shoulders, I took a couple of deep breaths. Tried out a new mantra.

Slow inhale: *Yes, you are embarrassed.*

Slow exhale: *But comedy is tragedy plus time.*

"What are you doing?"

"Breathing."

"I can see that. Are you going to be okay? Do I need to call the doctor?" Had there always been an edge of anger behind Ken's conversations with me? A sneer behind faux concern?

Yes. So much for my vaunted bullshit detector. It hadn't worked on Trista, either.

"But Trista seemed so genuine." My words felt and sounded foreign.

"She may be, but she hired you because I asked her to. I wanted to keep an eye on you, see what you were doing. She thought it would be fun because she really does despise her husband. Probably despises you, too, since you're banging him."

Another flare of shame and anger all rolled into one, but I sent those feelings to the vault. They could be felt later. Better to be as rational as I could be, and Ken's assumption was telling.

If I hadn't seen Blake Malone and my Malone standing together in the same room, my imagination would've concocted a gnarly story of how Malone had betrayed me, but I knew the answer was far simpler than that: My ex simply wasn't good at his job.

In fact, my ex was so inept that his attempt to humiliate me had instead sent me a paying client. He was so inept that when the time came to serve papers, that client had ditched him in favor of me.

I stood a little straighter with that knowledge. "I'm not sleeping with Blake Malone."

He snorted. "No need to lie about it, honey. I have the pictures to prove it. Got one through your apartment's vertical blinds last night. You getting railed on your dining room table. I had no idea you liked it like that. I mean, we have a table right over there. All you had to do was ask."

Reflexively, I glanced at the antique dining room table that had been a gift from Ken's grandmother. Nausea hit me in waves, the momentum of power swinging back to him. Not only was the thought of sex with Ken now utterly repulsive, but the feelings of violation took me by surprise. I squeezed my eyes shut. Was this how people felt when they saw the pictures I'd taken of them? Of course, the difference was that I hadn't been doing anything wrong. My ex had, though.

"You had no right to do that," I said through gritted teeth. "So help me, if you ever come near me again on anything akin to surveillance, I will have you arrested for harassment so fast you won't know what hit you. Trespassing, too, if I can manage it."

"You mean harassment like when you put all those flamingos in that poor guy's yard?"

And Ken wasn't as stupid as I had thought.

"That was different!" Even I could tell my words held little conviction.

"Was it?"

Dammit, he was right. I had been on a job for Denise Dobbs, but it wasn't a private investigator job; it was as her petty personal assistant. Technically, what I had done could be construed as harassment. Technically. If someone wanted to waste a lot of time and money to take it to court, they could. Unfortunately, Denise's husband struck me as one of those people who had time and money to burn.

Wait a minute. Somewhere in my law classes I had come across a handy phrase for what was going on here. "That's a false equivalence. Any mistake I made does not excuse the mistakes you made. No one hired you to surveil me. *You* did not have 'permissible purpose.' Delete those pictures."

"I wasn't surveilling you. I was surveilling him."

I thought about correcting him, but some instinct stopped me. If he wanted to believe I was sleeping with Trista's husband, then so be it. Let him simmer in his own ignorance. If he tried to humiliate me with those pictures, then I could sue him.

But all this had to end now. "Ken, you don't want to go down this road with me. I'm going to tell you once: The threats are over, the games are over, our relationship is over. If, however, you come for me or for my friends or my family, I won't be petty. I will be vengeful."

He laughed. He had the audacity to laugh at me. "Sure you will. I let you have the title because I do think you're petty enough to call the IRS on me, but I guess ol' Malone's doing something right based on watching you last night. Too bad he'll have moved on to another woman in three months like he always does."

He's not talking about your Malone.

No, but my Malone had built an expiration date into our relationship. He might still be a tomcat, but he wasn't a cheater.

So far as I knew. Since my BS detector was on the fritz, what did I know about anything or anyone?

"Hey," Ken was saying. "When he leaves, I'll be here waiting. We'll be even then. We can start over then."

Ah, so that was his play. I'd caught him cheating. He thought he'd caught me "cheating." This all came back to wanting someone to take care of him, his house, and his business after Eloise got smart a lot quicker than I did.

A laugh burbled up. "No."

"What do you mean 'no'? I signed the car over to you!"

"Sure did, because that's the right thing to do, the fair thing to do. But you betrayed my trust, so we wouldn't be 'even.' It doesn't take a genius to see that the only reason you want me back is because I kept things running. I was the woman who did it all. I kept your house clean, *and* I kept your accounting straight, but here's the funny part."

"What's the funny part?" Ken asked once it became obvious his participation in the conversation would be required.

"You're not even that good of a private investigator."

"What?"

"You heard me." Time to try some rhetoric of my own with a redirect. "Whatever happened to Eloise anyway?"

That question wiped the smile off his face.

"We didn't last a month. I proposed because she was a little skittish after you groped her, but then some friend of yours came and told her a bunch of lies about me."

"Interesting."

That had to have been Salcedo, but she'd never mentioned it.

"Not interesting. Horrible. She was . . ." He closed his eyes, smiling wistfully. "So young and firm and—"

"Pliant."

His eyes snapped open.

"Yes, Ken. Your secret is no secret to me. Somehow, you charm women into your bed, but what you really love is being the boss, directing their lives for them. Maybe what happened with us is that I was no longer a challenge. You beat me down until it wasn't as much fun anymore to bend me to your will. I'm glad Eloise escaped your clutches."

His mouth opened and closed, but he couldn't manage anything other than "You take that back!"

"No," I said. "I don't believe I will."

You know you're having a bad day when going to the tag office is an improvement over where you were before. As I stood in line, a riot of feelings swirled within, and I didn't care for that one bit. Sure, there was the schadenfreude of imagining what Ken would do when he discovered I had messed everything up in his office. There was the joy and pride of getting the car title without having to apologize or pay him any money. Relief that I wouldn't have to deal with him ever again.

But knowing Trista had initially lied to me cut me deep, and the scar from Ken's betrayal was still fresh. Mortification that he'd seen me having sex with Malone joined the party. Fear that I would have to deal with him again. Anxiety that I could've jeopardized my private investigator license over the flamingo stunt.

Feelings were, in my opinion, highly overrated.

0/10. Did not recommend.

Gradually, that swirl of emotion morphed into resignation, frustration, boredom, and irritation. I'd forgotten to bring a book with me, something I usually did when I knew there would be a line. I would've played on my phone, but the battery was almost dead thanks to my surveillance marathon earlier in the day. My stomach growled, reminding me that I hadn't eaten lunch, either.

Happy early birthday to me.

But when it was all over, relief became the predominant emotion because the car was in my name and the registration paid. Even better? My checking account still had plenty left for loan payments and rent and whatnot. I turned in the direction of Trista's house.

Oh, she'd played her part well. She'd pretended not to know who I was or what I was about, had gone along with my Anonymous McGee—at least, until I went to her house for the flocking, at which point it seemed safe enough to get to know each other.

Or so I had thought.

I didn't want to believe Ken, but I remembered that she'd said she wanted to hire me to serve papers because she didn't trust the other guy to do it.

Well, I guessed not since the other guy was Ken, and he had yet to figure out that there were two Malones.

Ken had pointed her to my Malone, and he would've served divorce papers to the wrong person, something Trista must've realized when she saw Malone's tattoo in my doorbell cam footage. The more I thought about it, the angrier I got. By the time I made it to Trista's house, my rage monster was threatening to come out again, but at the sight of Trista's three daughters entering the house with knapsacks and artwork, I put my rage monster on a leash.

I got out of my car and called "Hey" to stop Trista before she reached her front door.

At the sight of me, she froze.

"I'd like to have a word with you," I said.

She nodded. "Ken texted me, so I thought you might. Let me get the kids settled, and we can talk on the back deck."

She led the way into the house, and we followed the sounds of giggling, indignation, and teasing, both good-natured and otherwise. The girls were in the kitchen getting snacks and talking about their day at art camp. If they were curious about me, they didn't let on. Trista pointed to a door on the other side of the kitchen, and I made my exit to a screened-in porch.

Waiting gave me time to calm down, but it was still a slow process.

Finally, she joined me outside, looking more tired than she ever had.

She certainly wasn't offering mimosas today.

"So," she said.

I attempted a stare but could only come up with a squint. The roof over the screened porch didn't do much in the way of shielding us because it faced west. The sun came at us sideways, giving us the full brunt of a summer afternoon in Georgia. A trickle of sweat slid down my back. Times like this, I was sure hell was humid.

But I would desiccate from dehydration and drift into the wind before I said another word. My glare was doing the talking.

She sighed and took a seat. I did the same.

"About a year ago I first suspected something was up with Blake. I'd gone to school with Ken, a year or two behind him, so I hired him to see if my husband had a mistress."

So odd to think that I had probably handled that invoice and never thought a thing of it. That had been a lifetime ago, before I met my Malone. It also made sense of why Trista hadn't wanted me to find the mistress. She already had someone looking for her.

"He told me Blake was living in that apartment. I didn't question it because I knew Malone Construction leased one. Blake and I had, ah, taken advantage of it when we were first dating."

"So the thought that he might be entertaining someone else there stung all the more?"

"Of course it did!"

"Tell me this, Trista. I never thought you were working against me. I thought we were kindred spirits. Was any part of that real?"

"What's real? The bitterness is, and has always been, real. What I asked you to do? It may have been Ken's idea, but the idea of getting even the smallest bit of revenge on Blake gave me great joy even if I couldn't imagine a scenario in which you would actually succeed."

"Let me guess: You were going to stiff me on payment?"

"No, no. I mean, that was Ken's suggestion, but he only wanted me to keep tabs on you. I reasoned that I'd be happy to pay you if you somehow managed to get the job done."

"And then I showed you the video."

"I could've died when I realized Ken wasn't even following my husband. When it came time to serve papers, I saw that you were more reliable than Ken, which, honestly, I should've known. Jackie recommended him, and I shouldn't have trusted her either, bless her heart."

"But you did report back to him on what I was doing?"

She winced. "At first. I told him you were going to do something for Denise and covertly sent him a picture of the flamingos, but I didn't tell him anything after that, I swear."

Interesting. Ken had been happy to let me believe Trista had been on his side all along.

Of course, my BS detector was irrevocably broken, so what did I know? Too bad there was no extended warranty for women's intuition.

We sat there in the sun, sweating. I couldn't help but notice she hadn't offered me anything to drink.

"Well, I wash my hands of anything and everything having to do with the Malone family," I said as I stood. "And for the record, I'm not mad. I'm just disappointed."

"Disappointed?"

"Yes, I think I took one job for a guy. The rest were all for women. Sure, I did it because I needed the money, but I envisioned Little Miss Petty as a way for women to help each other, and here you were spying on me the entire time."

"Not the entire time. And it was just a favor for a friend."

"A friend? So you and Ken are buddies?"

"Fine for a friend of a friend."

"And you knew he'd cheated on me, right? You still wanted to help your friend after that?"

She looked away. "I guess I wasn't putting two and two together. He didn't mention that you were his girlfriend, just his former business partner."

"Left the girlfriend part out, did he?"

"That's why you said you'd been traded in for a younger model. I should've seen that."

"Exactly. I trusted you. I commiserated with you. I did a silly job for you, yes, but when you called, I answered. Speaking of, why the heck did you call me when the FBI raided your house? Why not call Ken?"

"Because I knew you were competent. And you already knew about Blake, so it wouldn't be as embarrassing as calling one of my other friends."

"'Other friends,' huh?" I chuckled a little. "So you'd started to think of me as a friend, too? I considered you one. Not necessarily someone

I had all that much in common with, but someone I wanted to help. But friends don't spy on friends. Friends don't team up with the ex of a friend."

"But we weren't friends then, and I didn't know he was the ex!"

"But you knew about the business part. You could've told me."

"You wouldn't have believed me!"

I leaned back. "I probably would've believed you. You forget, I knew Ken far better than you did."

"Well, I didn't know I could trust *you*, now did I?" she snapped.

And that was the crux of the problem.

"I didn't know if I could trust you, either, but I did. And, yes, I needed the money. Yes, the whole thing is probably ridiculous, but it's also ridiculous that I'll end up paying twice as much for my student loans as I borrowed. It's farcical that I had to put a car loan in my partner's name because my father ruined my credit. Ludicrous that same partner would then refuse to give me the title even though I made the payments. Shameful that I put so much work into his business and our house, but I don't get jack because we weren't officially married. But also crazytownbananapants that your husband can clean out all your joint accounts even though you *are* married. I could go on, but I won't. What I'm trying to say is that this world wants us to think we're in a competition for male attention, but, really, we need to stick together. I trusted you."

"Well, that's your mistake. Although I suppose a part of me knew you were more trustworthy than my other so-called friends, who are now gossiping about me on tennis courts and over Facebook after the FBI raid. You're living in a fantasy world, if you think women can trust each other. How many good women friends do you have? True friends. Ride-or-die friends."

"Funny you should mention that," I said. "Not long before you came to me, I met two women who fit the bill. If I didn't have many friends before, it was partially due to the odd hours of my job but mostly due to seeing the world in just the way you described—not that

I realized it at the time. Heck, I have one neighbor who brought me a casserole and another who watches my cat. I am surrounded by women who have my back."

Her face contorted as her anger melted into sadness.

"Where do you find them?" she asked, seeming honestly perplexed.

"Trista, to have friends like that, I guess you have to be one. You have to be vulnerable enough to trust even when the world says you shouldn't."

She took in a ragged breath. "I do apologize. If I'd known then what I know now, I would've never agreed to spy on you."

"Apology accepted." The words left my mouth of their own accord, but they felt right even as they surprised me.

Her eyes met mine, her mouth an O of shock. "Really?"

"Really."

She studied the worn boards of the porch. "Before you go, I need to write you that last check."

Chapter 36

I thought about my words to Trista all the way back to my apartment. Was I the kind of friend who was loyal and trusting? I liked to think so, but it was rather humbling to realize I'd somehow inspired such loyalty from Havisham and Salcedo.

But could I trust myself to know if they were true friends? Could I trust that part of me that said Malone was different, that he might be the unicorn of a man I'd been searching for?

It would figure that I'd find a good man, only to have him not want the same kind of relationship I did. What was I even doing with my life? Messing around with Malone as though we were going to ride off into the sunset together someday? He'd never promised anything serious. I'd thought I was the kind of person who could hit it and quit it, but apparently, I had feelings after all.

I was being ridiculous to think that heterochromia and having read a popular book meant anything. Who knew if his favorite shape was a star, and I was pretty sure he'd never kissed me under a blue moon, but none of that was important. It was silly, the ramblings of a grown woman referring to something a fictional *child* had said in a movie. Heck, Havisham had met her cowboy, but he was neither a billionaire nor a philanthropist.

So far as you know.

The whole day had left me thirsty, cranky, and completely disillusioned with humanity.

As I pulled into the parking lot, I saw a moving van backed up to our breezeway, and my heart lodged firmly in my throat.

I rubbed my breastbone.

If it hurt this much to see the moving van, how much more would it hurt when he actually left?

A clean break. Yeah. I needed to make a clean break of it.

After a couple of deep breaths, I walked up to his door and knocked.

"There you are!" he said as he pulled me close for a kiss. "What took you so long?"

"I had to make another stop after the tag office."

He grimaced. "As if the tag office isn't bad enough. But don't you worry. We are celebrating tonight. You got the title, and thanks to you, I had a major breakthrough. Let me open this bottle, and I'll let you pick the pizza."

"Malone—"

He opened the fridge and took out a champagne bottle, talking as he unwrapped it and took off the cage. "Finally, finally. I found that last puzzle piece, and you know, it was your puzzle piece that helped me figure it out—"

"Malone—"

"At first, I was thinking Wyoming or the Caymans, but . . ." Here he paused to pop the cork. "Liechtenstein! Mountains. For some reason the mountain on the puzzle piece reminded me of Liechtenstein. And there is no way he would've figured that out on his own. But do you know who does know about Liechtenstein? Selena! All thanks to you! You weren't kidding when you said you'd do something worse than punch her. I'd say going to jail for helping Blake embezzle money is going to be a whole lot worse."

I put a hand on his shoulder. "Malone."

He paused, and something about my expression made him frown. "Yes?"

"I don't think this is a good idea."

"Since when has champagne ever *not* been a good idea?"

"No, us."

My heart pounded against my chest as though trying to tell me to stop talking. Malone remained frozen. Champagne flowed into the sink before he absently sat the whole bottle in there, wisps of carbonation rising from the top. "Can I ask what brought about this change of heart?"

"No reason," I whispered, my past and my present colliding in ways I didn't like.

"Oh, there's gotta be a reason."

I forced myself back into the present. "No, my ex and I used to call it 'No Reason Champagne.' I do have reasons, very good ones."

"Please tell me it's not to get back together with him."

"No! Why does everyone think I would do that?"

"Because, I don't know, you were with him for a reason."

"I don't remember what it was at this point. No, the moving van. You're moving."

"Not today! That's for Mrs. Q. Her daughter finally talked her into moving into a place where she won't have to climb the stairs."

Ah, that.

"No, but someday you will move, Malone. Unless . . ."

I gave him space to talk about a branch office, as he'd considered for Selena. Instead, he said, "Unless what?"

"Nothing."

"Well," he said, "they do make phones and planes and such. I don't love the idea of long distance, but—"

"Is that really what you want to do?"

"No." He rubbed the back of his neck.

"Then what are we doing here?"

He crossed his arms over his chest. "You tell me."

I needed him to say it first. Why couldn't he understand that I needed him to say it first? Every time I'd put myself out on that limb in the past, someone had sawed it off and let me fall.

Well, not Havisham or Salcedo.

Have you really known them long enough that you can guarantee they won't do something similar someday?

Damn, today had done a number on me. I was hungry and dehydrated and confused and disheartened and—

Malone became blurry in front of me, and I felt the first dull stab of a migraine behind my left eye.

Ugh. Of course—I'd spent all that time in the car, then dealt with Ken, then visited the tag office, and then gone to Trista's house, where she didn't offer me so much as a glass of water.

"I can't do this right now," I said, holding a hand over my left eye. "I gotta go lie down."

Malone's expression changed to one of concern. "Are you okay?"

"Migraine. Stress. And I didn't drink enough water today." Now my vision blurred and filled with black globs. Malone's head seemed to be a foot away from the rest of his body.

"What do you need?"

"I have meds in my apartment. Hopefully, that and a nap will do the trick," I said, turning to go.

"You can stay here. Let me play nursemaid." The hope in his voice tugged at the heartstrings that only a month ago I would've sworn I didn't have.

Tempting. Too tempting.

"No thanks. I can handle it."

"But you'll call me if it gets worse?"

"Yeah," I said, almost irritated by how much he cared. How dare he pretend he cared that much about a headache when he wouldn't take the first step to suggesting something more in our relationship?

That's not fair, Stella. He said there were planes and phones.

Yeah, but then he admitted he didn't want to do long-distance.

I made my way across the breezeway, fumbling with the lock because I couldn't see straight to insert the key. BB meowed at me, and I had to take short, careful steps to make sure I didn't step on her because the black blobs in my vision were growing larger and taking on a sort of technicolor aura.

In mere minutes, the pain would begin in earnest.

After popping an Imitrex, I stumbled into the bathroom and wet a washrag to put over my eyes, then trudged to the bedroom, kicking off my pants and wriggling free from my bra before slipping into bed. BB jumped up with a little trill and circled around my pillow before curling up beside my head. I didn't have the energy to move her.

She began to purr, and it did feel slightly better. Enough for me to wonder about Malone. He was really going to make me say it first, wasn't he? I couldn't. No way. Never once had I been the first person in a relationship to say "I love you," and I had no intention of starting now. Not when my track record was abysmal.

The one time I'd declared my affection first was the one time I'd tried to make someone stay by declaring my love. Instead, I'd ruined everything—

No, absolutely not going back down that particular stretch of memory lane.

Oh, hell. Why not reevaluate that night while you're already in pain?

My career in karmic facilitation might have started at age six, but I achieved peak pettiness at the age of nine. And that pettiness brought my entire world crashing down.

Mom and Dad had always been on-again, off-again.

When you get pregnant at the age of sixteen, you aren't exactly mature—and girls tend to mature faster than boys, so that should give you a good idea of how immature my father still was.

We lived in an old, cramped house in Austell, one that wasn't particularly well maintained. My father had plenty of time on his hands for home maintenance, but he hadn't had the will since losing his job at the Lakewood Assembly Plant. Mom worked two jobs. We pretended to be a happy family whenever company was around, but they argued long and late into the night, and my father often smelled of body odor and beer.

Every now and then, he'd feel fatherly and talk to me about football or baseball. Every six months or so, he'd think to take me out for ice cream. But usually, he napped, drank beer, went to play poker with the guys, or, and this was his favorite pastime, he would sneak out to a strip club.

One summer afternoon, my mother made the mistake of leaving a wad of cash on a kitchen counter. She'd just gotten back from her second job, waitressing, and she was too exhausted to think straight. She trudged down the hall, leaving the odor of burned coffee and bacon grease in her wake.

Five minutes after the creak of the bedsprings indicated my mother had flopped onto the bed, my father was at that kitchen counter thumbing through her cash.

"Where are you going, Daddy?"

"Uh, to the bank."

My eyes narrowed. "The last time you said you were going to the bank, you went to watch women dance. That's what Nana said."

"Well, you shouldn't eavesdrop. And don't believe everything your nana says," he said as he placed the money in his pocket.

"You shouldn't steal Momma's money. She worked hard for that."

He muttered something about getting his rocks off, but that wasn't an expression I understood yet. I only knew it had something to do with seeing the women dance and take off their clothes, which was something Momma had whispered to Nana when she thought I wasn't listening.

"Listen, Stella. You go watch television and maybe we'll get some ice cream when I get back. Wouldn't that be nice?" His question was marred by a long, loud Natty Light–induced belch. He looked down the hall, waiting for my mother to appear, but she was too tired for that.

"Why don't we go for ice cream now?"

"Can't just now." He was already at the door.

Tamika, my friend at school, once told me that sometimes you could get someone to stay if you told them how much you loved them. Did I love my daddy? He was my daddy, so of course I loved him. I definitely wanted him to stay. I took a deep breath and said, "Daddy, I love you, and I would like for you to stay here."

He paused, hesitating at the door. "We'll go when I get back. Just you and me."

A promise of ice cream, one that might never be fulfilled, was not a declaration of love. If I could love him because he was my daddy, then why couldn't he love me because I was his child?

As an adult, I understood more about addiction and how the allure of shoe models could beat out a trip to get ice cream with your daughter.

But that didn't explain why he couldn't say even a half-hearted "Love you, too."

Something broke in me that day, a tie for my worst day ever.

I turned on the television, but the more I thought about it, the more unfair it seemed that my mother could work so hard only to have my father take her money. But what could I do about it? I was a kid. I'd played the only hand I'd been dealt, and my love hadn't been enough to keep him home.

That's when snippets of overheard conversations began snapping together like puzzle pieces.

You see, eavesdropping was my passion. As an only child, there wasn't much else to do. Not much earlier, I'd overheard my father talking to one of his buddies about how he had the hots for a particular dancer at the Taj Mahal, and I had filed that information away, not even sure what I would do with it.

Now I knew. If someone did something wrong, you called the police, right?

I found an honest-to-goodness phone book, and I called the local police department. Even then, I knew it wasn't a 911 situation. Fortunately, the woman who answered the phone was a mother herself.

Once she'd determined that I wasn't in immediate danger, she patiently listened as I explained that my father had stolen my mother's money and probably gone to a strip club called the Taj Mahal because he wanted to see a girl named Amber.

Not only was this woman kind, but she was also smart. The vast majority of adults wouldn't have taken me seriously, but she asked my father's name. Willie Stark rang a bell as someone who might have a warrant or three out for his arrest, so, after she hung up the call, she went searching for any possible warrants. The rest, as they say, is history.

My father went to jail. My mother carted me off to Nana's and then spent more of her hard-earned money on Daddy's legal fees. Eventually, she got tired of standing by her man. I lived with her a little while and met Skip's owner. Then, when she ghosted me, I went back to Nana's, where I stayed until I graduated from high school.

Mom never told me to my face that I was the reason why our family was broken up, but I overheard her tell Nana that I'd ruined her life.

Nana had immediately hissed, "For heaven's sake, Marie, she's a *child.* She was trying to protect you."

But the damage to our relationship had been done, and that day was the other in a tie for the worst day of my life. From that day forward I became, in my mind, Stella Stark: the girl who doesn't deserve nice things because she ruins lives.

As for my father? He served his time and then moved to Florida. I actually met Ken when I hired him to find my father. He was a better PI back then, or maybe he was motivated to take advantage of the fresh-faced college student who'd walked into his office. It was hard to say.

The end result was that he found my father. By then, Willie Stark had a new family, including a different little girl he took for ice cream.

He met me at an ice cream shop in Pensacola and bought me a caramel sundae before he told me as gently as he could that he didn't want to have contact with me. He knew he should forgive me because I was just a kid, but prison had been a horrible place. Seeing me reminded him not only of how awful those years had been but also of how badly he'd failed his first child and his first wife. He just couldn't do it.

Also, his new wife didn't want to meet me and didn't want me to meet my half sister.

I cried a lot in the days and weeks after leaving Florida. Then, one day, I found it hard to cry at all.

Tears seeped from my eyes as, in the present, I rolled over, willing the memories to leave and the painkillers to kick in. The pain was so intense that nausea had come to join the party.

Finally, my migraine meds kicked in, so I could slowly slip into oblivion.

Chapter 37

When I woke up the next morning, I had the pain at the back of my neck that always lingered after a migraine. BB was gone, but someone in my living room was speaking in a low voice.

Immediately, I was out of bed, looking for a weapon, remembering that my Taser was in the drawer of the coffee table.

Judo alone it would have to be.

I had 911 cued on my phone, my finger poised over the button, when I opened the door to see Malone.

"Feeling better?" he asked.

BB had settled into his lap and must've been the creature he was talking to.

I closed the phone app. "Why are you here?"

He frowned. "I was worried about you. Especially when I saw you hadn't shut the apartment door behind you. I decided to camp out here to make sure you were okay."

My heart melted ever so slightly, but that melting was followed by an ache. Ice cream melted, too. And folks might take you for ice cream every now and again, but ultimately they would leave you. Sometimes they might even tell you you're not enough while your ice cream is melting because you've lost your appetite.

"I'm fine."

He chuckled. "This is not my first rodeo, Stark. Never once has a woman ever been fine when saying 'I'm fine.' Let's start with the migraine. How's that?"

"Down to the pain in the back of my neck."

He patted a spot on the love seat beside him, and I sat. He began massaging my shoulders and my neck, and I made an indecent sound.

He stopped. "Is that a bad cry or a good cry?"

"Good cry."

He continued massaging. "So what happened yesterday?"

"I only got the title to my car after I sorted all Ken's mail and threatened to sic the IRS on him if he didn't sign it over to me. Then he told me that he hired Trista to spy on me. After getting my tags renewed, I went to see her. She wasn't as remorseful as I might have hoped. Then I saw the moving van, and—"

The thought of you leaving hurt so badly that I wanted to rip off the Band-Aid and get it over with then and there.

Only I didn't say that last part.

Instead, Malone filled in the gap. "You thought I was leaving?"

"Yes."

"Do you really think I would leave without saying goodbye?"

My migraine threatened to return. Those weren't the words I would've chosen to hear. I'd been hoping for something along the lines of "I like you as a person, not just a booty call."

"C'mon, Stark, I wouldn't do that," he finally said.

I turned around so I could face him. "But you are leaving soon, aren't you?"

He sighed deeply. "Chateau wants me to start a case in Denver after the July fourth holiday. Then I have to get back home to California to make sure no one's burned down the office while I've been gone."

"I see."

"I figured out what Blake did and where he stashed the money. The only thing left to do was to find him, and you did that for me."

"About that . . ." I absently rubbed my breastbone since an ache bloomed underneath. By helping Malone find his cousin, I'd hastened his departure.

He looked at me expectantly.

"Hand me a dollar and pretend you gave it to me yesterday morning."

"I don't have a dollar."

"Do you have any money on you?"

He reached into his back pocket for his wallet and handed me a twenty.

"Thank you. This is for that case I took. You know, the one where I searched for your cousin?"

He tapped his chin. "Oh, yes! I absolutely remember hiring you to do that."

"Was I right about Selena?"

He sighed. "Yes. Knowing Blake's accomplice helped me find those missing pieces to the puzzle. Both of them were arrested earlier this morning."

"Good," I said.

He stood and started pacing. "But I feel like such a fool for not even considering her. *She* is smart enough to know about Liechtenstein. *She* had access to anything Blake could've ever wanted."

"That was my thinking as well," I said in a soft voice.

"And convincing her to string me along and then dump me had to be a bonus for Blake."

"You know for sure she did that?"

His eyes met mine, one fire and one ice. "The dates don't lie. He hired someone to do the initial attack, but not long after we started dating, Blake suddenly knew what I was going to do before I did it."

"I'm sorry, Malone."

"Could've been worse. We could've married."

I winced.

"I guess I didn't want to believe she'd do that to me. They didn't interact at all at the gala." He scratched the back of his head.

"I noticed that, too. When you have that much money on the line, you can rationalize avoiding each other until you're safely out of the country."

"I still can't believe she would do something like that!"

I braced myself. Here was the point where he would turn on me, as people seemed so frequently to do.

Instead, he went back to the love seat and sat down beside me. "You're a genius, Stark. It was right under our noses, but you are the one who figured it out."

"Because you don't want to believe the worst in people."

He read between the lines I'd just spoken. "I'm not as good as you make me out to be, Stark."

"That may be true, but I'm far more cynical than you think."

His phone rang, and he cursed colorfully. "This had best be the last work call I ever have to take while we're together."

After mere seconds he turned to me. "Gotta go in."

"You go." I checked my watch. "I have to go to the bank before they close at noon."

"Then we'll meet back here to celebrate."

I forced a smile. "Something like that."

He walked over to kiss me on the cheek and then walked to the door. I trailed behind him. When his hand touched the knob, he stopped. "Oh! I almost forgot. Addie came by before you woke up. She brought something for us."

"I'm scared to ask," I said.

"Don't be," he said with a smile. "Hold out your hand."

I did as he said, and he slid a friendship bracelet on my wrist. Addie had made it with elastic, using both colored beads and white ones with black letters. My bracelet said A N T I - H E R O.

As if Little Miss Petty would be anything but.

Then my eyes caught Malone's bracelet, one he'd put on his wrist, no doubt without thinking twice about whether it was manly or not. His said K I N G O F M Y H E A R T.

I sucked in a breath, dizzy at the memory of how flippant I had been while standing in the Waffle House parking lot saying that wearing a friendship bracelet unironically would be a sign that—

Oh, what did the universe know about anything?

"Really sweet of her, don't you think?" Malone was saying.

"Yeah, she's a good kid."

"Okay, I hate to leave you, but I need to take care of this. Then I'm going to turn off my phone when we reconvene this evening."

"Yeah, same," I said, even though I knew I was prolonging the inevitable.

"I'll get new champagne," he said. "I'm afraid the bottle I opened last night went flat."

There would be no need for champagne, but I didn't say so.

Going to the bank felt like such a 1990s thing to do. While almost all my clients had paid me through Cash App (yes, my username was $LittleMissPetty), a few paid me in cash. I also had the hundy from Jackie and what Havisham had loaned me.

If the teller thought I had obtained the cash through nefarious means, she didn't mention it. I made a deposit and then went home to log on to the portal for my student loans and pay off everything I could. I took care of fees, got current with my payments, and then frowned at the principal. How could I possibly still owe so much?

I shook my head, then made sure my rent was paid for the month. That left me with . . . not a lot.

But, hey, the car was mine. More jobs were headed my way. On the whole, I'd done a good job of making something out of nothing.

At least, as the Beatles once sang, I'd done some with some help from my friends.

I felt both heavy and light. Light because I'd somehow managed to pay off my late fees but heavy because I knew I needed to talk to Malone. I'd give him a chance to say it first. If he could say it first, then I would reciprocate. If he couldn't say it first, then I would know he'd never looked at our arrangement as anything other than temporary.

That decided, I could check my mail without fearing another form letter threatening me with some kind of penalty. Outside I went, smiling at the memory of running into Malone and then pretending to look at that Lands' End catalog.

As if it would ever be cold enough to wear flannel pajamas in Georgia.

The mailbox creaked open, and I took out a stack. Some was actually addressed to me, but much of it was marked "Current Resident" or had the name of a previous tenant. Then there was a white envelope addressed to me.

From the Georgia Board of Private Detectives and Security Agencies.

What the heck could they be sending me? I was up to date on my license.

I hadn't even made it back into my apartment before the phrases "reviewed a complaint" and "non-disciplinary private admonition" had me sitting on the second-to-the-bottom step. My heart pounded. My mouth ran dry.

Up until that moment, I don't think I had realized how much I enjoyed my job. For a while it had been too intertwined with my relationship and carried all those negative associations. Now that I had even more freedom to pursue the jobs I wanted to pursue, I had begun to enjoy it.

Well, other than the camping.

But the threat of having my license suspended made me rethink crickets and flamingos and sewing the flaps shut on tighty-whities.

Someone—and I had a pretty good idea who—had submitted an anonymous complaint to the board suggesting that I had been trespassing on Dobbs's lawn and harassing him with the flamingos. Based on the timing of this letter, the Douchecanoe had tattled on me immediately.

And he knew he had when we spoke.

Fortunately, the board had a sense of humor and had chalked the entire incident up to "poor judgment," but it all added up to "unprofessional conduct" nonetheless.

Ken had to have been the one to have submitted the complaint because he was the only one who knew about my day job. Also, Trista's delight that day had been genuine. Well, best I could tell. But even Trista probably didn't have the first clue that Georgia had a regulation board for private investigators. Nor would she think to connect the flamingos to being a private investigator.

Once again, Ken had proven himself far pettier than I'd ever been.

Until now.

Heart pounding with rage, I took out my phone and searched for a number for the IRS.

A quick search of the website showed no number to call. I couldn't email to refer someone for an audit, either. Uncle Sam wanted paper. I found an official form called an "Information Referral" that would have to be printed, placed in an envelope, stamped, and sent.

Okay then.

Little Miss Petty would pretend it was 1994 and conduct her business old-school—as soon as she remembered where, other than the post office, she could buy some stamps.

Well, that and if she could coax her printer into actually working.

But this would be her last official act of pettiness.

If I'd learned anything these past few weeks, it was that I didn't need to be in charge of meting out consequences, logical or otherwise. Collecting evidence? Absolutely. But I would have to effect change from the right side of the law—spirit or otherwise—from this point on.

Chapter 38

To say I didn't want to have this conversation with Malone would be the understatement of the century, but it had to be done. In his case, it had been fun. It had been real. It had really, really been fun, but I couldn't afford to get attached to him only to have him leave. My heart couldn't take it.

When he came through the door, he said, "I thought about your headache. Champagne might not be the best thing, so I got ice cream."

I froze.

Tears stung because here was ice cream to ruin yet another party, and it was all the worse because Malone was being thoughtful.

"You don't like ice cream?" He frowned.

"No, it has nothing to do with the ice cream." *Even if ice cream keeps showing up on my crappiest days.* I took a deep breath and said what had to be said: "Malone, this isn't working for me."

He leaned against the counter—why did the man have to be so good at leaning?—and asked, "What do you mean?"

"Listen, I'm not the kind of girl you take home to Mother, so—"

"Whoa, who said anything about that?"

Further proof that he considered me a fling.

"No one, but I think I've gotten more attached to you than I have to Brené Brown. Only, she's stuck with me now, and you aren't. I'm as shocked as anyone to discover that I, apparently, like strings."

He nodded. "That's fair."

"You have ruined me for all other men when it comes to sex, but there's more to a relationship than sex, right?"

Now even our beautiful moment on my dining room table was tainted by the image of Ken sitting outside with his camera.

"Yeah, I guess you're right, but we have phones. They make planes."

"So you said, but do you want to sign up for another long-distance relationship?"

"No," he said, a little too quickly.

"Well, I think our situationship has run its course then. The benefits have been amazing, but one can't live on pizza alone."

"Right," he said.

"Why don't we just stop whatever this is before it hurts any more than it already does?"

Fight for me, please!

His eyes met mine, and I drank in their unique beauty because I knew I wouldn't be looking into them again. He waited a good while before finally saying, "If that's what you want."

My whole chest throbbed as if my heart wanted to claw past its rib cage and go with Malone instead. "Yes, that's what I want."

It's not in the least what I want.

He got to the door and stopped. "Are you sure?"

I nodded, but I had my fingers crossed behind my back to negate the lie. "Don't forget the ice cream."

He got the bag and paused beside me on his way out the door. He inhaled deeply, and I waited for him to speak, but he shook his head as if getting rid of the thought. Instead, he leaned down to kiss my cheek. "Goodbye, Stella Stark. Remember your worth. Anyone who doesn't see you as a goddess doesn't deserve to be with you."

At the door, he turned a second time. "I think . . . I think I'll go to Denver early because . . ."

He didn't finish that thought, and he didn't have to. I nodded my agreement.

Long after he left, I still stood by the door, absently rubbing my breastbone.

I felt hollowed out.

In the midst of a bone-crushing weight of sadness, I tried to chuckle, but the sound came out more as a hiccup sob.

Over time the worst day in a person's life could change. I knew that now.

The next day I found a bag tied to my doorknob. Inside was my purple thong, along with a note:

It's such a nice set. It would be a shame to break it up.

Chapter 39

"You are such an idiot," Havisham said.

"What's going on over here?" asked Betty. "I'm too old to break up fights. That's why they moved me out here, away from where all the nightclubs are."

"We're not going to fight," I said.

"Oh, we might fight," Havisham said.

Salcedo, who was sitting beside me tonight, reached across the table to put a hand on her forearm. "Let her be. She's had a rough couple of days."

"Of her own making."

"I am right here, so you don't have to talk about me in the third person," I said before turning to Salcedo. "And you're going to take down the website, right?"

"Yeah, if I have to."

"Well, I can't afford to lose my main job due to ethics complaints, now can I?"

"That's ridiculous." Havisham practically spit the words out.

"Maybe so, but I gotta eat, and I gotta pay you back. Also, I'm the one who had the breakup, so what's eating you up?"

She tried to smile, but it came out as more of a grimace. "I found my billionaire cowboy philanthropist, and I was counting on you to prove to me that this whole signs-from-the-universe bullshit might have something to it."

"You, of all people, know better than to look for signs from the universe," I said. "And Trace isn't a billionaire cowboy philanthropist anyway."

"How do you know?"

"Because I know," I said, even if I hadn't actually looked him up.

"Well, he's a multimillionaire cowboy philanthropist, and I would say that's close enough."

Wide-eyed, I looked to Salcedo for confirmation. She shrugged.

I waved away the discussion. "Whatever. If I were younger, maybe I would've begged Malone to give us a chance, but I needed him to make the first move. I gave him the opportunity. He didn't take it."

"How exactly did it go again?" Salcedo asked.

I told them about the conversation again, even though my chest ached at the thought of it.

"So he said, 'If that's what you want'?"

"Yes."

"Stark, he was waiting for *you* to make the first move," Havisham said.

"Well, I wasn't about to. Nothing good has ever come of my putting myself out there first. Not with my father. Not with Ken. No thank you. And long-distance wouldn't work anyway. I don't like planes, I don't like starting over, and I don't like being made a fool. I don't have the time, energy, or money to start over. Cat lady it is."

Havisham's eyes widened. "Wow, Stark. That was so cynical, you're making me sound like Pollyanna."

Salcedo frowned. "Stella. You're clearly miserable. Why don't you go to him?"

"No. I ran after my dad, and he cut me out of his life. I once went back to Ken after a breakup, and you see how that ended up for me. Besides, what do I know? My bullshit detector is obviously broken beyond repair. Trista was in cahoots with Ken the whole time."

"What?" asked Havisham and Salcedo together.

This necessitated telling them about the entire day from start to finish.

"And to think I gave that woman some chardonnay on the house," Havisham said.

Salcedo put a hand out as if to remind her that wasn't the most important part, and then she turned to me. "You shouldn't have been making decisions immediately after all that. Also, you need a therapist."

"No shit. How am I going to pay her? Can't even barter with acts of pettiness now without fear of having someone call to complain. No, I'll have to read my book and talk it over with my emotional support cat."

"Yeah, well, Brené Brown would tell you to take a chance on love," Salcedo said.

"The cat or the author?"

"Both."

"Maybe if Malone had mentioned the word 'love' even once, I would listen to the author. Or even the cat."

"Well, did you mention it first?"

"No. I never have, and I never will."

Havisham whooped. "Never? You asking for the universe to mess with you a little more? I said I'd never own a bar. What have I been doing all these years?"

"Know what? I'm going home."

"You do that. You're out of sorts," Havisham said.

"Thanks so much. Next, y'all are going to tell me we aren't friends anymore, either."

The tears hit me hot and heavy, and I tried to slide from the booth, but Havisham grabbed my arm. "Stella Stark, sit your ass down."

Meekly, I obliged.

"Look me in the eye."

I did.

"Do I strike you as the kind of person who would ever lie to you?"

"No."

"Or the kind of person who would arbitrarily decide I didn't like you?"

"No."

"You're damn right about that. I can pretty much count on one hand the number of people I actually like, and I like you. The only way you'll get rid of me is if you dump me or if I keel over."

"Thanks, Havisham."

"Me three," Salcedo said. "I like the fact that neither of you stand on ceremony. You say what you think. You do what you say. You don't do things for the sake of appearances."

"That's beautiful," Havisham said. "I think I almost shed a tear."

"Oh, don't make fun of me or this moment," I said between hiccuping sobs.

"I'm not! I'm a salty old broad because I hold all those tears in, but—oops! I just lost one."

"I love y'all," Salcedo said with a smile as she put an arm around my shoulders.

She said it with an ease I envied desperately.

"There you go, Stark. Cry it out," Havisham said gruffly.

"Y'all done made the baby cry," Betty said. She called over her shoulder, "Jasper! Get over here and sing this girl a song."

"I ain't singing no song!"

Their argument made me laugh even in my tears and told me the world would keep on spinning, even if the days were dull for a while.

Chapter 40

I'm not proud of how I wallowed the weekend after Malone and I consciously uncoupled. Salcedo had found another college student to room with instead of me, which was both good and bad. Bad that I had nothing to distract me but good she wasn't there to watch me mope. BB and I sat on the couch together watching *Murder, She Wrote*. I brought some treats for the kitten because she seemed jealous of my popcorn. She was also surprisingly understanding when I said things like "This episode is like *Gaslight*, which is funny because Angela Lansbury was in that movie" or "Look! There's Victor from *The Young and the Restless*!"

The next day, however, I had to get to work. Backgrounds weren't going to check themselves. Papers weren't going to serve themselves. Rent sure as heck wasn't going to pay itself.

By that afternoon I wanted nothing more than to return to my Jessica Fletcher marathon, but Havisham called.

"Stark, get your ass over here."

"I don't wanna."

"I'm shorthanded, and I need you."

I poured kibble out for the cat. "I can't mix drinks. You know that."

"True, but you can bus tables."

"Fine."

Thirty minutes later I walked into Finnegan's with a sour expression, only to be greeted by a chorus of "Surprise!"

Oh.

My birthday.

"Sorry we have to celebrate early, but on July fourth the place is going to be covered up. This way you can have Finnegan's to yourself," Havisham said.

The fact that Havisham had closed the bar for me gave me squishy feelings. I, however, did not like feelings, so instead of saying thank you, I said, "It's a real pain sharing a birthday with America."

Havisham studied me for a moment. But like knows like, so she wasn't offended. "You think that's bad, try having to share the spotlight with Jesus."

"You were born on Christmas Day?"

She grinned. "And that's your first birthday present because I usually don't tell *anyone* that."

I surveyed the crowd: Trace, Havisham's multimillionaire cowboy philanthropist, was there. Nana had brought Lucius Malone as her date. Salcedo came stag, but I knew she was now dating someone.

Odd to feel alone when with my favorite people.

"I can't believe you shut down the bar just for me," I said.

"Bah, I deserve a night off every now and again. Gives me an excuse to put up the 'Closed for a Private Event' sign, too. That usually entices someone to book an actual private party."

The small number meant we could easily sit at two tables pulled together and chat. When Havisham disappeared, I leaned over to whisper in Nana's ear, "Lucius Malone? Really?"

"He was my prom date back in sixty-four. Why do you think I've wanted to go to that gala all these years?"

I couldn't deny that Nana looked happier than I'd seen her in a long while.

Havisham reappeared with a sheet cake that held forty candles, each of them aglow.

Forty glowing candles? Both a fire hazard and an impressive sight to behold. From my seat at the end of the table, I could feel the heat.

"Make a wish. Make a wish," Salcedo started to chant, and Nana quickly joined her. Even Trace and Lucius eventually joined in.

I made a wish, an absolutely foolish wish, and then I did the best I could to blow out all forty candles. It took two tries.

"Aw, now your wish won't come true," Nana said.

I didn't have the heart to tell her that snowballs in hell had a greater chance of not melting than my wish had of actually coming true. I refused to look at the door. My wish had been that Malone would show up and declare his love for me.

Instead, we had cake, and then Havisham declared it was time for my presents.

She placed three huge gift bags in front of me.

"Green, Malone? You boys may not want to stick around for this one," she said gruffly. "This is not for the faint of heart."

"I think I can take it," her cowboy said as he crossed his arms over his chest.

In contrast, Lucius looked concerned but also clearly didn't want to be shown up. "I think I'm worldly enough to handle anything you have planned."

"Okay, don't say I didn't warn you."

"Havisham, what have you done?" I asked.

"Me? We. *We*—Salcedo, your nana, and I—have created a survival kit for your forties," she said. "You pull out the item, and I'll explain. If I have to. Start with the bag that has balloons on it."

I looked from her to the first gift bag. It seemed so innocent with its large balloons in primary colors and the brightly colored tissue paper sticking up from the bag, so why did I feel a growing sense of trepidation at what I would find inside?

I removed three sheets of tissue paper and drew forth a four-pack of reading glasses.

"Sometime in the next decade," Havisham said, "your eyes are going to decide not to work. It'll happen overnight. Then you'll need a pair of glasses in the kitchen so you can read recipes. And another for your purse so you can read menus. Another on the coffee table for when you want to look at your phone or read a book. And another—"

"I get it. What if I have trouble seeing distances instead?"

"Probably gonna be close up," Nana said as she held up her own pair of readers.

I reached inside and found . . . tweezers. "What's with the multipack?"

"Oh, you'll need one for your bathroom and one for your car—great natural light to see those chin hairs," Havisham said. "Maybe a pair for your purse, should you find yourself in a bathroom with especially good lighting."

I fixed her with a stare. "I don't think I want to be forty."

"Too bad. You're only thirty-nine for another day or so."

Next, I found sunglasses, sunscreen, a magnifying mirror, retinol, and a cleanser that would help with wrinkles without making acne worse.

Salcedo moaned, "Don't tell me I'm going to keep getting zits while also getting wrinkles. That's ridiculous. I thought zits stopped when you became an adult."

The older women stared her down. I told Salcedo as gently as I could, "I regret to inform you that the acne will continue even if the morale improves."

"Keep going," Havisham said.

I had to stand up to reach down into the bag because it was so deep. There I found a giant bottle of ibuprofen, super tampons, a portable neck fan, an eye mask / Bluetooth headphone combo, and a heating pad.

"For the love, is there anything *fun* about being forty?"

"That's what the next bag is for," Havisham said.

I turned my attention to a second gift bag, floral this time, and rummaged around inside to find a silk pillowcase.

"Good for your hair and for fighting wrinkles while also being a luxury," Nana said.

Next, I found deluxe chocolates and CBD gummies. Salcedo laughed. Trace muttered something about calling him if I wanted the good stuff.

"Nice," I said with a tight smile as I pulled out a T-shirt with a vintage Nancy Drew cover photoshopped to have the title *It's Not Voyeurism If You're Solving Mysteries.*

I would've loved this shirt a lot more if it didn't remind me of Ken's spying, which, in turn, reminded me of Malone. That dull ache behind my breastbone was back, but I kept going through the bag, hoping my smile was still in place.

A bottle of Veuve Clicquot. A gift certificate for a massage. A journal with a sticky note that said, "Start recording all your wisdom—the world will need it."

"Well, thank you, everyone," I said as I surveyed the two piles in front of me, some bad but mostly good. Such was life: a grab bag of both. But the thoughtfulness of the presents warmed me from the inside out. "I really don't know what else to say."

"Oh, there are a couple of more things in that second bag," Havisham said with a wicked grin that told me I wanted to leave whatever was at the bottom of the bag right where it was.

With a sigh, I reached past the tissue paper that remained to find . . . a vibrator.

I stared her down. "Havisham."

"Just two more little gifts, Stark. I believe in you."

With a deep sigh of resignation, I removed the vibrator from the bag and laid it on the table. The women squealed with delight. Trace burst into laughter. Lucius cleared his throat and blushed.

"One more," Havisham taunted.

Muttering something about getting this over with, I tossed all the remaining tissue paper on the table until I came to a jumbo box of condoms. I placed them gently in the midst of the tissue paper.

Well, I wouldn't be needing those anytime soon. The vibrator? Inspired gift, that.

"Aurelia, you forgot the lubricant," Nana said.

My cheeks heated. There was a sentence no one ever wanted to hear from her grandmother. Even Lucius, who might benefit from Nana's foresight, was studying the Liverpool flag as if it were a Monet.

"I can take care of that," I said. "In fact, I think I'm as prepared as I'm ever going to be. Thank you, everyone. And please don't ever buy me sex toys ever again."

Trace spewed his beer. Lucius shifted in his seat.

"Wait! You gotta open the third bag," Salcedo said.

I was afraid of where the night might go from the vibrator. "I'm feeling pretty gifted out. I mean, I'm grateful, but—"

She smiled. "Good things come in threes."

"That's why I named this place Finnegan's," Havisham said.

Finnegan's reminded me of Malone, too. He was the one who'd explained a mulligan for a mulligan to me. So cruel to give me condoms and to remind me of him.

Of course, everything reminded me of Malone.

"Fine," I said tentatively. "Lord, preserve me from anything else embarrassing."

I fished through tissue paper in the third bag and pulled out a coin purse in a fuchsia paisley print. The pattern was definitely not my style, but I settled for a different observation instead. "What the heck is small enough to fit in here?"

"That's where you can store your fucks since you will no longer have that many to give," Havisham said. "That's one bonus of turning forty."

Nana cracked first, her laughter inspiring everyone else's. "That's a good one, Aurelia."

"Please, call me Havisham."

"And you can call me Jefferson."

Oh no. Since meeting Havisham, I'd feared what would happen if these two got together, and now it had. The world would never be the same.

Salcedo cleared her throat. "But that coin purse was also made by Vera Bradley. The founder of that company was over forty when she started the business."

"Uh-oh. There's going to be a message to all of this, isn't there?"

"Very good, Stark! Look at you figuring out that happiness is being a lifelong learner." Havisham held up the chocolates. "Let these remind you of the famous episode of *I Love Lucy* where Lucy and Ethel eat all the chocolates from the assembly line. Because Lucille Ball didn't achieve fame until that sitcom."

"Let me guess . . . she was forty?"

"She can be taught!" Havisham then picked up the bottle of champagne from earlier. "The Widow Clicquot may have started her champagne house before she was forty, but she didn't come up with her revolutionary riddling method, nor the delightful idea of rosé, until she was forty. Or very close to it. Now back to the third bag with you."

I reached into the bag and came out with a copy of *Beloved.*

Salcedo spoke this time. "Toni Morrison was thirty-nine when she published her first book. She was over forty when she won the Pulitzer Prize for this one."

Next, I pulled out a paintbrush. "I think y'all know I'm not much of an artist."

"That you know of," said Nana. "Alma Thomas was sixty-nine when she started painting, and Grandma Moses was seventy-seven."

"Is this like Mary Poppins's bag?" I asked as I drew out a pair of black leggings.

"No," said Havisham. "Stop trying to ruin this poignant moment. Not only are leggings comfortable, but these were designed by Vera Wang. She was over forty when she started her fashion empire."

Now having to stand again to reach the bottom of the bag, I picked up *Mastering the Art of French Cooking.*

Nana, who could cook well if she wanted to, said, "Julia Child graduated from culinary school when she was thirty-nine and didn't get her own television show for another ten years. And *Mastering the Art of French Cooking* later served as an inspiration for Ina Garten, who didn't publish her first cookbook until she was fifty."

I wanted to say something like "*The Art of Microwave Cooking* would be more my speed," but I didn't. The thoughtfulness behind these gifts touched me in spite of myself.

"Come on, you're almost finished," Salcedo said softly.

I looked at these familiar faces. Even Trace leaned forward as if he wanted to know what would come next.

I picked up a DVD of *A Wrinkle in Time* and looked at everyone in confusion.

"Ava DuVernay didn't pick up a camera until she was in her thirties," Salcedo said. "And she got her first Oscar nomination when she was forty-two but didn't direct this movie until four years later. But that's not all."

She paused, letting the anticipation build.

"Madeleine L'Engle's novel, the one that was a basis for this movie? Written after she was forty. At the age of thirty-nine, she contemplated giving up writing because it was taking time away from her family with little to no return, but then she got the idea for her most famous book, *A Wrinkle in Time*."

"I hope y'all don't want me to write a book," I said.

"Oh, for heaven's sake," Havisham said as she stood and walked briskly to her bar and then behind it. From Salcedo's confused expression, I could tell this wasn't part of the scene they had rehearsed. My favorite bartender soon returned with a copy of Agatha Christie's *Murder in Mesopotamia*.

"Agatha Christie? I can solve mysteries, but I sure as heck can't write them."

"No, that's not it," Havisham said with a smile. "This whole bag of gifts is about not believing it when society tries to tell you you're over the hill or that you should give up. L'Engle almost gave up on writing, and Christie almost gave up on love."

"Havisham," I said in warning.

"Agatha Christie's first marriage ended in divorce," she continued as if she hadn't heard me. "Two years after that divorce was final, Dame Agatha was taking a ride on the Orient Express. She visited an archaeological site for the fun of it, and there she met Max Mallowan."

"I'm not a dame."

"She wasn't either at that time, and she wasn't looking for love, but young Max Mallowan must have been persuasive, because he became her second husband. This is the first book she wrote after meeting him. She was forty. He was twenty-six."

"Dang, girl. Rob that cradle!" Salcedo said.

"You gotta do what you gotta do," Nana murmured. Out of the corner of my eye, I saw that she was squeezing Lucius's hand even though they were the same age.

"I mean, it's working out great for me," Trace said. "That cradle was getting dull anyway."

"Havisham, my situation is different."

"I'm not telling you what to do," she said. "I'm just saying . . . sometimes we all need a mulligan. Or a Finnegan. Maybe even a Branagan."

"A do-over for a do-over for a do-over?"

"Neither love nor life is golf. We get as many opportunities as we need," Havisham said as she slid her arm around the waist of her cowboy. "If we're brave enough to try again, at least."

Salcedo's eyes cut between Havisham and me. She could sense the tension and asked, "How about champagne, everyone?"

The next morning, I awoke to a presence very close to my face, a fuzzy presence that purred.

I opened my eyes and saw, in the morning light, that even my emotional support cat was now taunting me. BB's eyes had changed as she matured. The eye behind the patch of black on her face was green. The eye on the other side, the side with white and yellow, was blue.

"Really? Not you, too."

I rolled out of bed and went to the bathroom, but what was wafting through the ceiling somehow? "All Too Well."

Chapter 41

It was the ladybug bracelet that did me in.

For the next month, I moped around while doing the usual jobs for Attorney Lawless. I had enrolled in a new set of paralegal classes. Still went with Havisham and Salcedo to the Waffle House, but not as often as we used to because Salcedo was back in class and Havisham was serious about her cowboy.

Even better, he'd worked through college as a bartender, so a little refresher and a pouring license and he was ready and able to help Havisham around the bar, a place where I felt increasingly like a third wheel.

Then one day I checked the mail, and there was a smaller padded envelope. Inside was a bracelet with ladybugs, nothing too expensive but not too cheap, either. A note simply said,

This reminded me of you. M.

I clasped the bracelet on the same wrist that held my gift from Addie, then turned over the envelope to look for a return address. There was the address for Malone's apartment, written in the same exacting handwriting I recognized from his walls.

San José.

He must've finished the Denver job, and he was back in the apartment I'd found the day I searched his name on Tracers while looking for his phone number.

Ladybugs might not have been a declaration of love, but going to an actual post office to mail something certainly was.

The next thing I knew, I was searching for plane tickets. One look at the price and I snapped the laptop shut. "I can't swing it, BB."

My kitten, who was looking more and more like a cat, sat beside me, tail wrapped around her front feet. She meowed.

"No. It's too expensive."

She blinked at me and adjusted her feet, rewound her tail, and then stared at me intently, her two eyes now even more distinctly different, one blue and the other yellow green. She said nothing.

She didn't have to. Not when her eyes reminded me of Malone.

"You can't use my own tricks against me."

Still, she stared.

"I don't like to fly."

Too bad, her eyes seemed to say.

"What if he has another girlfriend already?"

Then he wouldn't be sending you a bracelet, now would he?

"Unless he's like all the other guys I've met."

She tilted her head to one side as if to say, *You know better than that.*

"Fine. You're right. That's what credit cards are for, but I can't resurrect my pettiness career to pay them off, so *you* need to think of a new side hustle. Think you could get internet famous?"

She yawned.

I started the process of picking out a flight but grimaced at the last-minute price. "How do I know if he's even there, BB?"

She lightly bit me, her not-so-subtle request for pets. Absently, I petted her while trying to navigate my laptop with one hand. When I paused in my petting, she meowed.

"I am absolutely not texting him. I need to see his expression when I tell him. I need to *see* if he's happy to see me or not."

She looked over her shoulder, which I decided was her version of a shrug.

"Fine. You're right. If he's not home for some reason, then I'll wait. Or maybe say screw it and go to wine country. I've always wanted to visit, and I'm sure as heck not getting to the South of France anytime soon."

I booked the flight and a rental car for the next day and considered googling "Am I mentally unstable if I'm having entire conversations with my cat?" but decided I didn't want to know the answer to that particular question.

Almost twenty-four hours later, I wearily sat in my rental car, secure in the knowledge that I still didn't like flying. Even worse, I did not feel sexy at all. I felt gross in the late-August heat. I was tired from my early wakeup call and from spending so much time in either an airport or a plane. I still had almost forty-five minutes to go.

You should've texted him.

Maybe. It was ridiculous. Who shows up on someone's doorstep? Uninvited, at that?

In the outskirts of San José—yes, I did know the way, courtesy of GPS and the return address label—I had an idea. It was either a wonderful idea or a terrible one. Honestly, "wonderful or terrible" could've described the entire trip.

All I knew was that I wouldn't be able to live with myself if I didn't at least ask him the question, and that's how I ended up at his front door on a Wednesday evening holding a pizza box.

You're gonna feel like a prize idiot if he has someone over. Or if he isn't there at all. Or—

"Stark!"

His precious, handsome face said it all: eyes twinkling, grin broadening. God, how I'd missed that face.

"Malone."

"I see you have a pizza box."

"I do. Inside there is, believe it or not, a pizza."

"Interesting. Would you like to come in?"

"That I would."

His apartment was stunning, mid-century modern, tidy but not fussily so. The Dodgers game was on the television in the living room, but he turned that off before joining me at his dining room table.

"What brings you all the way to California?" he asked carefully.

"I've given the past few weeks a great deal of thought," I said, "and I was wondering if you would be interested in renegotiating our benefits package."

He frowned. "Just benefits?"

"Well, I would like to add an exclusivity clause to it, which is sorta backward, and this analogy is going sideways. Dammit, Malone, I miss you."

He crossed the distance between us in seconds, his arms around me and his lips on mine. We kissed as if we hadn't seen each other in a lifetime, and truly, that's the way it felt. He shoved the pizza box to the side and sat me on the table. My whole body shuddered in pleasure at the memory of tables past.

Ken's memory tried to intrude, but I shoved him away.

Malone had his hands on the hem of my shirt.

"Anchovies."

"Stark," he said in a warning voice.

"No, there's something I need to say to you first."

"Okay," he said cautiously.

"Something I've never said first to anyone ever."

His eyes widened ever so slightly, and while looking down to gather my courage, I caught a glimpse of his friendship bracelet. He still wore it, just as the ladybug bracelet had joined mine.

I looked up into his beautifully arresting eyes and said, "I have fallen in love with you."

His whole body relaxed. It was as though I could see all his anxieties and apprehensions melt away. "Stella Stark, I fell in love with you the minute we bumped into each other in the breezeway."

"Well, why didn't you just say so!"

He shrugged. "You were looking for a man in finance."

"No, I was looking for a forensic accountant who has a *Star Trek* tattoo. I just didn't know that yet."

"Hold on, let me see if I can find one." He turned to go, and I grabbed his arm.

"Malone?"

"Yes?"

"I don't know how any of this will work, but I want to try. I want more than 'pizza with benefits.'"

"And I want to give it to you," he said. "Literally and figuratively."

"I might be wearing a purple bra."

He crossed his arms over his chest and gave me his sternest look, the eyebrow above his blue eye arched. "I must see it. Those are the rules."

"That you made up!" I said even as I took off my shirt.

"Stark, I will build you an entire pizzeria if you come to bed with me now and don't leave that bed until next week."

"You drive a hard bargain, but sold."

The next thing I knew, Malone had thrown me over his shoulder. Through the curtain of my hair and out the window of his kitchen, I saw . . . a big, beautiful blue moon.

Later, I lay in his arms, thoroughly kissed, and grinned at the wonder of the moon shining down on us while the King of My Heart took a well-deserved snooze.

Epilogue

Not quite one year later

"Well, Stark, I've been saving something for this very moment," Havisham said as we gathered at Finnegan's to celebrate both my completion of the paralegal certificate and her marriage to Trace. She'd taken no chances he might jilt her; they'd gone to the justice of the peace.

Judging by the way he looked at her, though, she had nothing to worry about.

Malone, who'd flown into town for the week, pulled me close. I could tell he was thinking marriage, but he'd said nothing. He was a blessedly patient man.

I wasn't going to say never. I'd learned my lesson about taunting the universe.

Finally, Havisham popped up behind the bar with . . . the bottle of champagne that I'd brought in with me on what she and I now lovingly called That-Night-I-Accidentally-Touched-A-Boob.

"I can't believe you kept it!"

"Of course I kept it," she said as she popped the cork. "It wasn't mine. It was yours. Even that night I had an idea we might make something good come from the bad."

"See? You're a Pollyanna after all," I said as I took the flute she offered me.

"What perfect timing," Malone said.

"Oh?"

"Remember when Selena flipped on Blake to get a lighter sentence? That expedited his trial—well, I'm sure Grandpa made some calls too—and now my least favorite cousin is off to prison."

"Probably a Club Fed," Havisham muttered as she handed him a glass.

The idea didn't give me as much joy as I'd thought it would. "It's a shame Trista couldn't recover more of their assets."

"About that," Malone said.

"Yes?"

"I may or may not have shared some pertinent information with Trista's divorce attorney."

"All aboveboard?"

"Technically?"

I couldn't hide my grin. My Malone wasn't going to break the law, but he shared my sense of justice.

"Sorry I'm late," Salcedo said as she breezed through the door. "I was finishing up a paper and totally lost track of the time."

"Your timing is perfect," Havisham said as she poured another glass of champagne.

"Is that . . . ?" Salcedo asked, pointing at the bottle.

"Oh yes," Havisham said.

Salcedo looked at me, her eyes dancing. "What are we toasting?"

"Love," I said, raising my glass toward Havisham and Trace, then looking up at my favorite forensic accountant.

"And justice," he said.

"*Poetic* justice," Havisham said as we all raised our glasses a third time.

"And being just a little petty," Salcedo added.

Our toast concluded, we locked up Finnegan's to head for a Waffle House after-party. We were past due in bringing some burly boyfriends to visit Betty and Jasper.

Once outside, I stopped. "Is that another blue moon?"

"A supermoon, even," Malone said. "Almost ten years before you'll see another blue moon, so drink it in."

"Huh."

"That's a really loaded 'huh,' Stark."

"Say, how good are you at flipping pancakes?"

He grinned. "An expert. Want me to make you some tomorrow?"

"Definitely. What's your favorite shape?"

He put a hand on my forehead. "Are you okay?"

"As well as I've ever been. Shape, Malone."

Bless him, he stopped to give my question thought.

"Well, for my next tattoo, I was thinking about an asterisk, so I'm gonna have to go with a star."

I inhaled sharply. A star. "Why an asterisk?"

"Lots of reasons, but mainly because it can mean 'wild card,' and that reminds me of you."

"Not a banana pepper?" I asked cheekily, even though my insides felt gooey.

"Nah."

I grabbed his hand, and we walked in the direction of my car. "Listen, Malone. I know California doesn't have any Waffle Houses, but I was wondering . . ."

"Yes?"

"How would you feel about my coming to stay with you?"

By this time, we'd reached my Corolla, and Malone leaned against the car and pulled me to him. "And here I was going to scout out places for a possible Atlanta office of Chateau Cybersecurity while I was here."

"Really?" My heart swelled in such a way I knew I didn't want to leave my friends behind.

"It was going to be a surprise, but you beat me to the punch."

"So it's time to renegotiate the benefits package?"

"I'd be willing to update our contract to a more binding document," he said carefully.

My heart hammered. It was a different sort of proposal, but then again, I was a different sort of woman. "I could be persuaded."

"I'll enjoy persuading you," he said before kissing me under that big, bright, blue supermoon.

The universe had spoken.

Acknowledgments

Ironically, I don't feel petty in the least. Well, not in this particular moment. Maybe this book exorcised that demon? Only time will tell. I will say that some books are easier to write than others, and this one definitely falls into the "other" category simply because life has a way of lifing. This book would not have happened without a veritable village of people, so let's round up those usual suspects.

Sarah Younger, it's no exaggeration to say I would not have finished this book without you and that I might not even still be writing without you. Thank you. You are the GOAT, and now you have the pillow to prove it.

Lauren Plude, thank you for taking a chance on my whackadoodle ideas and for how you make them better. I'm afraid I didn't figure out where to put the crochet plant this time, but it will find its story.

Sasha Knight, thank you for your careful eye and for putting up with my architectural metaphors.

For both Lauren and Sasha: I appreciate deeply your dedication, your expertise, and your cheerleading all along the way.

Montlake team, thank you. Cover design, copy editors, marketing. You're the best!

Special thanks to private investigator Hannah Comer for answering about a million questions and looking at this book at its most unpretty. I assure you that she would *never* do some of the things Stella does.

Similarly, Brian Ong tackled my forensic accountant questions with patience and grace.

Adele Buck, thanks for talking with me about paralegal certificates and whether legal research was anything at all like doing proofs in geometry.

Tracy Rhodes, thank you for talking me through some additional process-serving and private-detecting questions.

If you, gentle reader, should find any mistakes pertaining to, well, anything, then those are mine and mine alone.

Valerie Bowman, God bless you. You read the ugly-duckling draft, gave some keen insights, and talked me off the ledge at least once. One day you might regret sharing a table with me at Romancing the Books, but I hope not.

Tanya Michna, your meme game is on point, as were your notes on the first draft. Thank you for cheerleading and for being the Statler to my Waldorf.

Jamie, I always value the care you put into critiques and the depth of your insight. Thanks for that, for the chats, and for introducing me to Brian.

Sonali, thanks for helping me get to Stella's wound while you were weeding. I'm over here trying to figure things out, and you're multitasking!

Lisa, Tracy, Virginia, Priscilla, Barbara, and Amy—thank you for your encouragement and for cheering me on.

Immense gratitude to Kim. It takes a special person to be both spiritual adviser AND chief petty officer.

Kelly Christine, thank you for helping me with the Swiftie aspects of this story. I feel I should reiterate that any mistakes related to Tay-Tay? Definitely mine.

Demerice Smith and Sofia Warfield, thank you so much for reading the first draft and sharing your thoughts. Your editorial letters were very well thought out.

Thanks always to my mother, who reads and comments and corrects and has been doing so for years. This part of my process is crucial so that when a scandalized reader asks, "Does your mother know what you write?" then I can say, "Absolutely. She helps me make sure my winders are windows, et cetera, et cetera."

Sabrina Carpenter (and Dunkin', I suppose), thanks for introducing me to brown sugar shaken espresso. Approximately 73 percent of this book owes its existence to brown sugar shaken espresso, and I will happily accept credit at Dunkin' for this shameless plug.

Maggie, thank you for the lovely insulated cup that often held the aforementioned beverage and kept it from sweating all over my desk.

April Smith, thanks for donating to LiFT 4 AUTISM. Your character may only show up briefly, but I did take out a billboard for her.

Thanks to author Beverly Jenkins, from whom I first heard "Karma is only a bitch if you are." She might have seen it in a meme, but she delivered it with style.

A serious thanks to Brené Brown—the author, not the cat. I've read *Daring Greatly* three times. It might sink in one day. Your podcast helped keep me sane during the pandemic, and I'm working my way through your other books. You were there for me in my own midlife unraveling, and I hope you take having a cat named after you as an honor, which was my intention.

Speaking of, thanks also to Richard Russo, who cracked me up in *Straight Man* with "Finny, the goose, not the man" and "Finny, the man not the goose." My version is meant as homage. Y'all need to go read *Straight Man*, if you haven't already.

Marietta Schools Foundation—thank you for answering my crazy question about whether Marietta High School had a prom in 1964. Here's looking at you, Laura and Stacey.

The fine folks at Elkins Chiropractic (Mitch, Kim, Diane): Thanks for keeping me well adjusted. Literally. Possibly figuratively. Hey, Diane, I'm drinking out of my "This is what a published author looks like" mug right now. (Thank goodness no one can actually *see* what this published author looks like right now.)

Connor, uh, thanks for that time we were driving to the University of Delaware and you had us listen to Taylor Swift for something like seven hours straight? Pretty sure that trip is responsible for that particular plot element of this book.

Lorelai, thanks for always being willing to fetch caffeine and for helping me brainstorm ways to be petty. I only regret I couldn't think of a way to incorporate your idea of slices of American cheese in random places.

Kiddos, thanks most of all for being you.

Jim, Jane, Bill, and Terri, thanks for being excellent parents and grandparents. If I had a complaint, it would be that it's awfully hard to come up with the bad fictional parents I sometimes need because y'all are so good.

Ryan, whenever my hero does something that a reader thinks is too good to be true or something a man would never do, chances are you have done that very thing. Thanks for holding me up while holding down the fort.

Booksellers and librarians, thank you. You're doing the Lord's work each time you help someone find a good book. I cherish each picture of one of my books on a library shelf. The cold cockles of my English major heart warm anytime a bookseller recommends me. (Or any book, really.)

Finally, thank *you*, gentle reader. Thank you for reading, reviewing, telling your friends, or even telling your cat. A book isn't a book without an audience, and I hope you've enjoyed this one.

About the Author

Photo © Mai Phung and Brian Smith

Sally Kilpatrick is the *USA Today* bestselling author of eight novels and counting, including *Nobody's Perfect* and *The Happy Hour Choir*. She has won multiple awards, including the 2018 and 2019 Georgia Author of the Year. Sally empty nests in Marietta, Georgia, with her ever-understanding husband and decidedly unimpressed cats. Her hobbies include reading, travel, wine, and running in an effort to make up for the wine consumed. She has yet to meet a house she didn't want to tour. For more information, visit www.sallykilpatrick.com.